"KILL HIM! KILL MEAT NOW!

Hickok instinctively blasted the rifleman first, his hands a blur as they drew the pearl-handled Colt Pythons, his right Magnum booming, and the rifleman staggered as the slug penetrated the middle of his forehead and blew out the back of his head. The man toppled to the ground as Hickok spun, his left Python cracking, the shot catching a woman wielding a butcher's knife in her right eye and spinning her body completely around before she fell onto her face.

Inside the SEAL, Geronimo clawed at the door handle. "They're Wacks!" he shouted, flinging the door open and jumping to the ground, the FNC Auto Rifle already at his shoulder as he aimed at a line of charging cannibals and squeezed the trigger. The Auto Rifle burped, and four of the crazies dropped.

Blade joined the conflict, leaping from the driver's seat, the A-1 pressed against his right hip as he fired, the heavy slugs tearing into a group of attacking Wacks and decimating them in a crimson spray of blood and flesh.

THE ENDWORLD SERIES
by David Robbins:

DAVID ROBBINS

ENDWORLD

CITADEL RUN

LEISURE BOOKS ∞ NEW YORK CITY

DEDICATED TO:

Judy, and Joshua,
and all of our future children;

the cherished memory of two loved ones,
Evelyn and Tyson Miller;

the dear man who gave us Creevis and Lukablavitz,
Jim Gordon;

the memory of Jack Shaefer:
no one will ever do it better.

A LEISURE BOOK

Published by

Dorchester Publishing Co., Inc.
6 East 39th Street
New York, NY 10016

1

"I sense danger," the Empath announced for the benefit of the three other occupants of the green vehicle.

Immediately, the muscular driver of the van-like transport applied the brakes, bringing the SEAL to an abrupt stop in the middle of the road. His brawny hands deftly twisted the steering wheel, angling the vehicle, enabling him to see in both directions without turning in his seat. His penetrating gray eyes scanned their immediate vicinity as he ran his left hand through his thick dark hair. The driver wore green fatigue pants and a black leather vest, and he was armed with a pair of Bowie knives, one strapped to each hip. "Are you certain, Joshua?" he asked the Empath.

Joshua nodded, his long brown hair bobbing on his narrow shoulders, his brown eyes partially closed as he concentrated his mental powers on the emanations he was receiving. He wore a blue shirt and brown pants, the front of the shirt covered by a large Latin cross he wore suspended from around his neck. "I'm positive, Blade. I'm picking up definite hostility, although I am unable to pinpoint the precise source."

"Maybe your battery needs recharging, pard,"

commented a blond man in buckskins, a lean figure with broad shoulders and a matched set of pearl-handled Colt Python revolvers in the holsters of his gunbelt. His right hand stroked his sweeping blond moustache as he looked around. "I don't see a critter stirrin' out there."

"Just this once, Hickok," groused the fourth occupant of the transport, a stocky Indian with brown eyes and black hair, wearing frayed green pants and a shirt, both constructed from an old canvas tent, "I wish you'd use normal English like the rest of us. If I hang around you long enough, I'm likely to start talking like you do."

"So what's wrong with the way I talk?" Hickok demanded.

"Oh, nothing, really," responded his friend. "But I don't want my wife to think I'm a dimwit."

"Are you implying, Geronimo, old buddy," Hickok said, glancing at his closest companion in the entire world, "that I'm a dimwit?"

Geronimo chuckled. "Does a bear crap in the woods?"

"I don't need this aggravation," Hickok stated, feigning annoyance. "I get enough of it from *my* wife, you know."

Blade gazed fondly at the gunman, grinning. Hickok was seated in a bucket seat directly across from him. Between them was a console, and behind them was another seat running the width of the vehicle. Geronimo sat directly behind Hickok, Joshua behind Blade. The rear section of the SEAL was devoted to storage space.

The SEAL.

Blade stared at the dashboard. Thank the Founder for the transport! Without it, traveling over the countryside would be extremely precarious, what with the ravaging mutates, the scavengers, and all the other deviates waiting to kill you at a moment's notice. Kurt Carpenter had been the Founder, and he had wisely foreseen his beloved Family's need for a superior vehicle, a mode of transportation capable of withstanding the structural stress, the hostile environment, and the harshly altered terrain existing after World War III. Carpenter had spent millions on the design and building of his prototype, incorporating various unique features and special capabilities. His Solar-Energized Amphibious or Land Recreational vehicle was now known by the acronym SEAL. The transport's body was composed of a nearly indestructible tinted plastic, enabling anyone inside the SEAL to see outside clearly, but preventing someone outside the transport from viewing the interior. Carpenter had known that gas and oil would be difficult to obtain after the collapse of civilization, so he had instructed his scientists and engineers to power the SEAL by solar energy, utilizing two solar panels attached to the roof. The energy was converted and stored in a bank of six revolutionary batteries positioned in a lead-lined case under the vehicle. Four huge tires, constructed of an impervious synthetic, enabled the SEAL to traverse obstacles conventional vehicles could never overcome. After the SEAL had been produced, Carpenter had employed the services of several military specialists, skilled mercenaries whose talents could be purchased for a high enough price, and had had them install certain advanced weapons systems in the prototype.

Kurt Carpenter, Blade thankfully reflected, had seldom missed a trick.

"So what's the plan?" Hickok asked Blade. "Do we cool our heels here or keep going into the Twin Cities?"

Blade pondered the gunfighter's query. As the head of Alpha Triad, the Warrior unit comprised of Hickok, Geronimo, and himself, Blade was responsible for making decisions and directing their actions. Indeed, as the chief Warrior for the entire Family, Blade was dedicated to preserving the security of the Home, their thirty-acre survival site in extreme northwestern Minnesota, and insuring the safety of the Family, the descendants of Kurt Carpenter's initial survivalist group.

"It must be close to noon," Geronimo noted, gazing out at the late October sky. "Plenty of time for us to contact Zahner and the rest."

"And don't forget Bertha," Joshua added, casting a thoughtful glance at Hickok.

Hickok noticed the look. "Why'd you stare at me when you said that?" he gruffly inquired.

Joshua shrugged and quickly diverted his attention to the road ahead. "No reason," he answered.

"You sure?" Hickok pressed him.

"Leave him alone," Blade interjected. "He didn't mean anything. Just because you're nervous about seeing Bertha again is no . . ."

"Who's nervous?" Hickok interrupted. "Bertha will understand. It'll be a piece of cake."

"If you ask me," Geronimo amended, "you'll be wearing cake all over your face when she's through with you."

"I didn't ask you," Hickok glumly retorted. He angrily glared at the buildings in front of them. "Blast it! Why'd I agree to come back here? I should be at the Home with my missus, eating her cooking and taking it easy. Why'd I come back?" he inquired of no one in particular.

"Because you had to return," Blade stated, his mind reviewing the reason for Alpha Triad's previous trip to the Twin Cities of Minneapolis and St. Paul, a distance of some three hundred and seventy miles from their

Home. About two months ago, the Family Leader, a wise, wizened, elderly man by the name of Plato, had sent Alpha Triad and Joshua to the Twin Cities for urgently needed medical and scientific equipment and supplies. Plato had hoped Minneapolis and St. Paul would still be intact, untouched by the scavengers and the looters, at least enough to permit Alpha Triad to locate the items needed in abandoned hospitals or universities. Unfortunately, the Leader's assumption had proven to be erroneous. Alpha Triad had found the Twin Cities in a virtual shambles. Most of the buildings had been standing since Minneapolis and St. Paul had been spared a direct hit during World War III, but the structures had been in utter disrepair, with a few exceptions, and the contents of all the buildings had long since been used or destroyed by the four factions fighting for control of the Twin Cities.

Blade sighed. A lot could happen in a century, and in the one hundred years since the Big Blast—as the Family usually referred to the Third World War—the Twin Cities had been ravaged by the constant warfare between the four feuding groups.

"I just saw something move," Geronimo declared, leaning forward and pointing ahead and to their right. "Behind that overgrown excuse for a hedgerow."

"Wacks, maybe?" Hickok speculated, retrieving his Navy Arms Henry Carbine from the console.

"Couldn't tell," Geronimo replied.

The Wacks! Blade grit his teeth and suppressed a shudder. During his last trip here he'd been captured by the Wacks and had almost lost his life. In fact, all four of them had nearly bought the farm. He mentally envisioned the layout of the Twin Cities, preparing himself.

The former metropolis was divided up into four

different turfs by the four factions. The Wacks were based in southern Minneapolis, and were the descendants of the former residents of the Minnesota Hospital for the Criminally Insane. They were pitiful, demented cannibals, scrounging for any food they could find, attired in rags and armed with everything from bricks to pitchforks. The second group was called the Horns, and they occupied most of St. Paul. They were a strict religious sect, the descendants of a church leader who had stubbornly refused to evacuate his congregation when ordered to do so by the Government at the outset of the war. The third clique was called the Porns by the residents of the Twin Cities, and they controlled western Minneapolis. They were the descendants of a drug and pornography kingpin. The final faction, holding most of northern Minneapolis, was the Nomads, made up of former Horns and Porns, people weary of the incessant fighting and longing for a better life.

"I don't see the reason for any alarm even though I sense danger," Joshua was saying, interrupting Blade's reverie. "We did achieve a truce among the Horns, the Porns, and the Nomads, didn't we? We promised them we'd lead them out of the Twin Cities and aid them in beginning a new life, possibly in one of the small towns situated near our Home. They all eagerly embraced our proposal. So why should you be so tense?"

"We're Warriors, Josh," Hickok answered. "We're trained to expect the worst."

"How sad," Joshua said, frowning. "Surely you must realize how warped your orientation is, speaking from a totally spiritual perspective."

"You may have a point, Big Words," Hickok admitted, "but this warped orientation of ours has kept us alive. Don't knock it until you've tried it."

"I have tried it," Joshua reminded the gunman, "and

I didn't like it."

"Can we save this philosophical discussion until later?" Geronimo suggested. "I just spotted someone behind that tree over there." He indicated a large maple to their left.

"Orders, Blade?" Hickok requested.

Blade pondered their course of action, studying the nearby trees and shrubs, searching for signs of movement, for any indication of hostility. Joshua did have a point; they had arranged a temporary truce among three of the four groups, so it was unlikely they would be attacked by the Porns, the Horns, or the Nomads. The Wacks, the crazies, were another matter. But did they range this far north?

The SEAL was parked in the center of State Highway 47, between 73rd and 71st Avenues, not all that far from where the Nomad camp was located, on the eastern shore of Moore Lake in Fridley.

What to do? Blade asked himself. They couldn't be more than two miles from the camp. Should they simply continue on their way and disregard whoever was lurking outside? After all, with the transport's impervious body, they were relatively secure from any assault. He was about to gun the engine when he remembered a pertinent fact; no one in the Twin Cities knew about the SEAL! When Alpha Triad had visited the Twins last, they'd hidden the vehicle as a safety precaution before venturing into the city. So, if they were now in Nomad territory, the ones outside could well be Nomads unaware of the SEAL's connection to the Family.. The Nomads might well believe that the transport was operated by Government troops, the soldiers known as the Watchers.

"You daydreaming?" Hickok goaded Blade.

"He's probably thinking about Jenny," Geronimo

wryly observed, referring to Blade's wife. "His hormones are undoubtedly going haywire. After all, he hasn't seen her for two whole days."

Blade ignored their barbs and lifted his Auto-Ordnance Model 27 A-1 from the console. The A-1 had been modified by the Family Gunsmiths so it could function on full automatic. Hickok, the Family's leading expert on firearms, had personally selected the A-1 for Blade. It was a re-creation of a gun known as a Thompson submachine gun, and Hickok had chosen it because the A-1's awesome firepower would tend to compensate for Blade's lack of marksmanship. In addition to the A-1 and his Bowies, Blade carried a Dan Wesson .44 Magnum in a shoulder holster under his left arm.

Geronimo was armed with his inevitable tomahawk tucked under the front of his leather belt. An Arminius .357 Magnum was in a holster under his right arm, and he held an FNC Auto Rifle in his hands as he alertly surveyed the surrounding area.

Joshua had been provided with an M-16 confiscated from one of the Government soldiers, but the rifle was lying in the rear section of the SEAL, a testimony to Joshua's detestation of all weaponry.

"We'll try and contact them," Blade said, slowly rolling down his window.

"Keep your head down," Hickok advised. "If they're packin', they'll blow your head off, pard."

Blade lowered his chest over the steering wheel and turned to shout out the window. "Hey! We know you're out there! We come in peace! My name is Blade! If you're Nomads, let us know! We won't harm you!" he promised.

"You know," Hickok mentioned, "the Nomads never saw you, only Josh and me."

"Hickok is in here with me!" Blade yelled. "Do you remember Hickok?"

"How could anyone forget him?" Geronimo interjected. "Flamboyant personalities like his are hard to forget."

"Well, thank you, pard." Hickok beamed.

Geronimo snapped his fingers. "Oh! I'm sorry! I meant to say flamboyant stupidity."

"There doesn't seem to be any response to your greeting," Joshua noted to Blade.

Blade rolled his window up.

Joshua reached for the door handle.

"And where do you think you're going?" Hickok promptly demanded.

Joshua paused. "To step outside and meet whoever is out there."

"Stay where you are," Blade ordered.

"But this is why I'm here," Joshua protested. "Didn't Plato send me along as an ambassador of the Family?"

"Yes, he did," Blade conceded.

"Didn't Plato want someone who would extend the hand of friendship instead of the barrel of a gun?" Joshua queried.

"Yes," Blade allowed.

"Someone who wouldn't be inclined to shoot first, then ask questions later?"

"Yes," Blade reluctantly acknowledged.

Joshua smiled. "So it's obvious I'm the one to greet whoever is out there." He started to open the door.

"Stay where you are," Blade repeated.

Joshua stopped, glancing at the massive Warrior, his brow furrowed. "I don't understand. I thought you just said . . ."

"I admit everything you've said is true," Blade said cutting him off. "Plato has designated you as the

Family's official good will ambassador. . . ."

"So?"

"So I can't let you step outside." Blade motioned for Joshua to sit back in his seat. "Joshua, you're our ambassador, true, but you're also one of the six Empaths in the Family, one of the half-dozen blessed with inexplicable psychic capabilities. You may be the youngest and least experienced of the Empaths, but you're still able to perceive things a normal person like Hickok, Geronimo, and I can't."

"Did I hear right?" Geronimo spoke up. "Did you just call Hickok normal?"

The gunfighter pretended to glare at Geronimo.

"You told us moments ago you sense danger out there," Blade said to Joshua. "Danger is our province, not yours. You will remain in the SEAL until we ascertain if your psychic impression was accurate."

"I'll go," Hickok immediately volunteered. "I'm tired of sitting in this buggy. I could use a little action."

"You'd better let me go," Geronimo stated. "If whoever is out there gets a good look at Hickok's ugly puss, they're liable to turn around and run off before we get the chance to talk to them."

"Funny, funny, funny," Hickok muttered.

"Hickok goes," Blade decided.

The gunman glanced at Geronimo and laughed in triumph. "He obviously picked me because I'm the better Warrior!"

"No," Blade shook his head, winking at Geronimo. "I selected you because Geronimo is the better cook. If anything happened to him, I'd have diarrhea all the way to the Home if I had to eat your cooking."

Geronimo chuckled and playfully slapped Hickok on the back.

Hickok sighed as he opened his door. "It's true what

they say. Greatness is never appreciated in its own time."

"Hickok!" Joshua exclaimed, leaning forward.

"What is it, Josh?"

"Why don't you leave the rifle here?" Joshua recommended. "A show of arms might frighten whoever is out there. It could intimidate them into taking violent action."

Hickok looked at Blade.

"It's up to you," Blade told him. "I'd suggest you take it, though."

Hickok noted the hurt expression on Joshua's face. He slowly placed the Henry on his seat. "Geronimo must be right," he said. "I must be stupid." He stared at Joshua. "I'll do it, pard, for you. Just don't ever tell any of the other Warriors back at the Home. They'll think I've gone off the deep end."

Joshua grinned, delighted at this unexpected turn of events. "Thank you, dear brother! Now what about your Pythons too?"

Hickok locked his blue eyes on Joshua's brown. "Remind me, Josh, that one of these days we've got to sit down and have a real loooooong talk about the realities of life."

"Watch it out there," Blade said.

Hickok nodded and slid from the SEAL, closing the door behind him, his back to the transport, facing the nearest vegetation and scanning for the slightest hint of a threat.

Nothing.

Just the trees and the bushes, the leaves waving in the wind.

Hickok nonchalantly hooked his thumbs under his gunbelt and strolled away from the SEAL. Maybe Joshua was right. Maybe, if they showed they were friendly, whoever was out here would reciprocate.

What could it hurt to try?

A twig snapped behind a large bush about twenty feet away, to his right.

Whoever was out here wasn't being too secretive about it.

Hickok grinned. Just what he liked. A klutzy ambusher!

There was a shuffling sound from behind a tree off to his left.

Hickok paused. He was entertaining second thoughts about this bright idea of Joshua's.

Was someone out there whispering?

Hickok didn't like the setup one bit, but he decided to give Joshua the benefit of the doubt.

More whispering.

"Howdy!" Hickok cheerfully called out. "My handle is Hickok! We're here on a peaceful mission!"

There was a brief silence, then it sounded like dozens of people were whispering all at once.

Hickok cautiously moved toward the large bush. What the blazes were they doing? Having a conference?

A tall man suddenly stepped from behind an oak. He held a rifle in his hands, the barrel pointed at the ground.

Hickok tensed, resisting an impulse to draw his Colts.

Not now!

Give them the benefit of the doubt.

The stranger wore a tattered, dirty blue shirt and torn, faded jeans. He was grinning, revealing a gap where two of his upper front teeth had once been.

Well, look at this! Hickok returned the smile, amazed. Joshua was on the right track, after all! If you showed a little friendliness, you were bound to make friends.

The man took several tentative steps in Hickok's direction.

"Howdy!" Hickok said again. "I'm Hickok. I'm pleased to meet you."

Still grinning, the man nodded his head.

"Do you understand me?" Hickok asked.

The stranger continued to nod.

Yes, sir! Hickok still couldn't believe it. Making friends was a piece of cake!

The tall man was now only ten feet from the Warrior, continuing to nod his head.

What was with this bozo? Did he have a nervous condition, or something?

"I'm Hickok," the gunman repeated.

"That's pretty," the man finally spoke.

Pretty?

"What can I do for you?" Hickok inquired. "What is it you want?"

The man stopped and raised his rifle. "To eat you, dummy!" He suddenly turned his head and shouted at the top of his lungs: *"Kill him! Kill meat now!"*

Without warning, screeching and screaming, over two dozen men and women burst from cover, charging toward the man in buckskins.

2

The boy was sitting on the top railing of the fence attached to the rear of the family barn, idly watching the bull make amorous advances at one of the two heifers his father had recently purchased, when he heard the low voice address him.

"Hello."

Startled, the boy almost lost his grip on the wooden rail. He twisted, frightened, afraid the soldiers had arrived undetected and would learn their secret. His green eyes were wide as he froze, gaping at this man in blue standing not five feet away, a slight smile creasing the man's ruggedly handsome features.

"Hello," the man in blue said greeting the boy again.

Confused, the boy nervously ran his left hand through his tousled blond hair. His father was on the south side of the barn, chopping wood for the fireplace in their log home. Inside the house, his mother was preparing their noon meal. Her cheerful whistling carried on the breeze through an open window in the kitchen.

"I apologize if I caught you off guard," the man in blue said.

Where were the dogs? How had this man gotten past

the two dogs? The boy wanted to call for his father, but
he was fearful the man in blue might shoot his dad. This
man carried lots of guns and other weapons, more
weapons than the boy had ever seen on one person, including the soldiers from the Citadel. Was the man in
blue from the Citadel? the boy wondered. Somehow, he
doubted it. There was something about this man, something special, although the boy coudln't put his finger on
it. The boy gazed into the man's clear blue eyes and was
reassured by the friendliness he detected.

"I was watchin' the bull," the boy explained.

"It's wise for a man to keep his eyes on what's going
on around him," the big man in blue remarked.

The boy grinned. This man seemed to understand
things real well. He marveled at the man's blue garment,
a strange one-piece affair with a shirt and pants somehow sewn together at the waist, both dark blue in color.
The man's hair and long moustache were a striking
shade of silver. He carried some kind of smallish
machine gun in his hands. Under his right arm, in a
shoulder holster, was a pistol, and in another holster
under his left arm was a revolver. As if all the guns
weren't enough, the man in blue also had an oddly
shaped sword in a scabbard attached to his leather belt
above his left hip. On his other hip was a fifteen-inch
survival knife.

"If you have some to spare," the man stated softly, "I
could use some water."

What should he do? The boy wanted to call his father,
but he was still wary, reluctant to trust his feelings about
this man, expecting it was a trap set by the soldiers. He
was about to muster his courage and shout for his dad
when the issue was taken from his hands.

His father came walking around the corner of the
barn, his axe slung across his broad right shoulder.

"Adam, I want you to take the wood. . . ."

Even as Adam's father was rounding the corner, the man in blue had spun, sweeping his machine gun around.

"Don't shoot!" Adam yelled in panic. "That's my dad!"

For what seemed like forever, Adam watched the two men stare at one another, measuring each other. Adam's father, completely stunned by the presence of the newcomer, recovered quickly. He finally smiled and nodded. "We weren't expecting company," he casually commented. He idly began brushing at his flannel shirt.

The man in blue slowly lowered his machine gun. "I won't trouble you. I just wanted a refill for my canteen."

Adam suddenly remembered there was a stream only two hundred yards from the house. This man must have passed it on his way in. Was he lying about the water? Was it a trap, after all?

"We have a pump up near the house," Adam's dad mentioned. "You're welcome to drink your fill, stranger."

The man in blue gazed at Adam, then his father. "You two are quite a match. The same hair, the same eyes, even the same brown shirt and jeans."

"Adam is my pride and joy," Adam's father said proudly.

"I like to do things the way my dad does them," Adam chimed in.

"It's good," the man commented, "to have a family, people you know will love you no matter what."

"Don't you have any children?" Adam asked.

The man in blue shook his head. "Not yet."

"You do have a family, don't you?" Adam innocently inquired.

"Adam!" his father interrupted. "Don't ask so many

questions. It's not polite."

"I don't mind," the man said. "Yes, Adam, I do have a family. A very big Family."

"I'm forgetting my manners," Adam's dad said. He shifted his axe from his right hand to his left, then extended his right as he walked up to the newcomer. "My name is Seth Mason. This is my son, Adam. That songbird you hear is my wife, Gail."

Adam watched the two men shake hands, and he wondered why his dad glanced down at their grip, apparently surprised by something.

"Follow me and we'll get you that water," Seth offered.

The man in blue followed Seth around the barn. As they passed Adam, his mouth dropped open. What in the world! On the back of the stranger's shirt, stitched into the very fabric, was the black silhouette of a skull.

What did it all mean?

Adam jumped from the railing and darted after the two men, keeping a close watch in case the man in blue might try to harm his parents.

The house was located thirty yards from the front of the barn, which faced due east. The Mason log home was a modest affair, only one story, with four rooms: the kitchen, a spacious main room for eating and family activities, a large bedroom for the parents, and another one about half as big for their son.

The water pump was situated ten yards from the front porch.

Seth Mason stepped to one side as the man in blue walked up to the pump.

Adam ran over to his father and stood beside him.

The stranger removed a canteen from a green case affixed to the back of his belt. He leaned his machine gun against the pump and started working the handle.

Almost immediately, fresh water cascaded from the spout onto the ground. The man placed his open canteen under the spray of water and started to fill it.

Adam saw his mother emerge from the house, wiping her hands on a white towel, her green eyes anxiously fixed on the stranger at the pump. Her long red hair was tied into a ponytail, and she was wearing her yellow blouse and jeans, as well as her knee-high black boots. She stopped at the edge of the porch, still staring at the man in blue.

"Seth . . ." Gail Mason said, her tone sounding worried.

"There's no problem," Seth promptly assured his wife. "Just a man who's thirsty, is all."

The man in blue straightened and nodded at Gail Mason. "Mrs. Mason. You have a fine son and a nice home." He screwed the cap onto the canteen and replaced it in its green case.

Gail frowned as the man retrieved his machine gun.

"Thank you for the water," he said, gazing at each of them in turn. Without another word, he wheeled and walked off.

Adam watched him go, feeling inexplicably upset. He liked this peculiar stranger and wanted to get to know him better, but he knew how his father felt about people they didn't know, which made it all the more surprising when his dad took a few steps forward and raised his right arm.

"Wait a minute!" he shouted.

"Seth!" Adam's mom whispered. "What do you think you're doing?"

Seth glanced at Gail. "Trust me on this, honey." He looked back at the man in blue, who was calmly standing twenty feet away, watching them.

Adam could plainly see his mother was unhappy

about something.

"We're just about to sit down to our midday meal," Seth announced. "We have more than enough. You're welcome to join us, if you'd like."

The man in blue came toward them, his gaze resting the entire time on Adam's mother. He stopped at the pump. I'll join you if it's okay with *you*," he stated directly to Gail Mason.

Adam saw his mom get a funny look in her eyes. She swallowed hard and nodded. "It's fine by me. Just don't track dirt on my carpet." She whirled and entered the house.

The man grinned and motioned for Seth and Adam to precede him up the steps.

Seth took Adam's right hand and led him onto the porch and into their log home, walking to the dinner table, where Gail was waiting with a large dish in her hands.

Adam, perplexed, watched the man in blue cautiously enter the house, acting as if he expected to be attacked. He moved to the left of the door as soon as he was inside, his back to the wall, his machine gun held level with his waist and pointed at one of the bedroom doorways. The man carefully studied every piece of furniture in the room, then crossed to the bedrooms and peered inside both of them, evidently satisfying himself they were empty. He did likewise with the kitchen, then stepped to the head of the dinner table and stood behind the one chair affording a complete view of the main room, the bedroom doorways, and the front door. Adam knew that was the chair his dad usually used, and he wondered why his father didn't say something about it. Instead, his dad took the chair at far end of the table. Adam opted for the chair to the left of the man in blue, leaving his mother the seat on the other side of the table.

"You can have a seat," Gail said. "I'll dish it out for you."

The man sat down, positioning his machine gun in his lap.

"I don't think you've told us your name," Seth politely remarked.

"My name is Yama," the man in blue revealed.

"Yama?" Adam giggled. "That's a weird name! I've never heard that name before."

Adam's mother, in the process of scooping mashed potatoes onto their individual plates, visibly tensed.

"How old are you, Adam?" Yama softly inquired.

Adam sat up, tall and straight. "Eight," he said, trying to deepen his voice as he spoke.

A barely perceptible grin touched Yama's face.

"Adam," Seth stated sharply. "What have I told you about lying?"

Adam squirmed uncomfortably in his chair. "Well, I'll be eight in a month. Isn't that close enough?"

"Close enough for me," Yama commented, watching Gail ladle out some peas. "You certainly are mature for your age, but there's something you haven't learned yet."

"What's that?" Adam questioned.

"That just because something is new or different, something you've never encountered before, doesn't make it weird. A man learns to keep an open mind about things, to rely on his common sense and the guidance of the Spirit within him. Do you understand?"

Adam nodded. "I think so," he replied, as his parents exchanged puzzled expressions. "I'm sorry I made fun of your name, but where did you ever get a name like Yama?"

"I selected it."

"You picked your own name?" Adam inquired incredulously.

Yama nodded, placing his elbows on the table and lacing his fingers together.

"How can you pick your own name?" Adam queried.

"It's a common practice at the place I'm from," Yama explained. "The man who founded, who started, this place a long, long time ago was worried we'd forget what things were like before the Third World War. This man left us a lot of books, a whole library, and we're encouraged to go through these books and select the name we want for a special ceremony."

"Special ceremony?" Adam repeated.

"It's called our Naming. We go through it on the day we turn sixteen. Whatever name we pick, that's how we're known for the rest of our lives. At first, we used only names from the history books, but now we use names from just about any source. My own name, Yama, for instance, comes from a book on the Hindu religion. . . ."

"The what?"

"It comes from the name they gave their King of Death. It wasn't my first choice, but Ares was already taken and I refused to be named after a planet. Yama fits, though. It's higly appropriate, considering my vocation."

Adam's brow was furrowed. "I'm not sure I follow you, Mister Yama."

"Just Yama."

"What's a Hindu?" Adam asked. "And an Ares? Does everybody take a name as strange as yours?"

Yama chuckled. "Not everyone. Some of my closest friends have more normal names. One of them is called Hickok, after a gunfighter who lived way back in the days of the Old West. Another is named Geronimo, after a mighty Indian warrior who refused to knuckle under to oppression. And one of them is known as Rikki-Tikki-Tavi. . . ."

Adam broke into unrestrained laughter. "Rikki . . . what?"

Yama smiled. "Rikki-Tikki-Tavi. He took his name from a story about this animal that defends its home and family from deadly snakes."

"Where are you from, Yama?" Adam wanted to know.

"Food's out," Gail promptly announced. "Adam, don't you disturb . . . Yama . . . while he's eating."

"Ahhhhh, Mom," Adam mumbled, reaching for his fork.

Yama looked at Seth. "Would you do the honor of giving thanks to the Spirit for our sustenance?"

Seth's mouth dropped open for a second, then closed. He glanced at his wife. "There's no way this man can be from the Citadel."

"I am not from the Citadel," Yama assured him.

"But how can we be sure?" Gail asked nervously.

"Is something wrong?" Yama questioned them.

Seth Mason appeared to be in the midst of a momentous decision. He looked from Gail to Adam to Yama, intently staring at the latter as if he were attempting to actually read Yama's mind. Finally, he nodded, closed his eyes, and said their grace. "Lord, we thank you for this meal. We thank you for all of your blessings. We ask that you lead our footsteps daily and preserve us from harm. Amen."

"Amen," Gail added, opening her eyes and gazing at Yama in stark fear.

Seth locked his eyes on Yama. "Well, if you're going to do it, go ahead. Get it over with!"

"Get what over with?"

"Turn us in," Seth said, an edge to his tone. "Kill us. Whatever it is the Doktor sent you to do."

"The Doktor didn't send me," Yama stated gently. "And why would I want to kill you?"

"For giving thanks to our Lord," Seth responded.

"For giving thanks . . ." Yama repeated, and his bewilderment was readily apparent to the other three. "I wasn't informed of this aspect. Explain."

"You don't know?" Seth questioned.

"Know what?"

Seth glanced at Gail. "See? I told you he isn't from the damn Citadel! Now I even doubt he's from the Civilized Zone." He looked at Yama. "Before I say any more, I need to know some things about you. Would you consent to answering a few questions?"

"If I can," Yama promised.

"You've got to understand," Seth went on. "I must be certain about you. I have this gut feeling, but it isn't enough where the safety of my family is concerned." He paused. "Are you from the Citadel?"

"No," Yama replied.

"From the Civilized Zone?"

"No."

The Masons exchanged amazed glances.

"We'd heard there are people out there," Seth said, "but we never expected to meet one. Where are you from?"

"I'm sorry, but I can't reveal that information."

Seth pondered for a moment. "Okay. I won't press the point. But can you at least tell me what you're doing here?"

"If my calculations are correct," Yama answered, choosing his words carefully, "and the map I was provided with is accurate, then I estimate I'm about twenty miles from the Cheyenne Citadel. Is this right?"

"You're nineteen miles northwest of the Citadel," Seth confirmed. "Why?" he added hastily. "You're not thinking of going there, are you?"

"I must."

"Don't do it!" Gail Mason interjected.

Yama looked at her.

"You're crazy if you try to enter the Citadel," she elaborated. "They have guards at all the entry points, and they check the identity of everyone going in. Do you have an identification card?"

"No," Yama admitted.

"Besides," Seth mentioned, smirking, "no one in the entire Civilized Zone wears clothes like yours. You'd stand out like a sore thumb. You'd draw soldiers like carrion draws flies."

Yama sat back in his chair, his eyes narrowed. "Why are you telling me all of this? You live in the Civilized Zone. Aren't you obligated to report my presence to the proper authorities?"

Seth laughed, a bitter, grating sound, devoid of all genuine mirth. "If you only knew! Do you have any idea what it's like living in the Civilized Zone?"

"I've heard some tales," Yama replied. "I stopped here with the hope of learning some more before I go into the Citadel."

"I'll tell you anything you want to know," Seth vowed.

"But why would you . . ." Yama started to speak, then abruptly stopped, his head cocked to one side.

Adam, ingesting all this astounding information in stunned silence, was the first to realize why Yama fell silent. "Listen!" he exclaimed. "The dogs!"

The pair of mixed-breed canines owned by the Masons were barking frantically.

"How did you get past our dogs, Yama?" Adam thought to ask him.

"They were dozing in the sun," Yama detailed. "I didn't want to disturb their beauty rest."

Seth Mason rose and hurriedly walked to one of the two windows in the main room. "Damn! It's a patrol! what are they doing here now?"

Yama rose so swiftly, so unexpectedly, Adam involuntarily jumped.

"If they find you here," Gail said to Yama, "they'll kill you."

"They will try."

Gail nodded her head toward Adam. "They may kill us too."

Adam found Yama's eyes on him for a moment.

"I don't want to pose a danger to your family," Yama stated. "I'll stay out of sight until they're gone."

Seth motioned for Gail to join him. "Let's greet them on the porch. Maybe we can talk them out of coming inside. Adam, you stay in here with Yama and don't you dare make a sound!"

Seth and Gail walked onto the porch, arm in arm.

Yama waved Adam toward the window to the left of the front door while he positioned himself beside the window to the right. Both of the windows were open, as was the wooden front door, although the screen door in front was closed.

Adam crouched below the window sill and cautiously peeked his eyes upward until he could see their front yard: the water pump, the red barn beyond, five of their chickens scratching in the dirt, his parents standing on the front porch, and just rounding the northern corner of the barn a tall soldier in his green uniform, carrying an M-16.

The first soldier was followed by another.

And another.

Horrified, Adam saw six troopers approach the Mason house. What was going on? Why were the soldiers here? They hardly ever came here! The nearest major road was a good ten miles to the south, and Adam's dad had often mentioned how he liked it that way, liked having a small ranch off the beaten track where they could remain free from the Government's constant prying and snooping. Except for infrequent trips into the Citadel for items and supplies the family couldn't produce on its own, and to attend Government-mandated functions and courses of instruction, the Masons avoided the Citadel like the proverbial plague.

So why were the soldiers here?

The six troopers had stopped about ten feet from the front porch. One of them, the tall leader, wore an insignia on his lapels. Little gold bars.

An officer, Adam knew.

"Hello, Lieutenant," Seth Mason welcomed them. "May we help you?"

The Lieutenant turned to one of his men. "Did you hear that? May we help you?"

The troopers all laughed.

Adam heard a sharp clicking noise and glanced over at Yama. The man in blue was doing something to a lever on his machine gun. Satisfied, he quickly crossed to the front door and stood by the right jamb.

The soldiers had all ceased laughing.

Adam, petrified, gazed outside.

The officer was extracting a piece of paper from a pocket on the left side of his shirt.

Adam noticed each of the troopers carried an M-16, but the officer also had an automatic pistol in a holster on his right hip.

"I'm Lieutenant Simms," the officer was saying.

"We're pleased to meet you," Seth said warily.

"That's what you think," Lieutenant Simms retorted. "Is this the Mason's residence?"

"It is," Seth verified.

"And are you Seth Mason?" Lieutenant Simms inquired stiffly.

"Yes, but . . ."

"Is this your wife, Gail?" the officer cut him off.

"Yes."

Adam, terrified, saw the officer point the M-16 at his parents.

"Good," Lieutenant Simms said. "Then by the authority vested in me by Samuel the Second, acting upon the specific directive of the Doktor, for heinous crimes against the State including violating the Biological Imperative, I hereby place you and your entire family officially under arrest and confiscate your property."

"What? You can't!" Adam's father took a step toward the officer.

Lieutenant Simms elevated the barrel of the M-16 until it was aimed at Seth's head. "Make another move, you lousy dirt farmer, and I'll blow your damn head off!"

3

Hickok instinctively blasted the rifleman first, his hands
a blur as they drew the pearl-handled Colt Pythons, his
right Magnum booming, and the rifleman staggered as
the slug penetrated the middle of his forehead and blew
out the back of his head. The man toppled to the ground
as Hickok spun, his left Python cracking, the shot
catching a woman wielding a butcher's knife in her right
eye and spinning her body completely around before she
fell onto her face.

Inside the SEAL, Geronimo clawed at the door
handle. "They're Wacks!" he shouted, flinging the door
open and jumping to the ground, the FNC Auto Rifle
already at his shoulder as he aimed at a line of charging
cannibals and squeezed the trigger. The Auto Rifle
burped, and four of the crazies dropped.

Blade joined the conflict, leaping from the driver's
seat, the A-1 pressed against his right hip as he fired, the
heavy slugs tearing into a group of attacking Wacks and
decimating them in a crimson spray of blood and flesh.

Hickok stood his ground, downing targets as rapidly
as they posed a threat: four, five, six more in swift
succession.

At least eighteen of the Wacks were down, dead or dying, when the remainder opted to retreat, breaking for the nearest cover and disappearing.

Blade and Geronimo joined Hickok and covered him while he reloaded the spent cartridges in his Pythons.

"I never expected to find the Wacks this far north," Blade commented.

"We shouldn't have to bother with finding the Nomads," Geronimo remarked. "All this gunfire will draw their attention and bring them on the run."

Blade nodded. "That's what drew them to us the last time." The four groups in the Twin Cities didn't own too many guns, maybe thirty firearms among them. Invariably, they would send scouting parties to ascertain the source of any firing. "We'll wait in the SEAL for them to arrive."

"What about them?" Hickok asked, nodding at the fallen Wacks, some of whom were still alive, groaning and crying.

"There's nothing we can do for them right now," Blade said. "There might be more of them lurking nearby, or the ones who escaped could be going for reinforcements. We'll play it safe and stay in the transport for the time being."

The three Warriors returned to the vehicle and climbed inside.

"Thank the Spirit only one of them had a gun," Geronimo mentioned. "What did the pathetic fools hope to accomplish using stones and knives and clubs against our firepower?"

"Some folks just never learn," Hickok declared.

Blade turned in his seat and glanced at Joshua. The Empath was gazing sadly at the dead and injured littering the ground, his mouth downturned, his eyes slightly misty. "Are you all right?" Blade asked him.

"Everywhere we go," Joshua said slowly, huskily, "it's the same thing. Killing. Killing and more killing."

"Oh, brother!" Hickok snapped. "Are we going to go through all of this again? It was them or us, Josh. You saw that."

"I realize your alternatives were markedly limited, given the circumstances," Joshua admitted.

"Decent of you, pard," Hickok cracked.

"I just can't become accustomed to all of this slaughter," Joshua said, looking at Hickok in despair. "Back at the Home we live together in harmony and peace, we cultivate spiritual growth and strive to promote loving relationships." He paused. "It's so different out here! Every time we come out into the world, it's the same thing! Someone is always trying to kill us! I've tried to adjust to it, to this survival of the deadliest, but I can't."

"You can't?" Hickok quizzed him. "Or you won't?"

"What do you mean?"

Hickok sighed. "I thought after our run to Thief River Falls and our previous trip to the Twin Cities, after you saw what the real world was like, you were beginning to see the light. Heck, pard, you even wasted some of our enemies yourself. . . ."

"I know," Joshua interrupted. "I know! I've tried to adapt! I really have." He paused. "Sometimes I think I would have preferred living before World War III, before the Big Blast, as we so quaintly call it. At least back then people weren't trying to kill you every chance they got!"

"I'm glad I wasn't born before the Big Blast," Hickok said disagreeing. "I've had some interesting talks with Plato and some of the other Elders about life back then, and I reckon I would have hated it."

"Hated it?" Joshua repeated. "Why?"

"Think back to our schooling days," Hickok said.

"Remember our history classes? We were told that people before the Big Blast couldn't pack their weapons on their person. Remember?"

"I recall it well," Joshua stated.

"It may not make no nevermind to you, pard, being the spiritual type," Hickok pointed out, "but when I heard that little bit of information, I thanked the Spirit I wasn't born way back then. I couldn't imagine not being allowed to strap on my Pythons whenever and wherever I wanted." The gunman frowned. "From what Plato told me, those folks back then were near regulated to death. They had more laws than a mangy dog has fleas! And why do you reckon it was that way? I'll tell you. Plato said there were two big reasons for all those laws. First, the folks back then suffered from a pitiful lack of self-control and discipline. They might have everything in the world they could possibly want, but guess what? They always wanted more. The parents and the kids were all the same. They thought life owed them a living. They thought they could do pretty much as they pleased, and half of them didn't follow half of the laws most of the time anyway. But the leaders kept slappin' on more and more laws to compensate for the absence of self-control on the part of the people." Hickok stopped and looked at Geronimo. "Any sign of movement out there?"

"Nothing," Geronimo answered, his eyes constantly sweeping their surroundings. "You keep talking. This history lesson of yours is . . . fascinating."

"The second reason for all the laws was the quality of leadership they had," Hickok continued. "Plato says they didn't select their leaders based on which one was the wisest, like we do. They voted in leaders based on which one had the cutest smile, the best clothes, or just a name they liked. Plato says they were actually paying these mediocre types thousands and thousands of dollars a year to make laws, and you can bet, when someone's being paid that much money to make laws, that's exactly what they're going to do, whether laws need to be made or not. . . ."

"Say, Blade," Geronimo interjected, "do you suppose we could ask Plato to permit Hickok to teach American History after we return to the Home?"

The gunman disregarded the sarcasm. "One last thing, Josh. You mentioned something about people back then not trying to kill you every chance they got. Well, pard, they didn't have to kill you, because back then they had other, subtler, ways of gettin' you. The ones in control, the ones with all the power, found it real easy to dominate the ordinary folks, what with all the laws they passed. The power-mongers could break you into tiny pieces, could take your home from you and even your own family, and do it all proper and legal-like, and there was nothing you could do about it. Folks back then were forced to conform—to fit into a dictated social mold, as Plato called it—whether they liked the idea or not. Oh, sure, they could buy all the things they wanted, and live in a fancy home, and have kids and all, but only so long as they payed their taxes on time and obeyed all the laws. But try to be different, try to be unique, try to be your own person, and they'd pounce on you quicker than a fox on a rabbit." Hickok shook his head. "No, sir. You can have those times. I'm plumb tickled to be living right here and now!"

Joshua stared out his window, reflecting on the gunfighter's words.

"You know," Geronimo chimed in, "I think that's the longest speech I've ever heard you give."

"I was a mite long-winded," Hickok acknowledged.

"What worries me," Geronimo said gravely, "is that it actually made sense! What do you think, Blade?"

"What worries me," Blade replied, "is that no one has

shown up yet. The Nomads had to hear the gunshots. We're not that far from their camp. Why hasn't someone come? What's going on?"

"Why don't we mosey on over to their camp and take a look-see?" Hickok suggested.

"I love a man who has a way with words," Geronimo said, chuckling.

"Hickok has the right idea," Blade said. "We're here to let these people know the Family has agreed to assist in relocating them in a town near our Home and to help them organize for their departure in the spring. The sooner we get this over with, the sooner we can all get back to the Home and our wives."

"I'm for that!" Geronimo heartily assented.

Blade started the SEAL and drove slowly forward, on the alert for any more Wacks. He was becoming increasingly disturbed by the absence of people, with the notable exception of the Wacks. What had happened? They should have seen someone by now!

As he drove, Blade reminisced. He remembered Hickok and Joshua promising the leaders of the Nomads, the Porns, and the Horns that they would return in a month with word on whether the Elders had accepted the relocation proposal. So what if they were a month or so late? Surely the leaders would have understood and been patient about the delay?

The leaders.

Zahner was the leader of the Nomads, the group in control of northern Minneapolis. The Nomads numbered about two hundred, the smallest of the three main factions.

A man named Bear led the Porns, literally handed the leadership after Hickok had eliminated their former leader. Numbering six hundred or so, the Porns were the largest group, but compared to the Nomads and the

Horns, they were the least organized.

The Horns were headed by Reverend Paul, with approximately four hundred followers based in St. Paul. The men always dressed in black, the women were inevitably modestly attired, and they all practiced a devout lifestyle as befitted their religious beliefs.

The exact population of Wacks was unknown, as was the identity of their new leader, if they had one. Blade had seen their last chief consumed by a mutated monstrosity.

"Do you think it's possible," Geronimo speculated, "the truce broke down, that the sides are at war again?"

"Could be," Hickok concurred. "We took too blasted long getting back here!"

"It wasn't our fault," Blade noted. "The Kalispell thing came up, and then Geronimo had that spot of trouble in South Dakota."

"It's good the Kalispell thing did come up," Geronimo added. "Otherwise, we might never have found the medical and scientific items Plato needed. As it is, because we did locate the equipment in Kalispell, we won't need to bother looking here in the Twin Cities. We can concentrate on the matter at hand and get to the Home that much faster."

"What do you intend to do about Bertha?" Blade asked Hickok.

"I thought we dropped that subject earlier," the gunman said bristling.

"I'm only asking as your friend," Blade emphasized. "You know that."

"Reckon I do," Hickok grumbled, "but I still wish everybody would stop bringing her up. Fact is, I'm not sure how to handle her. I've never had a problem like this before, and I sure as blazes never want one like it again!"

"Suit yourself," Blade said.

Hickok lapsed into moody silence, contemplating his problem. How the dickens was he going to tell a woman who loved him, Bertha, that while he was gone he had up and married another woman? With Bertha's personality and temperament, she might put a knife into his gut out of sheer spite!

How'd he ever get into this blasted fix?

Alpha Triad had rescued Bertha from some soldiers stationed in Thief River Falls. Bertha, a resident of the Twin Cities and one of the Nomads, had tried to find an escape route from the former metropolis. The soldiers from the Civilized Zone—the Watchers, as the people in the Twin Cities referred to them—had had the city bottled up, with troops stationed at strategic points along all the primary arteries. Zahner, the Nomad leader, had sent Bertha, one of his best fighters, to attempt to locate a way out of the Twin Cities and away from the incessant warfare among the different groups. She had been captured by the soldiers and was being held at Thief River Falls when Alpha Triad had saved her. Refusing to return to the Twins, she had gone with Alpha Triad back to their Home. Later, she had changed her mind and accompanied the Warriors and Joshua on their initial foray into the Twin Cities. She had been injured and Hickok had last seen her lying in a tent, bandaged, recovering from her wound but emotionally distraught over his aloofness.

But who could blame him for being aloof?

Hickok wasn't proud of his actions, but he'd had little choice. First, Bertha liked him far more than he liked her. Not that he didn't care for her, because he did, but more as a close friend than a lover. Secondly, he had been on the rebound, having lost a woman he did deeply love during a battle in Fox, Minnesota. He simply hadn't been ready for another heavy romance, not then anyway. And finally, he had learned that Bear, the man he had installed as Porn leader, was in love with Bertha and wanted her to become his mate.

So who could blame him for walking out on Bertha?

Who could blame him for finding someone else, a woman he did truly love?

Who could blame him for marrying this woman?

Bertha. That was who.

Who was he kidding? Bertha wasn't the type to take news like this in stride.

So how should he handle it? He wasn't all that experienced with women, and the prospect of hurting her distressed him. Blowing away an enemy was one thing; causing profound grief to a friend was another.

Hickok sighed.

There had to be a painless way of . . .

Blade slammed on the brakes so hard the entire transport lurched violently.

Hickok placed his hands on the dashboard to brace himself. "What the blazes are you doing?" he demanded.

"Look," Blade replied, nodding.

Hickok did.

The roadway ahead was covered with bodies, dozens of them.

"Dear Father!" Joshua exclaimed. "What could have happened?"

"We're going to take a look," Blade said, turning off the ignition. "Joshua, remain in the SEAL with the doors locked."

"But . . ." Joshua started to object.

"Do as I say!" Blade ordered. He glanced at Hickok and Geronimo. "Ready?"

"I was born ready," Hickok responded.

Geronimo nodded.

The three warriors cautiously emerged from the vehicle and advanced along the highway. Tall trees and shrubbery lined both sides of the road.

"Good spot for an ambush," Hickok observed.

"Looks like somebody already had that idea," Geronimo stated.

Blade could hear the wind rustling the leaves of the nearby trees. He cradled the A-1 in his huge arms, ready to react to the slightest sound or movement.

"Nothing to our rear but the SEAL," Geronimo declared, covering their flank.

They reached the bodies.

"What a mess!" Hickok commented. "Looks like somebody caught them in a cross fire."

The prone forms were shot to pieces; men, women, and even children were each perforated with multiple bullet holes.

"Doesn't look like they had a chance," Hickok deduced. "This guy still has a rifle slung over his shoulder. It must have happened so fast he didn't have time to bring the rifle into play."

Geronimo knelt and studied one of the bodies. "Couldn't have happened more than forty-eight hours ago, probably closer to thirty-six."

"Do you notice anything else?" Blade asked them.

"Like what?" Hickok answered.

Blade nudged a man dressed in black with the toe of his right moccasin. "I count fifty-two bodies. This one, from the way he's dressed, is obviously a Horn. Look at this other one, the one wearing the beads and the outlandish hair style. I could be wrong, but I'd guess that this one is a Porn."

"Horns and Porns together?" Hickok said skeptically. "I know there was a truce in effect, but they still weren't too fond of each other. What gives?"

"And what about the animals?" Geronimo brought up.

"The animals?" Hickok repeated.

"Yeah. Look at the bodies. None of them have been touched by the animals. There are a lot of wild animals in the Twin Cities, not to mention all of the rats. Why haven't some of them taken a few bites out of the corpses?"

"Something scared the animals off," Blade reasoned.

"Like what?" Geronimo queried.

"Your guess is as good as mine," Blade replied.

Hickok gazed at the body of a little girl with blonde curls and a ragged cavity where her left cheek had been. "So what do we have here? Horns and Porns and possibly Nomads together, which is downright peculiar. From the position of most of the bodies, I'd say they were trying to head out of the Twin Cities when they were ambushed from both sides. Whoever did this never heard of the word mercy."

"Do we keep going?" Geronimo questioned Blade.

"We gave our word to these people," Blade stated. "When the Family gives its word, it keeps it."

"If you want to get technical," Geronimo said, "it was Hickok who gave his word on behalf of the whole Family. We could just leave and send them a post card explaining that Hickok is off his rocker and no one should ever believe a word he says."

"I don't rightly know what a post card is," Hickok retorted, "but I do know when I've been insulted. Again."

"You're improving!" Geronimo grinned.

"We keep going," Blade directed. He wheeled and strode to the SEAL.

Joshua unlocked the doors to admit them. "Any idea

what hapened to all of those people?"

"None," Blade admitted.

"Where's your M-16, Josh?" Hickok asked as he slid into his seat.

"In the back," Joshua revealed.

"Better get it and make sure it's loaded," Hickok advised.

"I'd rather not," Joshua stated distastefully.

"Do it," Blade commanded, turning the engine over. He drove to the right, along the shoulder of the highway, avoiding the bodies. Once past the last of the corpses, he resumed driving on the pitted, cracked road surface.

"Where we headed, pard?" Hickok wanted to know.

"Same destination," Blade revealed. "Moore Lake. That's where the Nomads were camped, last we knew."

"Take a left here," Geronimo advised, consulting their map. "This is 61st Avenue. It should take us almost to the north shore of the lake."

Blade complied, his gray eyes continuously roving over the vegetation on both sides of the road. The SEAL's bulletproof structure would protect them from an ambush, but there was no sense in taking needless risks. He followed 61st Avenue until he glimpsed Moore Lake, and then left the roadway on a straight beeline to the water, the SEAL's gargantuan tires crushing every obstacle in their path.

The others were quiet, expectant, and tense, on guard for any trouble.

Blade hugged the shoreline as he cruised around the lake.

"No sign of any wildlife," Geronimo mentioned.

"Someone, or something, has been through this area not long ago," Hickok speculated.

"I've been thinking about those bodies," Geronimo commented, "about why the animals haven't eaten them yet. The only thing I can think of that would scare off all the animals over a prolonged period would be steady traffic on the highway or . . ."

"Or frequent, periodic traffic on the highway," Blade finished for him.

"You've been thinking the same thing I've been thinking," Geronimo said.

"Sure have," Blade confirmed.

"I don't understand," Joshua stated. "What do you mean?"

Hickok looked at the Empath. "They mean patrols, Josh. Regular patrols passing along the highway would scare off all the critters."

"You too?" Geronimo asked Hickok.

"Yep, pard. Me too."

"We'll know soon enough," Blade announced. "I just caught sight of some tents about a quarter-mile ahead."

All four of them focused on the terrain ahead as the transport bypassed a clump of boulders, circumvented a stand of trees, and arrived at their destination, a large field with a dozen tents situated in its center.

Blade braked the SEAL.

"There's no sign of life," Geronimo noted, his exceptionally keen eyesight permitting him to scrutinize the campsite closely. "Nothing. Just the tents."

"Possibly the Nomads decided to move their camp elsewhere," Joshua guessed.

Hickok laughed sarcastically. "Oh, sure, Josh. They moved their camp, but left all those tents behind!"

Blade eased the vehicle forward. He spotted a flock of ducks floating in Moore Lake. The scene seemed normal enough, except for the conspicious absence of the Nomads. Where could they have gone? What had happened to Zahner and Bertha?

The strong westerly breeze was intensifying as Blade

brought the SEAL to a complete stop and turned the transport off. He turned and stared at Joshua. "We're going to investigate. You will stay inside. . . ."

"But . . ." Joshua began.

Blade held aloft his right hand for silence. "I'm tired of giving you an order, Joshua, and having you object every time I do. Believe it or not, I have valid reasons for the orders I give. So when I tell you to stay put in the SEAL, you will damn well stay put in the SEAL! Understand?"

Joshua sheepishly nodded his assent.

"Do you see what happens when a man is denied some lovin' and affection for a couple of days?" Hickok asked Geronimo, grinning. "He gets all cranky with his pards."

"I think the poor boy needs a cold bath," Geronimo said joining in the sarcasm. "Hey! Maybe he'd like to take a dunk in Moore Lake?"

"Great idea!" Hickok enthused. "He could splash around with the little duckies! He'd feel right at home. He's as quackers as they are!"

The gunman laughed uproariously at his own joke, while Geronimo hid his face in his hands and shook his head.

"As I was saying," Blade resumed, his eyes twinkling with suppressed mirth as he looked at Joshua, "you will stay in the SEAL with the doors locked. If anything happens to us, get the SEAL back to the Home."

"But I've never driven it before," Joshua noted.

"A little practice and you'll get the hang of it," Blade told him. "Now this next part is very important. Under no circumstances whatsoever are you to open these doors for anyone but us. Do you understand that?"

"I understand."

"Are you positive?" Blade pressed him. "You must

not open the doors for anyone else, no matter who it might be. Do I have your word as a spiritual son of the Universal Spirit that you will obey me?"

"There's no need for that," Joshua said.

"Do I have your word?" Blade stressed.

"You have my word," Joshua pledged.

"Good." Blade looked at Hickok and Geronimo. "If you two are through making like Laurel and Hardy, let's go!" He opened his door and climbed from the transport.

"Who the blazes are Laurel and Hardy?" Hickok inquired as he followed Blade's lead.

"I saw a picture book on them in the Family Library," Geronimo clarified as he joined Hickok on the grass. "Laurel and Hardy were comedians way back when. They starred in something called movies. One of them was fat and the other one was thin."

"So which one am I?" Hickok demanded.

Blade walked around the SEAL and glared at them. "What the hell is the matter with you nitwits? In case you forgot, we're in hostile territory! And here you two are, arguing over which one of you is the fattest?"

"He weighs more than I do," Hickok mumbled.

"I do not," Geronimo rejoined.

Blade shook his head. "Married life has made you sloppy!" He turned and scanned the tents. Except for a few of the tent flaps whipping in the wind, all was quiet and deceptively peaceful. "Where is everyone?" he asked, half to himself.

Geronimo and Hickok were all business now. Geronimo walked a few yards toward the lake and knelt, examining the soft earth. Hickok covered them with his Henry.

"Some tracks here," Geronimo declared. "From the look of them, I'd say they were made by big vehicles, even larger than the SEAL. Probably not more than thirty-six hours ago."

"About the same time frame as the ambush back there," Blade observed.

"Think there's a connection?" Hickok questioned him.

"Could be," Blade responded, stepping toward the nearest of the tents. "Move out. Each of you take a tent. There may be a clue inside one of them as to what happened here, maybe something that will tell us where the Nomads went."

The three Warriors separated, each making for a different tent.

Blade approached the tent with supreme caution. The tent was old, patched in several spots, and constructed of a faded canvas. The wind was causing the flap to wave back and forth, almost like a giant hand beckoning Blade to enter. He spotted the remnant of a campfire about four feet from the tent flap, the ashes obviously cold and gray.

What *had* happened here?

Blade used the barrel of his A-1 to open the tent flap all the way as he stepped inside. In the instant it took his eyes to adjust to the subdued lighting, the muzzles of three M-16's were shoved within an inch of his face.

"Not one move!" barked a harsh voice. "If you try to resist, my men will do to your brains what I like to do to my eggs—scramble them!"

4

Adam Mason felt a tight knot in his stomach as the officer took several steps toward his father and mother, still training his M-16 on them.

"There must be some mistake!" Seth was saying.

"There was, all right," Lieutenant Simms growled, "and you were the asshole who made it!"

"There's no need to talk like that in front of my wife!" Seth said bristling.

Lieutenant Simms chuckled. "Where you're going, fellow, rude language will be the least of your worries."

"But why?" Seth demanded. "Aren't we entitled to know the specifics of the charges against us?"

The officer gazed at one of his men. "It's always the same, isn't it? They always have to know! As if they didn't already!"

"We haven't broken any laws!" Seth countered.

Lieutenant Simms lowered his M-16 and glanced at the paper in his hand. "You can act ignorant all you want to, farmer, but it won't do you any good."

"Please, officer," Adam's mother pleaded, "won't you tell us the reason for the charges?"

Simms sneered. "I'll humor you, lady, only because

48

you and I are going to have some serious fun later. But you know and I know you both are as guilty as they come!"

"Of what?" Seth demanded brusquely.

"Are you, or are you not, on the circuit of Dr. Nevins?" the officer asked them.

"Yes, we are," Seth answered.

"Then you admit that Dr. Nevins is your family physician?"

"He has been for years," Seth replied. "He comes around on his circuit about every six months and gives us our required physical. Why?"

"Yes, the good Dr. Nevins was efficient, wasn't he?" Lieutenant Simms said sarcastically.

"Was?" Seth asked.

"Don't you have a boy around here somewhere?" Simms asked. "By the name of Adam, according to the record?"

"He's around here somewhere," Seth responded. "Probably out playing in the fields."

"How convenient," the officer sarcastically snapped. "And didn't Dr. Nevins deliver the boy?"

"Yes, he did," Seth admitted, his voice lowering, sounding less defiant.

"Looks like the wind is going out of your sails," Simms said gloating. "You know what I'm getting at, don't you? Of course you do." He snickered, then turned markedly serious. "Quick! What is the requirement of the Biological Imperative, Section 10, Subsection C, paragraphs nineteen through twenty-one?"

"I'm not sure," Seth said uncertainly.

"Not sure? All citizens of the State are required to be completely familiar with all of its laws and regulations. Is this not so?"

"Yes," Seth replied, averting his eyes.

"I say you do know," Simms declared. "You knew what it was about eight years ago when Nevins delivered your brat. You knew damn well that every baby born with Type O blood, by law, must be reported to the Bilogical Center in Cheyenne! You knew damn well that the Doktor personally issued that directive! And you knew if you did report the birth, you'd never see your brat again! That's why it was never reported!"

"What proof do you have?" Gail Mason requested.

"The lady wants proof?" Lieutenant Simms snickered again and some of his men did likewise. "We have all the proof we need, bitch! An informant told us about kindly Dr. Nevins, how he was falsifying his records, how he wasn't reporting all the babies with Type O blood. The fool! Did he think he could get away with it forever? Well, we interrogated Dr. Nevins three days ago. Of course, he denied all of the allegations. But the moron kept a secret set of records at his home, hidden behind one of the walls in his study. We found it, and guess what? Guess whose name we found under one of the entries? Guess who gave birth to a baby boy with Type O blood and it was never reported to the Doktor? Guess!" Simms roared.

"Oh, Dear God!" Gail exclaimed.

"God?" Simms bellowed. "There is no God! Believing in a deity is also against the law! You know that!" He looked at his men. "If they keep opening their lousy mouths, by the time we get to the Citadel, we should have a list of charges against them as long as my arm!"

His men tittered.

Adam was absolutely petrified. What should he do to help his parents? What *could* he do? Maybe Yama would . . .

Yama was gone.

Adam gaped at the spot where he'd last seen the man in blue, wondering where he'd gone? Had he run away? Was that it? Somehow, he didn't think Yama was the kind of man to run away from trouble.

"Okay! Enough of the fun and games!" Lieutenant Simms raised his M-16. "Get your asses off that porch this instant! Keep your arms up, or you'll get a new navel!"

Adam held his breath as his father and mother began to move from the porch to the grass. They were on the second of the three stairs when a new voice was heard.

"If you are an example of the quality of military leadership in the Army of Samuel the Second," stated a voice Adam recognized, "then Samuel should consider tightening his recruitment standards."

By shifting his position, and aligning his eyes with the lower left corner of the window, Adam could see Yama standing calmly at the northwestern corner of the log house, his machine gun held loosely in his hands.

At the first sound of Yama's statement, the soldiers had immediately shifted, their astonishment plainly evident, their M-16's at their sides, taken completely unawares.

"Who the hell are you?" Lieutenant Simms demanded, finally able to make his voice function.

"Death."

"Death?" Simms reiterated, thinking the stranger was making some kind of joke.

"Yes, Death," Yama affirmed. "See?" He brazenly turned, enabling the troopers to see the silhouette of the skull on the back of his shirt, and then promptly faced them again, a thin smile on his lips.

"If this is your idea of a joke, buddy," Lieutenant Simms retorted, "it's going to get you in a heap of trouble."

"You have it backwards," Yama said.

"What do you mean by that?" Lieutenant Simms angrily inquired.

"*You* are in a heap of trouble," Yama clarified for him.

"Us? There's six of us!" The officer laughed. "You must be crazy! Drop that gun! Now!"

"I'd prefer it if you would drop yours," Yama told him.

"I'm not playing games!" Lieutenant Simms threatened. "What do you think you can probably do against all of us?"

"Kill you," Yama replied, crouching and leveling his machine gun, moving faster than a striking snake.

Adam heard the metallic chatter of Yama's gun and saw two of the soldiers, the ones nearest the man in blue, torn apart by the shattering impact of the heavy slugs ripping into their chests and abdomens.

The four surviving soldiers instantly returned Yama's fire, but he was already gone, leaping from sight behind the corner of the house.

"Damn!" Simms fumed, swinging his M-16 to cover the Masons again. "Damn! Who the hell was he?" he snapped, glaring at Seth.

Adam's dad shrugged. "We don't really know," he confessed.

"Bet me!" Simms shouted. He glanced at a stocky trooper to his right. "Harris! Take Morgan and track down the son of a bitch!"

"Do you want him alive or dead?" Harris inquired.

"Waste the bastard!" Simms ordered, his face contorted with the intensity of his fury.

Harris nodded and led Morgan, a young soldier with straw-colored hair, at a trot around the southwestern corner of the house.

Adam dropped to the floor, wondering what he should do next. His parents appeared to be okay for the moment, but Yama was in deadly danger. Those two men after him looked like they meant business!

He just had to see what would happen!

Adam scurried across the hardwood floor, scuffing his knees, and into his bedroom. He saw his window wide open and realized how Yama had exited the log home undetected. An oaken chest was directly under the window, and Adam climbed on top of the chest to peer out the window, keeping his body below the sill except for his eyes.

About an acre behind the house was kept cleared of all brush and used as the backyard. Several trees had been left standing to provide shade and a break against the wind. One of those trees was an old elm tree with a trunk almost four feet in diameter, situated only twenty feet from Adam's window.

There was no sign of Yama.

Adam detected movement out of the corner of his right eye and saw the two soldiers come into view, advancing cautiously, their M-16's at the ready as they searched for the man in blue.

Where was Yama?

The stocky soldier suddenly tapped his companion on the left arm and pointed at the base of the elm tree.

Why?

Adam followed their line of vision and couldn't believe what he discovered: Yama's machine gun was propped against the trunk of the tree, leaning at an angle!

The troopers were now walking slowly toward the tree, rightfully suspecting a trap. They separated as they neared the tree, and then both of them sprinted around opposite sides of the trunk simultaneously.

Adam tensed, expecting to hear the sound of their

M-16's blasting Yama to shreds. Instead, the soldiers looked disappointed as they moved over to Yama's machine gun and the stocky one bent over to retrieve the weapon.

What was going on?

Adam couldn't comprehend any of this.

The younger soldier abruptly looked directly above his head and started to bring the barrel of his M-16 up, but he was too late.

Yama plummeted from concealment in the branches of the tree, his unusual sword grasped by the hilt with both hands, and swung the long, curved blade downward even as he dropped.

Adam involuntarily gasped as the blade sliced into the young trooper's face, splitting it open from the forehead to the chin, blood gushing from the cavity and flowing copiously over the soldier's neck and chest.

The stocky trooper, Harris, was trying to straighten, his M-16 rising, when Yama wrenched his blade free from the young trooper and swung the sword much like Adam would swing his baseball bat when playing with his parents or some of the neighbor children. The curved blade caught Harris in the neck, in the throat, nearly decapitating him; his head flopped to one side, blood gushing from his severed arteries and veins, and he fell to the ground.

Adam watched as Yama wiped his sword clean on the back of the younger trooper's shirt. The man in blue scooped up his machine gun, replaced his peculiar blade in its scabbard, and ran off to the right, out of Adam's sight.

Where was he going now?

Adam crawled from his room and back to the window in the living room he'd peered through before, the one to the left of the front door. He could hear someone speaking as he rose to his knees.

". . . get this friend of yours," the officer was telling Adam's parents, "and then we'll take you to the Citadel for a personal interview with the Doktor. That's quite an honor. Not many get to meet the Doktor personally. Of course, not many live to tell about it afterwards, either." He snickered.

"What do you think is taking Harris and Morgan so long?" inquired the only remaining soldier anxiously.

Lieutenant Simms glanced at the southwestern corner of the house. "They should have found him by now, shouldn't they?" He nervously began chewing on his lower lip. "Maybe we should get out of here while the getting is good. We can come back with reinforcements and take care of that bastard in blue!"

"What about them?" the last trooper asked, indicating the Masons.

"Yeah. What about them? It's all their fault. They should pay the penalty for violating the laws of the State." Simms glared at Seth and Gail, fingering the trigger on his M-16.

Adam felt sweat on his palms, knowing the officer was going to shoot his parents. Where was Yama?

There was the grating pop of a single shot, and the other soldier grunted as his forehead blew out, ejecting a shower of blood and bits of flesh over the grass.

Adam saw Lieutenant Simms whirl, facing the southwestern corner of the house.

No one was there.

Simms covered the Masons again. "Where are you? I know you can hear me! You'd better come out in the open, where I can see you, or I'll waste the dirt farmer and his wife! Now!"

Adam held his breath, fearing Yama would expose himself to the officer's gun and be shot on sight.

"You have ten seconds!" Simms bellowed.

Still no Yama.

"Five seconds!" Lieutenant Simms shouted.

"I won't need that long," said a quiet voice, coming from the northwestern corner of the house.

Adam craned his neck.

Yama was standing near the corner, his machine gun trained on the officer.

"You shoot me," Simms told him, "and I can guarantee you I'll take them with me before I drop!"

Seth had his left arm around his wife and was holding Gail close to his body, as if sheltering her.

"Looks like we have a draw," Simms said.

"Would you like to settle it?" Yama questioned him.

"Like how?" Simms demanded.

"We put our weapons on the ground and finish it man to man," Yama proposed.

Lieutenant Simms grinned. "I like your style, stranger. If that's the way you want it, why not?"

"After you," Yama stated.

"Do I look nuts?" Simms retorted.

"Then on the count of three," Yama said. "One."

Adam observed the two men slowly crouch.

"Two."

Yama set his machine gun on the grass and Simms did likewise with his M-16.

"Three."

Both men released their grips and stood.

"And now the handguns," Yama directed. "One."

Again they followed the same cautious procedure.

"Two."

Yama laid his revolver and pistol on the ground as Simms placed his automatic at his feet.

"Three."

The men stood.

"What about that sword and knife of yours?" the officer queried. "I'm not carrying a blade."

Yama unfastened his leather belt and dropped the sword and survival knife.

Lieutenant Simms was grinning like a crafty fox after a successful raid on a chicken coop. He took two steps toward the man in blue. "Aren't you a bit curious about why I accepted your cockamamie idea?"

Yama shook his head.

"Well, you should be," Simms said.

Adam saw the officer position his body in some sort of weird squat, his legs at a slant to his torso.

"Three years running," Simms revealed, "I was regimental champ in hand-to-hand. Black belt."

Yama seemed unimpressed by the revelation. He advanced toward the officer until he was four feet away, then he too dropped into an odd crouch and held his hands in front of his body, his fingers forming rigid claws.

"So!" Simms was smiling. "You've had some training! Good. I wouldn't want this to be too easy!"

"It won't be," Yama assured him.

Lieutenant Simms suddenly made a grunting sound and swept his left foot up, aiming at Yama's head.

His movements smooth and coordinated, Yama stepped to one side, avoiding the leg blow, and spun, his own left leg lashing out and catching Simms in the stomach.

The officer doubled over and hastily backpedaled, quickly regaining his composure.

"Not bad," Lieutenant Simms commented.

Yama didn't respond.

Simms, irritated, unleased a series of sweeping kicks, none of which landed. Yama parried them with his forearms, giving ground slightly as Simms pressed his assault.

Adam was astonished. He'd never seen anyone fight like these two were doing.

They were standing still again, both in unusual postures. The officer appeared to be somewhat worried.

"You're a real bag of tricks, aren't you?" Simms quipped. "Now that I'm warmed up, what say we get this fiasco over with?"

The next flurry was almost too quick for Adam to keep track of. He could tell Simms was desperately attempting to break Yama's guard using a fascinating combination of hand and foot strikes, not one of which seemed to do any good. Yama, however, was backing off as he deftly blocked the blows. He abruptly found his back against the house.

Simms, winded, had stopped for a moment. "No place to go, eh?" he taunted. "Too bad. Any last words you'd like engraved on your tombstone?"

Yama still didn't answer.

Simms tried a combination strike, his left leg flicking out at the same instant his right hand, the fingers extended and hard, lanced toward Yama's throat.

Adam saw Yama twist his lower body, dodging the leg, as his left forearm came around in a half-circle and deflected the hand blow. Before the officer could recover his balance, Yama drove his right hand out and up, his fingers in a paw-like shape, driving it into the officer's nose.

There was a loud crunching noise and Simms staggered, crimson spurting from his collapsed nasal passages.

Yama never gave him a chance. The man in blue brought both of his hands close to his chest, the fingers forming into steely claws. He lunged, savagely sweeping upward, the heels of his palms slamming against his opponent's chin and forcefully snapping his head back.

Adam clearly heard a cracking sound.

Lieutenant Simms stiffened and took one giant, lurching step before crashing to the ground.

Yama walked to his weapons and reclaimed them.

Adam rose and ran outside, into his father's arms, hugging him close as his mom put her arms around both of them. "I thought they would kill you!" Adam exclaimed, tears filling his eyes.

"They would have, eventually," Seth replied, "if not for Yama." He gazed at the man in blue. "I don't know how I'll ever be able to thank you."

Yama walked up to the porch. "You're not out of the woods yet."

"What does he mean?" Gail inquired.

"He means more soldiers will come," Seth said.

"You really think so?" Gail questioned.

Seth stared thoughtfully at the fallen soldiers. "These men were obviously attached to the Biological Center, perhaps even auxiliaries in the Doktor's Genetic Research Division. Who knows? One thing is for certain: they were acting under direct orders. That means there are others who are aware of what we did. When this patrol fails to return on time, they'll send another one. Maybe even one of the Doktor's genetic deviates will come. We wouldn't last two seconds!" He sighed. "We can't remain here."

"You mean," Gail said in shock, the realization beginning to dawn on her, "we have to leave our home?"

"We've been waiting for this to happen since the day Adam was born," Seth stated. "We knew the risk we were taking, but what choice did we have? We weren't about to turn our infant son over to that madman. We knew we were going against the State and violating the Biological Imperative. That officer was right all the time."

"Why do they want babies?" Yama asked.

Seth's eyes danced with his smoldering hatred as he answered. "They don't want all babies, only those with Type O blood. The one who wants them is the Doktor, damn his soul to hell!"

"Why?"

"We don't know the real reason," Seth replied. "We've only heard rumors, horrible stories of him drinking their blood."

"The Doktor drinks blood?"

"I know it's hard to believe," Seth admitted, "but that's what we've heard. No one knows for sure because very few go into the Biological Center and come out again. Only those on official business are permitted entry."

"So what will you do now?" Yama queried.

"I wish I knew," Seth said forlornly.

"Could you stay with relatives or friends?" Yama suggested.

"The Government would find us," Seth explained. "They have extensive dossiers on every single citizen. They know who all of my relatives and closest friends are. There isn't a place in the Civilized Zone where we'd be safe."

"Then why not leave the Civilized Zone?"

Seth stared at Yama. "What did you have in mind?"

"Why not come to live with my people?" Yama proposed. "We would be happy to have you, believe me."

"Leave the Civilized Zone?" Gail asked, anguish in her tone.

"What other choice do we have?" Seth countered.

"I don't know," Gail said absently, "but there has to be another way! We couldn't live out there!"

"*He* does," Seth reminded her, pointing at Yama. "So do his people. If they do it, so can we."

Gail looked at Yama. "We've heard such terrible tales about life beyond the Civilized Zone! Are they true?"

"I don't know what you've heard," Yama stated, "and I'll be the first to admit that life isn't easy, but you'll be secure at the place I live, I can promise you that. You'll find many new friends and Adam will have dozens of new playmates."

'I don't know. . . ." Gail said doubtfully.

"Where do you live?" Seth asked Yama. "How far is it from here?"

"I'd like to answer your questions," Yama replied. "I really would. For the time being, though, I'd better not, just in case you're captured before my business here is finished. I will tell you my Home is hundreds of miles from your ranch."

"Hundreds of miles!" Gail exclaimed. "We'd never make it!"

"How did you get here?" Seth demanded.

"In a jeep my people confiscated from some of your soldiers who no longer had any use for it," Yama detailed. "It took me a while to learn the intricacies of driving, and we have to siphon additional gasoline from other confiscated vehicles, but the trip itself was relatively easy. I did encounter a few difficulties, but," he patted his machine gun, "they weren't too hard to handle."

"Could your jeep hold all of us?" Seth wanted to know.

"It could," Yama confirmed. "We'd need to travel light to conserve our fuel, but we could do it." He glanced at Gail Mason. "Don't worry. We won't get lost. My maps are accurate, and you'd be surprised at how light the traffic is."

"Did you run into many soldiers?" Seth inquired.

"No. As a matter of fact, for most of the trip I didn't see another vehicle. The highways, or what's left of them a century after the War, are still serviceable. There are collapsed and buckled sections, but we'll bypass them."

"What about the checkpoints?" Gail asked Yama. "We know the Army has checkpoints on all of the roads and highways into the Civilized Zone."

"The primary weakness of checkpoints," Yama said, "is their distinct lack of mobility. A good pair of binoculars and a two-mile detour over the countryside will overcome any checkpoint."

"You seem to have an answer for everything," Gail stated somewhat defensively.

"I'm still working on the meaning of life." Yama grinned.

"Answer me this," Seth requested. "You mentioned you have business to finish here. Are you still planning to go into the Citadel?"

"I must."

"You'll be killed!" Gail warned him.

"I have no option."

"We can't talk you out of going into the Citadel?" Seth queried.

"I must venture into the Citadel," Yama reiterated.

"Well, then let me draw you a sketch of the inside of the city," Seth offered. "It might come in handy once you're inside."

"You go ahead. I'll be right with you after I complete a necessary chore," Yama said.

"Chore?" Gail asked.

Yama indicated the bodies of the soldiers. "They need to be buried."

"I'll lend you a hand, Yama," Seth stated. "I've got some shovels in the barn. I'll be right back."

Seth walked toward their barn.

Gail, emotionally distraught, nervously rubbed her hands on her legs. "I think I'll clear the table. I don't think any of us are in the mood for food now anyway." She turned and entered the house.

Yama gazed at the boy. "You've been very quiet."

Adam nodded. "I've been thinking."

"About what?"

Adam pointed at the dead officer. "I think I've figured out why you named yourself after that King of Death."

Yama's expression became somber. "Very perceptive. Dealing in death is my business, Adam. I'm responsible for helping to protect the people at my Home, and this means I've had to perfect the craft of killing to a fine art. Yama is a fitting name."

"I've never met anyone like you," the boy said.

"There are others like me," Yama informed him, "at the place where I live. I'm not unique."

Adam stared at Yama in wonder, his youthful eyes brimming with unrestrained hero worship. "I'm going to be just like you when I grow up." He smiled, wheeled, and walked into the house.

Yama's face tightened as he strolled over to the deceased Simms. They were about the same size. He'd be able to wear the uniform when he entered the Cheyenne Citadel.

A crow cawing overhead arrested his attention.

This spying mission wasn't proceeding precisely according to plan. Plato wanted him to learn as much as possible about the Citadel and the nefarious Doktor. The Family required the information if they were to successfully combat the efforts by the Doktor and Samuel the Second to eliminate them. Realistically, the best method to acquire the desired data was to physically enter the Citadel. A question formed in his mind, unbidden, disturbing his equanimity:

Would he be able to get out again once he was inside? Only time would tell.

5

For an instant, Blade considered resisting, weighing the likelihood of downing the men in the tent before they plugged him. The probability factor was markedly slim. He allowed one of the soldiers to take his A-1 from him.

"It's nice to see you have some intelligence to go with all those muscles," commented the speaker with the harsh voice, a burly figure in a green uniform with gold clusters on his lapels.

A commotion erupted outside. There was the muffled blast of a solitary shot, the sounds of a struggle, someone shouting, "Get him!" and a loud thump.

"Outside!" barked the burly officer, and the three troopers covering Blade backed him out of the tent.

Blade noticed Geronimo standing in front of another tent, his hands in the air, surrounded by three more soldiers.

The officer was staring at a third tent. "Captain Rice! Any problems?"

The flap to the third tent opened and four soldiers emerged, three of them bearing an unconscious Hickok in their arms.

Blade started to move toward them, and the barrel of

an M-16 was pressed against his left temple.

"Don't move, buddy!" advised the trooper with the weapon.

Captain Rice, a lean man with a wisp of a moustache and a crooked nose, approached the first officer and saluted. "No problems, Colonel."

"What was all that noise?" the colonel demanded.

"We followed your instructions to the letter," Captain Rice explained. "Incredibly, the fool went for his guns! Three M-16's in his face and he went for his Pythons!"

"And the shot?" the colonel inquired, staring at Hickok.

"I couldn't believe it," Captain Rice stated, amazed. "The man is the fastest on the draw I've ever seen. He actually managed to clear leather before one of my men slugged him over the head. He even got off a shot. He's tricky, Colonel, real tricky. He handed over his rifle, no problem, but while I was taking it from him, momentarily distracted, he drew the Colts. Private MacLean jarred his arms as he fired, as MacLean tried to grab him, and the shot missed me by an inch. It was close. Real close."

The colonel grinned. "Hickok always did have more courage than brains." He turned and faced Blade. "Isn't that right, Blade?" he asked, pleased by the look of surprise flitting across the huge Warrior's features. "I should introduce myself. I am Colonel Jarvis. Does that name ring a bell?"

"Should it?" Blade responded.

"Possibly not, although I thought it might. You see," Colonel Jarvis said, putting his left hand on Blade's right shoulder in a deceptively friendly gesture, "I'm in charge of this district. You may recall running into some of my men in Thief River Falls? A few of them escaped and reported your activities there. You do remember what you did to my unit in Thief River Falls?"

Blade felt the colonel's sturdy fingers dig into his flesh, and he was impressed by the officer's strength. "Were those your men we went up against? They weren't very professional," he said baiting Jarvis.

"Oh, they were professional, all right," Jarvis rejoined. "But they made the crucial mistake of underestimating your abilities. I won't make that same mistake, I assure you."

"You did already," Blade taunted him, nodding at Hickok.

Jarvis's eyes narrowed as he gazed at the gunman. "Hickok is difficult to predict. He never does what you'd expect him to do, what any sane person would do." He paused. "He's developing quite a reputation. Did you know that? In fact, all of you are. Aren't you curious to learn how I know so much about you?"

Blade exaggerated his feigned indifference, pretending to yawn. "I already know."

"Oh?" Colonel Jarvis said doubtfully. "I'll bet you do."

Blade locked his eyes on Jarvis. "You're an officer in the Army of Samuel the Second, the dictator of the Civilized Zone, which is what's left of the former United States of America. Samuel the Second is the son of a man named Samuel Hyde. Hyde was the Secretary of Health, Education, and Welfare when the Third World War erupted, and he was the only member of the Cabinet to survive. Since Congress and the Supreme Court were wiped out, Hyde took over the reigns of government, declared martial law, and established a new national capital in Denver. Hyde died a few years back, and now his son is intent on reconquering all of the former territory of the United States, all the area outside the Civilized Zone. The Army has been used to keep tabs on all inhabited centers outside the Zone, using sophisticated technology to eavesdrop and maintain extensive files on each group you find. You know so much about us because you've been spying on the Family, on our Home, for years and years." Blade stopped, a gleam in his eyes. "Any more stupid questions?"

Colonel Jarvis was having a hard time disguising his astonishment. "I had no idea you knew that much about us."

"We know more," Blade informed him.

"But how?"

"Wouldn't you like to know."

Colonel Jarvis smiled. "We'll find out, sooner or later. But first, I'd wager you don't know the reason we're here, in the Twin Cities, and how it is we were waiting for you in these tents. Curious?"

Blade refused to reply.

"No need to answer," Colonel Jarvis said, grinning. "If I were in your shoes, or should I say moccasins, I would be intensely curious. Bear with me a while and you'll find out."

"I am curious about one thing," Blade mentioned.

"What?"

"Why are you being so courteous? Why not kill us and get it over with?"

Jarvis chuckled. "I'm a fighting man, Blade, like you and your fellow Warriors. My courtesy is simply professional respect, from one fighting man to another. As to the reason you're not dead already, you can thank Samuel for that. He's given orders to take you alive. You've caused him considerable grief, and Samuel is the type of man who firmly believes in an eye for an eye. I imagine he wants to pluck yours out."

"If I ever get the opportunity," Blade vowed, "I'll do

unto him as he intends to do to me."

Colonel Jarvis placed his hands on his hips. "We have so much to talk about, but first things first." He reached into a pocket on his shirt and extracted a black whistle.

Blade abruptly realized that Jarvis was the only soldier present not bearing a weapon.

Jarvis put the stem of the whistle between his thick lips and blew two sustained notes.

Immediately, from behind a stand of trees forty yards distant, a motor turned over with a sputtering roar. A few moments later a large truck, a troop transport, drove from concealment and toward the tents.

"My compliments," Blade said, deciding he might glean more information from Jarvis if he acted friendly to the officer. "This operation was extremely well planned. Your doing?"

Jarvis beamed, delighted at the unexpected praise. "Yes. We knew you were returning to the Twin Cities, but we didn't know when until one of our monitoring posts spotted your vehicle about ten miles outside the city. They radioed me, and I prepared my little trap." He paused and glanced over his shoulder. "Speaking of your vehicle . . ." He stared at the SEAL.

The troop transport braked to a stop a few yards from the tents, the canvas cover over the bed fluttering in the strong wind.

Colonel Jarvis looked at Blade and extended his calloused right hand. "The keys, please."

"I don't have them."

Jarvis nodded at Rice.

"Search them for the keys!" Rice commanded, and all three Warriors were subjected to a thorough search at gunpoint.

Blade was relieved of his Bowies and the Dan Wesson, while Geronimo was stripped of his Arminius and his cherished tomahawk. Hickock's Colts were already in Rice's possession.

"The keys aren't on them," Rice announced at the conclusion of the search, "nor did we find any additional weapons."

"That's odd," Jarvis noted. "I was under the impression you boys packed a lot of back-up hardware."

"Not this run," Blade revealed. "We've lost a lot of weapons in recent months, so this trip we decided to stick to the basics. Besides, we weren't expecting major trouble."

Jarvis glanced at Rice. "You are positive the keys aren't on them?"

"Yes, sir," Captain Rice responded.

Colonel Jarvis ran his right hand through his curly black hair, his brown eyes squinting in thought as he faced the SEAL. "The keys have to be here, somewhere. Possibly they neglected to secure the doors."

Blade gazed at the SEAL, thankful for the tinted plastic body. There was no way anyone would be able to see Joshua inside the vehicle, so Joshua was safe as long as he remained inside. But would he? Hickok wasn't the only one who could be unpredictable.

"Bring him!" Jarvis commanded.

Captain Rice and three soldiers escorted Blade to the SEAL, the colonel leading them.

Jarvis attempted to open the driver's door. "The damn thing is locked. Try the other side."

Rice promptly obeyed. "Locked over here too," he shouted.

"I don't understand," Jarvis admitted, stroking his pointed chin. "Is there a secret latch somewhere? You must have a way of getting back inside." He leaned forward and pressed his face against the plastic. "Can't see a thing!"

"Should we blow the doors open?" Captain Rice asked.

"Don't be an idiot!" Colonel Jarvis complained. "This vehicle of theirs is priceless! There isn't another one like it on the face of the planet. Samuel wants this thing in one piece. We'll find a way to get inside without blowing it open. In the meantime, post four guards here."

"Yes, sir," Rice said.

Colonel Jarvis turned to Blade. "I don't suppose you'd like to reveal how to get inside?"

"Sorry," Blade said shrugging. "Think of it as a challenge."

Jarvis grinned. "You must be hungry after your long trip. Would you care to join me for a late lunch?"

"Do I have any choice?"

"None."

Blade was hustled aboard the troop transport and forced to sit on the bed beside Geronimo and a prone Hickok. Five of the troopers and Captain Rice rode in the back with the Warriors, while Colonel Jarvis joined the driver in the cab. Four of the soldiers were left behind as guards on the SEAL.

"Where are we headed?" Blade asked Rice as the troop transport pulled out, heading south.

"I don't want to spoil the colonel's little surprise," Rice answered. "You'll find out soon enough."

Geronimo was examining Hickok. "He's got a bump on the noggin. It doesn't look to be too serious. Thank the Spirit they hit him on the head!"

The gunman moaned.

"I think he's coming around," Geronimo said, gently shaking Hickok.

Captain Rice produced a canteen. "Here."

Geronimo took the canteen, unscrewed the cap, and

splashed some water on Hickok's face.

Blade kept his eyes focused on the soldiers, hoping the truck would hit a rut or a hole and throw them off balance. If he could grab his Bowies or the A-1 from the pile near Rice . . .

Hickok's eyelids fluttered. He gasped as a handful of water dropped into his open mouth. "Blast! First an earthquake, and now I'm being drowned!" His eyes shot open and he caught sight of Geronimo. "I should have known! Enough with the water already!" He sputtered as he sat up.

"It was time for your annual bath anyway," Geronimo remarked as he replaced the cap onto the canteen.

"Where the blazes are we?" Hickok glanced around and discovered the soldiers. "Terrific! Couldn't you two take care of these wimps without me?"

Blade placed his right hand on Hickok's shoulder. "Are you all right?"

Hickok rubbed a tender spot on his head. "Yep. I'm fit as a fiddle."

"You sure?" Blade pressed him.

"Yes, Mother, thank you." Hickok glared at one of the soldiers. "You the one who slugged me?"

The trooper grinned.

"Just wanted to be sure," Hickok told him. "You and I have a score to settle, and I always collect on my debts."

The soldier swallowed hard.

"Where we headin'?" Hickok inquired.

"It's a big surprise," Blade let him know.

"Where's the SEAL?" Hickok asked.

"Still at the Nomad camp," Blade replied.

"And where's . . ." Hickok begun, about to question

Blade on Joshua's whereabouts. He caught himself in time.

"Where's what?" Captain Rice interjected.

"Where's my Pythons?" Hickok demanded, thinking fast.

"Right here." Captain Rice indicated the pile of Warrior weaponry. The Pythons were lying on top of the heap.

"Don't let anything happen to them," Hickok threatened, "or I'll hold you accountable when I get them back."

"You won't be getting them back," Rice assured him.

"That's what you think," Hickok stated.

Captain Rice looked at Blade. "Is he always this . . ." He tried to find the right word. "Belligerent?"

"We prefer to think of it as bullheaded," Geronimo chimed in. "It's an absolute miracle his eyes are blue and not brown."

"How can you joke at a time like this?" Captain Rice inquired. "Your lives are on the line and all you do is make fun of each other. It's incredible."

"It's all part of our Warrior training," Hickok said.

"Your Warrior training?" Rice stated.

"Yep. If we ever find ourselves in a situation where we're outgunned, we razzle-dazzle the enemy with our wit," Hickok declared.

"Of course, in Hickok's case," Geronimo noted, "once he loses his guns he's totally disarmed."

The troop transport had turned eastward some time before, and now the big truck reached State Highway 47 and bore to the left, bearing due south.

"Say, Rice," Blade thought to ask, "on our way in we came across a bunch of bodies. Was that your handiwork?"

Rice laughed. "Yes. They were trying to escape. The colonel decided to make an object lesson out of them."

The truck was barreling along the road at over fifty miles an hour. Blade realized escape would be impossible even if the transport did hit a big hole or a rut. Anyone attempting to leap from the truck at this speed would likely wind up with a broken neck. No one in their right mind would try such a feat.

Blade sighed, discouraged.

They would have to wait for the proper circumstances to make their bid for freedom.

The truck abruptly lurched wildly as the vehicle struck a buckled section of the highway. The men in the rear were tossed violently from side to side, jostling one another, as the troop transport became briefly airborne. The cab was elevated, the bed hanging at a sharp angle, for only an instant.

But it was enough.

Hickok, squatting on the floorboards, ironically retained a better balance than those sitting or standing. He dove forward, headfirst, sliding past the astounded soldiers, past the scattered pile of Warrior arms, grabbing his Pythons as he slid the length of the truck and over the open tailgate.

The truck descended with a bone-wrenching impact, knocking most of the troopers off their feet.

Blade tensed, about to make his break.

Captain Rice, still standing, waved his M-16 in the direction of the two remaining Warriors. "Don't either of you move!" he directed Blade and Geronimo.

The truck was coming to a stop.

"Hickok did it!" Geronimo said to Blade. "The son of a gun really did it!"

"I just pray he landed okay," Blade commented.

The soldiers in the transport had all recovered.

Colonel Jarvis appeared at the rear of the truck. "That damn driver wasn't paying attention to his driving! Is everyone . . ." He stopped, aware they were missing someone. "Where the hell is Hickok?"

"He escaped," Captain Rice explained, "when we hit the bump."

Colonel Jarvis spun, scanning the highway behind them. "There's no sign of him! Damn!" He turned and pointed at two of the troopers. "Go after him. Bring him back alive if possible, but don't hesitate to kill him to protect yourselves. Go! Go! Go!" he exhorted them as they jumped to the tarmac and ran off.

"I'm sorry, sir," Captain Rice said.

"It wasn't your fault," Colonel Jarvis snapped, watching the two soldiers. "The driver will be reprimanded when we return to headquarters."

"Should we tie them up, sir?" Rice inquired, nodding at Blade and Geronimo.

"Yes," Jarvis nodded. "You'd better. It wouldn't look too good on our records if another one were to escape."

"I hope we haven't ruined your day," Blade said pleasantly.

"Not at all," Jarvis assured him. "It's you who will have his day ruined very shortly."

"How's that?" Blade asked as two troopers secured his arms behind his broad back.

"When we reach our destination," Colonel Jarvis declared.

"The Citadel?" Blade fished for confirmation.

Jarvis shook his head. "No, dear boy. Much, much closer than the Citadel."

"Can you give us a hint?" Geronimo interjected.

Jarvis glanced at both of them. "Do either of you play golf?"

6

The burial detail completed, Yama was relaxing on the front porch, leaning against one of the porch posts, when Adam emerged from the Mason house. Seth and Gail were inside, Seth preparing a sketch of the Citadel and Gail fussing in the kitchen.

"Mr. Yama," Adam said, "can I talk to you a minute?"

"Didn't I say to call me Yama?" Yama questioned him.

"I'm sorry. My folks always say to be polite." Adam sat down on the top step.

"The place I'm from," Yama told him, "we're not allowed to call each other mister or miss."

"You're not? Why not?" the boy inquired.

"The man who founded my Home didn't believe in a lot of phony politeness and servility. He wanted everyone to enjoy equal social status in our Family. Everyone is given a title according to the work they do, whether it be Warrior, like myself, or Tiller, for those who tend the soil, or Carpenter or Artist or Empath or whatever. And, like I said earlier, we get to pick the name we want to use for the rest of our lives when we turn sixteen. So everyone has one name and one title and that's it. Do you understand?"

"I think so," Adam said thoughtfully. "It sounds like the way you do it is fair to everybody."

"It works for us."

"It's not that way here," Adam said. "In the Civilized Zone everybody is always bossing everybody else around. You saw those mean soldiers. My dad says it's even worse in the cities like the Citadel. He says that's why we live on the ranch, so we don't have to beg or . . ." Adam strived to recall the word his father had often used. "Or grovel." He grinned.

"Your family will never grovel at the place I'm taking you," Yama promised him.

"If we get there," Adam stated.

"Why do you say that?"

"I heard my mom and dad talking," Adam elaborated. "They aren't too sure we'll make it, especially my mom. She doesn't think you'll come back from the Citadel."

"I intend to return," Yama pledged.

"I hope so," the boy said affectionately. "I don't have a whole lot of friends, living way out here on the ranch and all."

"You'll make a lot of new friends at my Home," Yama informed him. "I think you'll like it there very much."

"Can I ask you something?" Adam ventured tentatively.

"What?"

"About all those guns and stuff. What kind are they?"

Yama held up his machine gun. "This is called a Wilkinson Carbine, converted to full automatic and adapted to hold a fifty-shot magazine." He touched the pistol under his right arm. "This is a Browning Hi-

Power 9-millimeter Automatic Pistol. The revolver under my other arm is a Smith and Wesson Model 586 Distinguished Combat Magnum."

"Wow!" Adam enthused, impressed. "You sure know an awful lot about guns. What's that funny sword called?"

"It's called a scimitar," Yama explained, "and my survival knife is called a Razorback."

"Someday I'm going to have guns and knives just like yours," Adam vowed earnestly.

"You should grow up to be like your father," Yama said, frowning. "Become a tiller of the soil. Put constructive purpose into your life. Don't fill it with death. Don't become attracted to the darker side of human nature."

"Having a ranch is boring compared to what you do," Adam declared.

Before Yama could respond, the screen door swung open and Seth walked outside, a piece of paper clutched in his left hand. "Here," he said. "I'm finished."

Yama took the paper and studied the crude sketch.

"It will give you some idea of what's in the Citadel," Seth mentioned. "The city isn't like what it used to be before the war. Cheyenne is much bigger now. The population swelled to over a million people after the Government forced evacuations from elsewhere in the country, mostly back east and up north. I think the Citadel is the third largest population center in the Civilized Zone. At least, that's what they tell us. Denver is the largest, but then it's the capital."

"Thank you," Yama accepted the map. "It will expedite my business in Cheyenne immensely." He didn't reveal he already had a detailed map of the Citadel, meticulously drawn by a recent addition to the Family, a creature once belonging to the Doktor's

Genetic Research Division.

"I still wish we could talk you out of going," Seth said.

"I'll be leaving soon," Yama divulged.

"So soon?"

"I must," Yama disclosed. "I want to enter the Citadel at night. The cover of darkness will augment my chances of success. If I leave soon, I should be there within four hours."

"When will you get back here?" Seth inquired anxiously. "The longer we stay here, the greater the danger to my family."

"I intend to spend only one night in the Citadel," Yama revealed. "If all goes well, I should be here by tomorrow noon at the latest."

"We'll be waiting," Seth stated. "We don't have any other choice."

"I can imagine how you must feel," Yama said sympathizing. "You're about to abandon the work of a lifetime, your home and relatives and friends. Don't despair. Considering the alternative, you are doing what is best for your loved ones."

"I certainly hope so," Seth said, his worry etched in his features.

"You shouldn't be in any great danger while I'm gone," Yama opined. "They probably won't send out another patrol to search for the one I terminated until tomorrow, possibly later if this patrol had others stops to make. I've hidden all of their weapons in your barn. Can you shoot?"

"We all can," Seth answered. "I have two hunting rifles and a revolver hidden under my bedroom floor. They're illegal to own."

"Good. So the M-16's will come in handy if you are attacked. But like I said," Yama added hastily, hoping to alleviate Seth's evident anxiety, "it's very unlikely they'll send anyone else out here for at least a day."

"Let's hope so."

Yama slowly stood. "I'd better change. Will you watch over my own clothes while I'm gone?"

"I'll do it," Adam eagerly volunteered.

"Are you planning to take your own guns or one of the M-16's?" Seth inquired.

"Why?"

"Well, you'd be less likely to draw attention if you're carrying an M-16."

"I know," Yama acknowledged, "which is another reason I'm going in at night. My skills are at maximum effectiveness using versatile arsenals. I can hide my revolver and pistol under the uniform shirt, no problem. In the dark, my Wilkinson shouldn't be too conspicuous if I carry it close to my leg."

"But what about your knife and sword?" Seth queried. "I've never seen a sword like yours before, and I'm sure no one in the Citadel has one like it."

"I'll put the knife in my left boot," Yama replied. "As for my scimitar, if I attach a leather strap to the hilt and loop the strap around my neck, close to the collar, I can suspend my sword down my back, under the shirt. No one will know I'm carrying it."

"Like my wife said," Seth remarked, "you seem to have an answer for everything."

"I'm trained to be imaginative, to devise creative solutions to difficult problems," Yama said. "Our teachers were always telling us to think fast, to think on our feet."

"You do it remarkably well," Seth complimented him.

Yama moved toward the barn. "I left the uniform I'll need in the barn. I'll change and be right back."

"Wait for me!" Adam called, and darted after the man in blue.

"You promise to take good care of my clothes?" Yama asked as the boy caught up with him.

"I'll stick them under my mattress," Adam said. "Nothing will get them there."

"Good. It took the Weavers a lot of time and effort to make my garment and I'd hate to see anything happen to it."

Adam attempted to match his stride to Yama's. "You be real careful in the Citadel. If they catch you, they'll kill you."

"I don't intend to get caught," Yama stated.

"Just be careful," Adam stressed.

The Mason dogs ambled around the southern corner of the barn.

"There's Huck and Tom!" Adam exclaimed, elated. He knelt and the two dogs, one brown and the other black and both more beagle than anything else, ran up to him and playfully licked his face and hands.

"Are you a Mark Twain fan?" Yama inquired.

Adam glanced up. "I have two of his books in my room. My dad had them when he was my age. They're hard to read sometimes but a lot of fun. Do you like to read?"

"Very much. Everyone at the place I come from, at our Home, likes to read. It's one of our favorite pastimes. We have hundreds of thousands of books in our Library, and you'll be welcome to read them at your leisure."

"Nifty! I'd like that." Adam stood.

Yama continued toward the barn. "Just remember to treat the books gently. Many of the pages are slightly discolored and will rip or crumple very easily."

"I'll remember," Adam pledged.

They entered the barn and walked over to one of the stalls. Earlier, Yama had draped the officer's uniform over one side of the stall. He leaned the Wilkinson against the wall and stripped off the shoulder holsters for the Browning and the Smith and Wesson, placing the handguns on the floor.

"Will I get to have guns like yours at this home of yours?" Adam asked.

"When you're much older, possibly," Yama answered, grinning. He started to remove his standard dark-blue garment.

"Brother!" Adam exclaimed in awe. "Where did you get all those muscles? You must be the strongest man alive!"

Yama chuckled, his highly developed musculature rippling as he moved. "I have a friend named Blade who has more muscles than I do. Many more."

"I can't believe that," Adam said.

"You'll see for yourself when you meet him," Yama stated. "And you'll meet another man named Samson. He has as many muscles as I do, possibly even a few more. So you see, I'm not the strongest man alive."

"One of the strongest, then," Adam persisted, "and it's a good thing too."

"Why's that?"

"Because you'll need a lot of strength to stay alive in the Citadel."

Gail Mason's voice interrupted their conversation. "Adam! Adam! I need you for a minute! Adam!"

"You'd better go," Yama urged the boy.

Adam walked to the barn door. "I'll be right back," he promised, and ran off.

Yama finished exchanging clothes. The officer's uniform was a tight fit, but it would suffice. He began arming himself as he'd planned, reflecting on his mission. Plato needed a firsthand report on the Citadel, and that was exactly what he would receive. And, Yama mentally vowed, not the soldiers, not the genetically created creatures produced in the Doktor's lab, not even the Doktor would prevent him from successfully completing his assignment. He might not be the strongest man alive, but he was a Warrior and the Warriors were noted for their tenacity.

So look out, Citadel!

He was on his way!

7

The troop transport arrived at their destination within five minutes of Hickok's rather abrupt departure. Blade noted that the big truck slowly braked to a smooth stop; apparently, the driver was extremely reluctant to further arouse the colonel's ire.

"On your feet," Captain Rice ordered.

Blade and Geronimo moved to the rear of the truck and jumped to the ground.

Twelve soldiers were lined up at attention behind the troop transport.

Colonel Jarvis appeared. "I told you to expect a surprise." He gestured to their left, grinning. "I trust you're not disappointed?"

The two Warriors turned, their expressions telling the whole story, unable to conceal their shock.

It was a stockade, a tremendous stockade situated in the middle of a field, constructed of huge posts imbedded in the earth and strand after strand of barbed wire encircling the enclosure to a height of twenty feet. Positioned immediately outside the stockade, at points corresponding with due north, east, south, and west, were four tall sentry towers complete with mounted machine guns and spotlights powered by a generator placed on the bed of another troop transport. Soldiers were everywhere, dozens and dozens of them, some milling about, at ease, off duty, while others manned the guard towers or stood at attention beside the barbed wire.

"Pinch me, Blade," Geronimo said.

"I see them too," Blade affirmed.

"Look at them all!" Geronimo commented, stunned.

Blade was looking, his mind unwilling to lend any credence to the sight his eyes beheld. How many were there? Five hundred? Eight hundred? A thousand? The stockade was literally crammed with a packed sea of humanity.

"Admit it," Jarvis urged, pleased with himself. "You never expected this!"

"Not in my worst nightmare," Blade confessed. He detected prisoners attired in black and others with Mohawk haircuts, and he realized what had transpired before Jarvis began bragging.

"Seven hundred and thirty-one," Colonel Jarvis proudly disclosed. "All that's left of the Horns, the Porns, and the Nomads."

"All that's left?" Geronomo questioned, astonished. "But there were about twelve hundred of them, all told."

"Not any more," Jarvis revealed. "The rest are dead. Oh, there may be a few still in hiding, but the majority of them now stand before you, my captives."

Blade discerned the obvious relish with which Jarvis said that last word.

"You wiped out almost five hundred lives?" Geronimo queried, horrified.

"It was simplicity itself," Jarvis said. "These pitiful wretches possessed so few firearms I was able to subdue them with only one hundred men."

Blade stared at Jarvis. "I know about Samuel's plans to reconquer the United States, but it was my understanding he's going after the larger populations outside the Civilized Zone first. Isn't that why his Army attacked the Flathead Indians in Montana? I know for a fact, and undoubtedly you do too, that there is a large free group in South Dakota called the Cavalry. So why are you here? Why did Samuel send you to the Twin Cities when there are larger free populations elsewhere?"

"Of course we know all about the Cavalry," Colonel Jarvis stated. "As a matter of fact, they won't remain free much longer."

"What do you mean?" Blade demanded.

"Sorry. That's another little surprise I'll save for later." Jarvis smiled.

Geronimo openly glared at the colonel. He was the one who had ventured into Cavalry territory; he was the one who had arranged for a treaty between the Family and the Cavalry, both forming what Plato had designated the Freedom Confederation; and he was the one who had married a Cavalry woman. The prospect of his newfound friends being subjugated by the army infuriated him.

"As to why we are here," Jarvis was saying, "we owe it all to you."

"Come again?" Blade said.

Colonel Jarvis pointed at the stockade. "The reason we're in the Twin Cities, the reason all those people are locked up, and the reason so many of them have already died is because of you."

Blade shook his head, unwilling to accept the blame. "No way!"

Jarvis put his hands behind his back and adopted a

stern visage. "I don't appreciate being called a liar! I'll explain it for you, so you'll see I'm telling the truth." He paused, watching the abject faces in the compound. "You see, Samuel was perfectly willing to leave these people alone, to continue monitoring their activities but otherwise allow them to live out their petty little lives in strained desperation. The Twin Cities population wasn't due to be reabsorbed for a year or two. But then something happened." Jarvis grinned at Blade. "Then we learned of your trip to the Twin Cities. We discovered your plans, how you intended to lead these people out of the shambles and aid them in establishing a new life near your accursed Home. We couldn't allow that. We don't want your Family becoming any stronger than it already is. So Samuel devised a brilliant strategy. Send out a special unit under my command to forcibly contain these degenerates and ship them to one of our Reabsorption Centers near Denver. . . ."

"Reabsorption Centers?" Geronimo repeated.

"Of course! You don't think we'd allow these depraved, maladjusted misfits to be absorbed into the general populace of the Civilized Zone without first reeducating them, without aligning their diminished mental capacities with the prevalent social consciousness required of all upright citizens, do you?"

"But how?" Blade needed to know. "How did you find out about our plans? From one of your listening posts outside our Home?"

"No," Colonel Jarvis responded. "Our high technology wasn't necessary this time. We used an informant."

"An informant! Was it someone from the Family?" Blade demanded.

"No. I'll let you meet him." Jarvis scanned the area. Blade, attracted by the rumble of the generator,

glanced to the southwest. About fifty yards from the
stockade was the truck housing the generator, and it
wasn't alone. Blade counted fifteen troop transports in
all, not including the one they came in. Evidently, the
Army intended to utilize the big trucks to relocate the
Twin Cities population.

"Ahh! There he is!" Jarvis had spotted someone
nearby, standing with a group of troopers. He waved,
beckoning the person to join them. "Here he comes
now."

Blade didn't recognize the informant. He was a small
man, with tiny dark eyes and a small, pointed nose. He
wore faded jeans and a torn blue shirt.

"Blade, Geronimo," Jarvis said as the grubby man
stopped at his side, "I'd like you to meet Rat."

The name rang a bell, but Blade still couldn't place
him. "Should I know him?"

"Probably not," Jarvis answered. "I believe it was
Hickok who encountered Rat on your first trip to the
Twin Cities. You and Hickok are the best of friends,
aren't you, Rat?"

"Where is he?" Rat asked in a squeaky voice. "Where
is the prick? You promised I could have him!"

"And I'm a man of my word," Jarvis declared. "Unfortunately, Hickok escaped on the way here and . . ."

"Escaped!" Rat shouted, nervously looking around
the field.

Jarvis laughed. "Relax. We'll protect you. We have
an agreement, remember? Besides, what can Hickok do
against all my men? He's one man against one
hundred."

Rat was rubbing the stubble on his narrow chin. "You
don't know Hickok like I do, Jarvis. We're not safe until
you have him in custody."

The colonel's eyes had narrowed at Rat's manifest

lack of respect. "It's Colonel Jarvis to you," he said angrily.

"No offense meant," Rat hastily apologized.

"I remember now," Blade mentioned. "Hickok told us about you. You were one of Maggot's crowd, the ones who used to run the Porns. Hickok said you managed to get away during his final fight with Maggot."

"Yeah, I escaped that bastard!" Rat snapped, his intense hatred for the gunman distorting his features. "I hid out. Some of my buddies gave me food and water and told me what was going on. They told me how Hickok made Bear the new head of the Porns. Most of the Porns went along with it because they hated Maggot's guts. But a few of us didn't like the idea one bit. And then I heard how Hickok was coming back, how he'd promised to lead everybody from the Twins. Mr. High and Mighty! Well, I knew I had to stop you guys, so I gambled and snuck out of the city."

"He contacted us," Jarvis detailed, "one of our outposts surrounding the metropolis."

"Yeah," Rat continued. "They were real interested in you guys. I offered them a deal. If they would help me become boss of the Porns, I'd help them get you."

"We modified the arrangement somewhat," Jarvis elaborated. "In exchange for the information he had concerning Alpha Triad, we offered him Hickok's head on a platter."

"You made a deal with this worm?" Blade inquired, calculating his insult would annoy Rat.

"Who are you calling a worm?" Rat demanded, peeved.

"When it suits our purpose," Jarvis said, "we occasionally establish pacts with . . ." He glanced at Rat distastefully. "Outsiders."

Blade recalled his trip to Fox and the Family's fight

with the Trolls. "Like you did with the Trolls?"

"Exactly." Jarvis nodded. "We have a lot of territory to reconquer. We can't be everywhere at once. We lack the personnel to place permanent listening posts near every inhabited town and hamlet. On the other hand, we don't want the people living outside the Civilized Zone to organize and oppose us, so whenever we locate a group like the Trolls, crude, primitive, savage barbarians devoted to looting and killing, we form a pact with them. In exchange for their continual harassment of the people in their vicinity, we supply them with a few guns and other items. It's an extremely effective system, because it fosters anarchy and disrupts any efforts at organization."

"And later," Blade deduced, "when Samuel is ready, you'll waltz right in and enslave everybody with a minimum of opposition."

"Deucedly clever, don't you think?" Jarvis asked.

"Yes," Blade conceded. "You don't miss a trick."

"We try not to," Jarvis said.

"You're not as clever as you'd like to believe," Geronimo said baiting the colonel.

"Why's that?"

"You haven't defeated everyone in the Twin Cities," Geronimo informed him.

"We'll catch Hickok. It's only a matter of time," Jarvis assured them.

"I wasn't referring to Hickok," Geronimo stated. "I was referring to the Wacks."

Colonel Jarvis laughed. "Those demented idiots? Who cares about them? They're not organized. They're a bunch of lunatic cannibals, nothing more, and they hardly pose a serious threat to the Civilized Zone. For your information, we did ambush about six dozen of them at that hospital they use for a base of operations.

Killed forty-nine, if I recall. We'll get the rest, eventually. There's no rush."

"So what now?" Blade asked. "Do you truck us all to the Civilized Zone?"

Colonel Jarvis gazed at the crowded stockade and thoughtfully stroked his jutting chin, his brown eyes squinting in the bright afternoon sun. "Yes, we do. But we have a problem in that respect. We have sixteen available transports. Even if I pack in these filthy swine like sardines, the most I can cram into any one truck is forty. That means my trucks can carry six hundred and forty prisoners, all told, and there wouldn't be any space left for my men. So the most I can take back with me is five hundred and forty prisoners. But we have seven hundred and thirty-one, which is one hundred and ninety-one too many. Let's round the figure off to two hundred. What do I do with the excess?"

"You could let them go," Geronimo offered. "I know Blade and I wouldn't object if you decided to leave us here."

Jarvis chuckled. "The only way I'll leave you here is if you are six feet under."

"Forget it, then," Geronimo said. "We haven't mastered the technique of breathing dirt."

"Sir," Captain Rice mentioned, "should we place these two in the stockade with the others?"

"Why not? They might find a few of their old friends inside. They can talk over old times."

"Before we go," Blade commented, "I'd like to know what you meant earlier."

"About what?" asked Jarvis.

"When you said something about playing golf."

"Oh." Jarvis swept the area with his right hand. "This land my men constructed the stockade on was once a golf course. Do you know what golf was?"

"I've seen some books in our Library on it," Blade divulged. "A game of some kind, where you went around smacking this dinky little ball all over the place with funny-looking clubs."

"Exactly. Well, this field was once known as the Columbia Golf Course, according to my map." Colonel Jarvis started to walk away, then stopped. "I'll see you later and we'll have that meal I promised. In the interim, you can enjoy the company of the Porns and Horns and Nomads." He paused. "Damn strange names! Where do you suppose they ever got names like that?"

"I know," Blade volunteered. If he continued to be marginally cooperative with Jarvis, the officer might become complacent and lower his guard long enough for them to make a break for it.

"You do?"

"The last time we were here," Blade disclosed, "we learned a few of the facts. It seems there were two main factions left here after the evacuation. One was in Minneapolis, the followers of a pornographer and drug dealer, mostly street people. The other group was a religious one based in St. Paul. The leader of the religious faction started referring to the pornographer and his band as, aptly, Porns. The Porns retaliated by calling the religious group the Horns."

"The Horns? It doesn't make any sense."

"It had something to do with insulting their sexual prowess," Blade revealed.

"Horns?" Jarvis pondered a moment. "Hornbill? Horned lizard? Horned? Horny?" He laughed, comprehension dawning. "Horny! That's it, isn't it? That's why they became known as the Horns!"

"So we were told," Blade confirmed.

"And when Zahner began his outcast splinter group

he called them Nomads because they didn't owe allegiance to anyone," Jarvis recounted. He glanced at Blade. "Thanks for the information. It will make my report complete. I'll see you later." He waved and departed, heading toward the northern sentry tower.

"He's awful polite for a fascist," Geronimo remarked bitterly.

"Move it!" Captain Rice barked.

The twelve soldiers surrounded the Warriors as Rice led them to a gate in the center of the western side of the stockade.

Blade saw a multitude of faces turning their way, watching them with hostile interest. What kind of reception would they get if they were tossed in there? After all, none of those people knew them. The three groups had met Hickok and Joshua, but not Geronimo and himself. How would they react to complete strangers in their midst? Considering the circumstances, they would view the Warriors with suspicion and fear. They might turn on the two newcomers and beat them to a pulp.

A pair of troopers stood at attention in front of the gate.

"Open it!" Rice ordered.

One of the soldiers removed a key from his left front pocket and unlocked a large padlock attached to a bar in the middle of the gate.

"I'd like to register a formal complaint," Geronimo said as the soldier swung the gate open. The other troopers present trained their M-16's on the gate, effectively preventing anyone inside from bolting.

"If you have a complaint," Rice stated, "I'll take it to the colonel. What is it?"

Geronimo nodded toward the crowded captives. "After all the trouble you went to just to capture us, the least you could do is supply separate cells with indoor plumbing.''

One of the soldiers cut their bonds, and they were rudely shoved into the stockade.

8

His blasted left shoulder hurt like the dickens!

Hickok hurried, striving to ignore the pain, his injury the result of his uncontrolled plunge to the road surface after bailing out of the troop transport.

Things weren't as bad as they appeared.

Sure, Blade and Geronimo were still in the hands of the Army. Sure, Joshua was alone in the SEAL a mile or so ahead. Sure, their plans had been shot to heck and back. But there was one bright spot on their horizon.

He had his Pythons!

Come what may, he was ready for it!

He was hastening toward Moore Lake. His only hope of rescuing Blade and Geronimo depended on reaching the SEAL. The soldiers were unaware of the special features incorporated into the vehicle, and the special armaments could be used to devastating effect.

All he had to do was reach the SEAL.

That was all.

If the jokers on his heels didn't catch him first.

He knew there were two of them and they'd been on his trail for some time. They'd probably found the point where he left the highway and dove into the woods.

Let 'em catch up!

He'd blow the varmints away!

Or would he?

Hickok leaned against a tree, slightly winded, checking for any sign of his pursuers.

Nothing yet.

What if he did shoot them? he asked himself. The shots would draw other soldiers, maybe even the Wacks, to his position. Gunfire would advertise where he was for anyone interested. So what should he do? Try to outrun them? Hide and hope they passed him by? Or take them out quietly?

Hickok glanced around, seeking a potential weapon. His eyes alighted on a broken limb five feet away. He walked over and picked up the branch. It was about four feet in length and relatively straight, with the thicker end blunt and ragged and the thinner part tapered into some semblance of a point.

Not much, but it would have to do.

He resumed running, deliberately applying extra pressure as he pounded his moccasins on the ground. His tracks had to be fresh and clear if his plan was to succeed. The element of surprise had to work in his favor, and it would if the soldiers were intently concentrating on his sign, on his footprints.

Time passed.

Hickok came across the spot he'd been searching for, an ideal location for an ambush. To his left stood the charred trunk of a tree, the apparent victim of a lightning strike. Only ten feet of the burnt trunk still stood. To his right, six feet from the tree trunk, was a giant boulder, the side of the boulder facing the trunk essentially flat while the other side was tapered and rough.

Perfect.

He ran around the trunk of the tree and stopped dead in his tracks. Slowly, carefully, he retraced his steps, walking backwards, meticulously placing his feet in the exact print or impression he'd made while first coming around the trunk. When he was between the trunk and the boulder he tensed his leg muscles, took a deep breath, and leaped as far as he could in the direction of the boulder. He landed in front of it and moved to the other side, scrambling up the boulder until he was just below the rim.

Okay.

Let them mangy wimps come!

They did.

Within minutes, Hickok heard them approaching through the underbrush. For a couple of supposedly professional military types, they made more noise than a pregnant horse! He clutched the branch and patiently waited, unwilling to risk a peek and jeopardize his chances.

"He's moving faster," someone whispered.

"Think he knows we're after him?" inquired a second man.

"No way. The jerk doesn't know his butt from a hole in the ground," replied the first voice.

There was a moment's silence.

"What's the matter?" asked the second man.

"His tracks stop."

"They what?"

"They stop right here," said the first man.

"How can tracks just stop in the middle of nowhere?"

"They can't," stated the first man, evidently the tracker. "I must have made a mistake. Let's go back a bit."

Hickok slowly counted to himself, and when he reached ten he launched his body over the top of the boulder.

Bingo!

The two soldiers were almost directly under the gunman, one of them kneeling and examining the tracks while the other was staring at the charred trunk. Something warned the second man, perhaps his sixth sense, but whatever it was he suddenly looked up and tried to bring his M-16 into play.

Hickok wasn't Rikki-Tikki-Tavi, the Family's exceptional martial artist, but he had been trained in hand-to-hand combat, spending years under the tutelage of a Family Elder with vast experience at infighting, and the gunman applied his knowledge now as his life hung in the balance. He lashed out with his right leg, his foot catching the standing soldier in the face and knocking him aside. The kneeling tracker glanced up, puzzled, his mouth widening in alarm.

The Warrior brutally rammed the pointed end of the limb into the trooper's left eye, imbedding the tip of the branch at least four inches into the man's skull. The soldier screamed and recoiled, grasping at the limb in a feeble attempt to extract it.

Hickok shot a glance over his left shoulder, just in time.

The other soldier had recovered. He'd lost his M-16 when kicked in the face, but now he whipped out a long knife from a sheath on his left hip and lunged.

Hickok released the branch and dodged aside, grabbing the trooper's wrist with both hands and driving the forearm down onto his right knee.

There was a distinct snapping sound and the soldier shrieked at the top of his lungs.

Hickok swept his right hand up and in, his fingers straight and hard, using the edge of his hand as he slashed the trooper across the throat.

Once.

Twice.

The soldier gurgled, his chin falling limply to his chest, as blood and froth spewed from his mouth.

Hickok glanced at the tracker. He was lying on the ground, on his back, the limb sticking upward as if it were trying to take root.

The second soldier moaned once, then fell, dead.

Hickok nodded in satisfaction. "A piece of cake," he said to himself. He bent over the troopers and rummaged through their uniforms.

Quite a collection!

He found wallets on both men, each containing paper money in varied denominations. He also discovered a handful of coins, each imprinted with the countenance of a stern man with a beard and a funny hat and the words "In Samuel We Trust" encircling the coin. One of the men, the tracker, had a photograph in his shirt pocket, a picture of the tracker and a pretty young woman and a small child, a boy of four or five years old.

Dear Spirit!

Were they the soldier's wife and son?

Hickok stared at the photograph for a long, long time, considering the ramifications. In all the fights he'd been in, all the gunfights and battles, he'd never given a thought to the relatives of the enemies he killed in combat. This trooper had had a wife and son! How would they feel when they learned he was gone? How many widows, the gunman wondered, had he made during the course of his illustrious career? He thought of his own wife of a couple of weeks, his beloved Sherry. How would she . . .

A bird singing nearby shattered his reflection.

He vigorously shook his head, his blond locks flying, ending his morbid introspection. As a Warrior, he couldn't afford the luxury of grieving over his opponents. He had to tell himself, over and over, his whole duty involved preserving the Home and protecting the Family. Nothing else mattered.

Besides, these men were soldiers. They knew they were in a deadly profession. They were aware of the hazards.

Hickok stood and glared at the tracker. Idiot! Why did you leave your family alone and neglected, just so you could get your thrills in the military?

Inexplicably angered, the gunman hauled off and kicked the tracker in the face.

Served the varmint right!

He scooped up their M-16's and spare ammunition, gazed at them one last time, then began jogging northward.

There was still plenty of daylight left.

Good.

He wouldn't stumble over a mutate on his way to the SEAL.

9

The first thing Blade noticed as he was thrown into the stockade was his miscalculation of the density. True, the captives were jammed inside in a compact mass, but there was a good foot or so between each person, enough room to move around somewhat freely. The second thing he noted was the intensifying of their malevolent expressions.

"What the hell is this?" a big man demanded as the gate was quickly slammed shut.

"Who are these two?" asked another.

"I don't know them," stated a woman.

"Neither do I," confirmed another. "Does anyone know these two clowns?"

Blade and Geronimo found themselves backed against the fence with precious little room available to maneuver should they be attacked.

A tall black man, taller even than Blade, sauntered up and jabbed the Warrior in the chest with his right index finger.

"Who are you, mister?" the black arrogantly inquired.

"Are they spies?" questioned an elderly woman.

"If they're spies, kill them!" suggested a thin man.

The black was powerfully built, attired in a pair of torn and aged jeans. He forcibly poked Blade in the chest again. "You'd best answer me, mother, or I'll take your head off!"

Blade looked at Geronimo, who grinned. "I was getting flabby sitting in the SEAL all day," Geronimo said. " I can use the exercise."

"What's that supposed to mean?" the black queried.

"It means," Blade told him, his voice low and gravely, "you'd better not touch me again."

"Oh?" The black smiled, his dark eyes twinkling in his handsome face. "Is that so?" He drove his finger into Blade's chest again. "What's going to happen if I do, white boy?" And again. "You aim to do somethin' about it?"

"Yes."

"Like what?"

Blade's right hand streaked upward and clamped on the black's neck. The black reacted instantly, swinging his right fist at the Warrior's head. Blade ducked under the blow and slammed his left hand into the black's crotch, gripping with all of his strength and heaving, lifting the man completely over his head.

The black was struggling and gasping, striving to break the Warrior's hold on his throat and groin.

The people in front of them suddenly backed away, pushing those behind them and eliciting curses in response.

Geronimo casually crossed his arms and smiled up at the black. "If I were you, friend, I'd apologize to Blade here before he gets mad. Believe me, you wouldn't want to get him mad."

"Did you say his name is Blade?" asked someone in the crowd. A man parted the front row and advanced toward them. He had an air of authority about him. His hair was brown, his eyes blue, his white skin tanned brown, and he was wearing a torn green shirt and beige pants. His black boots sported holes in their tips. He stared into Blade's eyes. "Is your name Blade?"

Blade simply nodded.

The man looked over his right shoulder at the people behind him. "These two aren't spies. This one is Blade, Hickok's friend."

The crowd immediately started muttering and whispering.

"Blade?"

"He's a buddy of Hickok's!"

"But where is Hickok?"

The spokesman glanced up at the wheezing black. "I think you can let Bear down now. He's afraid of heights, you know." The white man grinned.

"Bear?" Blade repeated. He lowered the black to the ground. "The one Hickok installed as leader of the Porns?"

"One and the same," said the spokesman.

Bear was doubled over, endeavoring to catch his breath and rubbing his tender throat.

"Who are you?" Geronimo asked the other man.

"I'm Zahner," he replied, offering his right hand.

"The head of the Nomads," Geronimo stated as he shook hands. "Hickok told us all about you."

"And you must be Geronimo," Zahner reasoned. "Yes, Hickok mentioned you two a lot. But . . ." He paused, studying the Warriors. "Don't take this wrong, but why aren't you dead? Hickok left us with the impression you'd been killed by the Wacks."

"He thought we were dead," Blade confirmed. "We'll tell you the whole story later. Right now, we have more important matters to discuss." He placed his right hand on the black's left shoulder. "Are you all right?"

Bear slowly straightened. "I'm fine," he replied, his voice a bit raspy. "Is Hickok with you?"

"He was," Geronimo answered, "but he tried to gouge a hole in the road with his head and we haven't seen him since."

"Say what?" Bear said, perplexed.

Blade abruptly realized they had an audience; Captain Rice and four troopers were standing just outside the barbed wire enclosure, listening to their every word. "Is there somewhere we can talk?" he asked Zahner.

Zahner nodded, understanding. "Follow me. There's someone I think you'd like to see."

The prisoners parted as the four men moved through the throng, knowledge of the Warriors' entrance into the stockade having already been rapidly spread by word of mouth. Zahner was apparently seeking someone. He continually scanned the crowd until they were nearly in the middle of the stockade.

"There she is!" Zahner stated. He cupped his hands around his mouth. "Yo! Woman! Get your big boobs over here!"

Blade and Geronimo gazed in the general direction Zahner was facing, and Blade spotted her first. A broad smile creased his features and he surged forward, his arms outspread.

There was a squeal of sheer delight and a woman hurtled through the press of people and leaped into Blade's arms. "Blade! Blade! You big dummy! You made it back!" She gripped him by the hair and planted a moist kiss on his lips. "You made it!"

"Bertha," Blade said softly.

Bertha was giggling, deliriously happy. Her thick, curly black hair glistened in the sunlight. Her skin was a dusky shade, not from prolonged exposure to the sun but because one of her parents had been white and the other black. Her amply endowed figure was covered with a grimy yellow shirt made from an old sheet and fatigue pants confiscated from soldiers in Thief River Falls months before. "It's so good to see you again!"

"And you," Blade told her. "But aren't you forgetting someone?" He nodded at Geronimo.

"Geronimo!" Bertha screeched.

Geronimo opened his arms to embrace her and was almost bowled over by the impact.

"You too!" Bertha elated. "I knew you'd come back, no matter what the others said. I just knew it!" She released Geronimo and looked around. "Where's White Meat?"

"He escaped on the way here," Geronimo revealed. "He'll show up sooner or later."

"Is he okay?" Bertha inquired, her agitation and concern transparent. "Was he hurt? How's he been? What's he been up to since I saw him last? Tell me everything!"

Geronimo glanced at Blade, both knowing they were thinking similar thoughts: should they tell Bertha Hickok was married to another woman? Independently they reached concurring conclusions; Hickok got himself into this mess, Hickok could get himself out.

"Hickok is fine," Blade stated. "Why not let him tell you what he's been up to when you see him?"

"I can't wait," Bertha said enthusiastically.

"He's all we've heard about for the past two months," Bear grumbled. "Hickok this and Hickok that! It was enough to drive you nuts!"

Bertha jerked her left thumb toward Bear. "Don't listen to Mr. Mouth! He's just jealous because I told him I wouldn't be his lady, that I was Hickok's and

Hickok's alone."

Blade mentally constrained his emotions to avoid displaying any surprise. "You don't say?"

"Yep. I figured it all out," Bertha said proudly.

"Figured what out?" Geronimo questioned her.

"Well, the last time I saw White Meat he was actin' real weird and I couldn't figure out why," Bertha explained.

"Acting weird, for Hickok, is normal," Geronimo quipped.

Bertha ignored him. "I finally figured out that Hickok must of thought Bear and I were an item. That's why he acted the way he did. Wait until he finds out Bear and I are just good buddies and nothin' more! Won't he be surprised!"

"That's an understatement," Geronimo said.

"I can hardly wait to see him again," Bertha said with yearning.

Geronimo leaned toward Blade. "I just hope I'm around when those two meet! I wouldn't miss it for the world!"

"You planning to take notes?" Blade joked.

"Now there's an idea!" Geronimo agreed. "Why didn't I think of it? I'll take notes and give them to Hickok's you-know-what after we return to the Home."

"Let me know what type of flowers you'd prefer at your funeral," Blade courteously commented.

"What are you two yappin' about?" Bertha wanted to know. She'd been preoccupied with memories of her adored gunfighter: the first time she'd seen him, when he'd rescued her from the soldiers stationed in Thief River Falls; their constant bickering and his restrained affection; and the sight of him in action against the troopers, his Colts pitted against their sophisticated weaponry. Lordy, that boy could shoot!

"Far be it for me to intrude upon true love," Zahner said sarcastically, "but don't we have more critical items to discuss?"

"We do," Blade agreed. "Hickok gave you his word, on behalf of the Family, that we'd be back to assist you in evacuating the Twin Cities. Well, obviously, we're here."

"You're a little late, ain't you?" Bear complained. "It's been about two months! Two months! Hickok said you guys would come back in a month!"

"It wasn't our fault," Blade responded. "The delay was unavoidable. We're genuinely sorry, but there was nothing we could do about it. There was no way we could have gotten here any faster."

"Too bad," Zahner remarked, gazing at the stockade and the soldiers. "You could have saved us a lot of anguish."

"The past is past," Blade philosophized. "We can't change it, but we can alter the future. We can lead you out of here and help you begin a new life near our Home."

Bear pointed at the enclosure. "Ain't you forgettin' one minor problem?"

"We haven't forgotten," Blade assured him. "Now, before we go any further, isn't there one of you missing?"

"Missing?" Zahner reiterated, puzzled.

"You're the leader of the Nomads," Blade said, "and Bear is the head of the Porns. Where's the chief Horn? I think Hickok and Joshua said his name was Reverend Paul?"

Zahner, Bear, and Bertha exchanged strange looks.

"Reverend Paul was butchered by these bastards!" Zahner stated harshly.

"How did they capture all of you?" Geronimo

inquired.

"It was easy for them," Zahner answered, confirming Colonel Jarvis. "One of the Porns . . ."

"Rat," Blade interrupted. "We know."

". . . led the soldiers into the Twin Cities in the middle of the night, using back alleys and sticking to sections he knew we seldom used or were unguarded. They had it all planned, nice and neat!" Zahner snapped bitterly. "They set up an ambush and jumped us halfway through our meeting."

"What meeting?" Blade asked.

"The three sides agreed to meet under a flag of truce," Zahner detailed. "All of us. Everybody. Except the Wacks, of course. We were tired of waiting for you guys to come back, and we were beginning to think you never would. We decided to talk it over and have a public vote on whether we would continue to wait, or whether we would attempt to leave the Twin Cities on our own." Zahner sighed wearily. "Rat knew of the conference. He told the soldiers, and the rest is history. It was a massacre! We didn't stand a chance! They surrounded us and opened fire with their automatic weapons. It . . . was . . ." Zahner stopped, choked with sentiment at the gory memories, unable to continue.

"It seemed like they were firin' forever!" Bear took up the narrative. "Men, women, and children were droppin' like flies! It went on and on and on!"

"When the shootin' was all over," Bertha elaborated, "they had us form a big circle in the field. Then they carted off all the bodies and got to work building this big fence. They had all the things they needed, like the barbed wire and such, right in the trucks. They knew what they was doin'."

"How long ago did this happen?" Blade inquired.

"Four days ago," Zahner replied. "They've been

feeding us only one meal a day. I overheard some of the soldiers talking yesterday, and they were saying they didn't think they'd be here too much longer. Evidently they're getting set to move us out soon."

Geronimo glanced at Blade. "I wonder why they waited almost two months to come in here. When did Rat tell the Army about us? What took them so long?"

"Logistics, probably," Blade deduced. "After Rat told them, whenever it was, the information had to be transmitted up through the chain of command all the way to Denver and Samuel. Samuel would have needed time to formulate his plan of action, and undoubtedly additional time was required to set everything in motion. Remember, Rat was expecting us to return to the Twin Cities in a month. Maybe the Army intended to ambush all of us on the road between here and our Home. Maybe, when we didn't come back on schedule, it threw their entire scheme off kilter. It's all sheer speculation at this point. If I get the opportunity, I'll try and milk Jarvis for the information."

"How did you know Rat led them in?" Bertha queried.

"We saw him," Blade said, "right before they tossed us in the stockade."

There was the sound of a commotion near the western side of the fence.

"What's that?" Bear asked.

"Only one way to find out," Zahner stated, and led the way toward the enclosure.

Bertha stayed close to Blade. "Do you really think White Meat will show up here?" she asked him.

"No doubt in my mind," Blade answered. "Hickok knows we're prisoners, and he'll tear the city apart looking for us."

"And what happens when he finds you?"

"Well, he'll be as surprised as we were to discover everybody being held in the stockade. Then he'll try and get us out."

"What can he do against all those guns?" Bertha asked.

"Hickok against one hundred soldiers?" Blade said thoughtfully. "I'd say the odds were just about even."

10

"I'm bored to tears standing around here watching this bucket of bolts," the young guard groused.

"You'd better not let an officer hear you," said one of his companions. "I can promise you that you wouldn't be bored at your court-martial."

"How long do we have to stay here?" the young soldier demanded. "It's starting to get dark."

"What's the matter? You afraid of the bogeyman?" taunted his companion.

"There ain't no such thing!" snapped the young trooper.

"Say! Who's that?" asked a third soldier.

As one, the four troopers assigned to watch the vehicle the Warriors arrived in at Moore Lake swung around, facing an intruder who was standing twenty feet away, near one of the Nomad tents.

"Who the hell is that?" queried the young soldier.

"It's him! He's one of them!" exclaimed the fourth guard. "The one called Hickok."

Hickok stood with his hands at his sides, near the pearl handles on his Pythons. He'd stashed the M-16's he'd taken from the two tropoers earlier behind one of the other tents. The four in front of him were exchanging worried looks and nervously fingering their weapons. Two of the soldiers had their M-16's slung over their shoulder, the third carried his cradled under his left arm, and the fourth was holding his in front of him, horizontally, at waist level.

"Howdy, boys!" Hickok greeted them. "Did you miss me?"

"What are you doing here?" one of the troopers arrogantly questioned. "What happened to the others?"

Hickok grinned. "I'm here because I'm going to get in that contraption behind you and go for a little drive. Unless, of course, you reckon you four can stop me."

"What do we do?" asked the young soldier uneasily.

One of the troopers, the one holding his M-16 in front of his waist, started to inch his right hand toward the trigger guard. "You know what we've got to do," he told the youngest.

"Didn't you hear what Hickok did in Thief River Falls?" inquired another of the soldiers.

"I heard," said a third, "he beat twenty of our guys with those Colts of his."

"Sounds like an exaggeration to me," remarked the one with his M-16 near his waist.

"Well, I overheard the old man the other day," stated the youngest. "He was talking with Captain Rice about how this Hickok and his friends wiped out the Trolls. Just the three of 'em, and they killed all of the Trolls!"

For a fleeting moment, judging by the frightened looks of the soldiers, Hickok thought he might be able to bluff them into dropping their weapons without a fight.

He was wrong.

"Just think how famous we'll be," said M-16 at the waist, "if we take him out. Our names will be in all the papers. There might even be promotions in it for all of us!"

Hickok could tell they were wrestling with a dilemma; should they meekly give in or go for the fame and fortune?

Fame and fortune won.

The one with the M-16 at waist level swung the barrel of his gun up, thinking he was fast, recognizing in his final fleeting moment of life on this planet that, compared to the Warrior gunfighter, he was as slow as the proverbial molasses.

Incredibly quick, Hickok's Colts cleared leather, the hammers already cocked as the Pythons leveled and roared.

Two of the troopers were simultaneously tossed backwards by the force of impact, the one with his M-16 in front of him taking a slug through the center of his forehead, while the soldier with the M-16 cradled in his arm was struck in the right eye. As the remaining two troopers endeavored to bring their weapons into play, Hickok's hands shifted slightly and the Pythons bucked and spat their projectiles of death. Each of the men took a shot in the head, and they fell as one to the ground.

Hickok twirled his Pythons into their holsters and nodded. "Piece of cake." He strode to the bodies and examined them to insure they were finished.

Something clicked to his right and he drew the Colts, crouching and stepping to one side in case he was already in an opponent's sights.

Joshua was standing there, the SEAL door wide open, sadly staring at the dead soldiers.

"You came close, pard," Hickok informed him. "Next time, don't sneak up on me like that."

Joshua absently nodded, still gazing at the troopers.

"You've done it again," he commented.

"You bet, pard," Hickok said. "It was them hombres or me. Any more of these simpletons around?"

"I don't think so," Joshua answered. "They've been the only ones here since Blade, Geronimo, and you were taken away."

"How come you're still here?" Hickok asked. "I thought the big guy told you to make tracks if anything happened to us."

"I couldn't just desert you," Joshua responded.

"So what have you been doing all this time?"

"Praying."

Hickok's eyebrows arched. "Doing what?"

"Praying for guidance," Joshua elucidated. "Asking our Spirit Father for His will. Striving to ascertain an appropriate course of action. Should I confront the four guards or . . ."

"It's best for you that you didn't confront them," Hickok interrupted. "They'd have blown you away for sure.

Joshua looked forlornly at each of the four corpses. "They won't be blowing anyone away ever again."

"Sure won't!" Hickok beamed. "Listen. We've got some serious traveling to do. Last I saw, the soldiers were taking Blade and Geronimo south. We're going to go after them and free them."

"Just like that?"

"Just like that," Hickok affirmed.

"How do you do it?" Joshua queried.

"Do what?"

"Always have such an optimistic, confident attitude? I don't comprehend how you do it," Joshua said.

"That works both ways, pard," Hickok rejoined.

"Both ways?"

"Sure. You're supposed to be the spiritual person in

the Family, aren't you? The one with all the answers about life and death? The one who is close to God? If you're so close to God, then how come you don't always have a optimistic, confident attitude?" Hickok asked.

Joshua seemed taken aback by the question. He started to speak, then stopped.

"Never mind, pard. Now's not the time for this kind of chit-chat anyway. Let's load up their guns and take off," Hickok proposed.

"Won't we bury them?" Joshua inquired.

Hickok chuckled. "You never give up, do you?"

"No, I don't." Joshua paused, watching the gunman collect the weapons. "We're not going to give them a decent burial, are we?"

"Nope. There's a lot of critters around these parts, lots of wild animals looking for a meal. Didn't the Spirit design some critters to go around and eat dead things? I wouldn't want to deprive them of their din-din, and I certainly wouldn't want to try and buck creative design, now would I?"

"You know something, Hickok?" Joshua asked.

The gunman glanced at the Empath. "What's that, pard?"

Joshua grinned. "You're not as dumb as you pretend to be."

"Blast!" Hickok exclaimed, sounding exasperated.

"What is it?"

"That darn Injun ain't here to hear you say that!" Hickok's face brightened. "Say, you wouldn't want to put that in writing, would you? Geronimo's never going to believe it unless I can supply some proof. What do you say, pard?"

"I think I'm beginning to agree with Geronimo," Joshua said. "You *are* nuts!"

11

"I've got a bad feeling about this," Geronimo declared.

"So do I," Blade agreed apprehensively. They were standing near the western gate in the stockade, Zahner, Bear, and Bertha alongside them, staring outside the enclosure at a large group of prisoners. The soldiers, under the direction of Colonel Jarvis, had taken several hours to remove a couple of hundred of the captives, herding the unfortunates chosen into a compact mass only a few dozen feet west of the stockade. All of the troopers had participated, with fifty training their weapons on the group being separated from the main body, while the rest of the soldiers kept their eyes on the compound.

"What are they up to now?" Zahner asked anxiously. "Do you think they're going to truck us to the Civilized Zone in stages?"

"Didn't anyone else notice?" Bertha ventured. "The bastards only took the oldest ones out of here and some of the young ones. Not the real little kids, mind you, but ones about ten to twenty. Didn't you see it?"

Blade had seen it, but hesitated to comment, reluctant to instill fear and panic in the prisoners. What was it

116

Jarvis had said earlier? Something about having two hundred or so captives too many? "What do I do with the excess?" Jarvis had remarked. What *was* he going to do with those poor souls out there?

Colonel Jarvis, with Captain Rice at his left elbow, approached the barbed wire.

"Here comes the chief prick himself," Bertha muttered. "Lordy, how I'd love to cram his teeth down his throat!"

"I see I have your undivided attention, Blade," Jarvis said greeting the Warrior as he stopped next to the fence.

"Don't do it," Blade said softly.

"But I must," Jarvis countered. "You know that."

"Do what?" Zahner interjected. "What are you planning to do with them?"

Colonel Jarvis clasped his hands behind his back and puffed up his chest. "You might consider this as object lesson number two. The first lesson was when those others managed to sneak out under the fence the other night. How many were there? Fifty-two, I believe?" He glanced at Blade. "Have you told them yet?"

Zahner clasped Blade's right arm. "Told us what? Didn't they make it?"

Blade averted his eyes and shook his head.

Zahner turned, his eyes blazing his hatred. "Damn you!" He lunged at Jarvis, his arms between the strands of barbed wire.

Jarvis deftly side-stepped, chuckling. "I'd behave myself, if I were you, Zahner. Or maybe you want me to haul more of your people out here?"

Zahner gripped the wire, heedless of the pain, his arms quivering, as a loud groan racked his body.

"Good!" Jarvis grinned. "That's a good boy. But I want to demonstrate how fair I can be. Notice." He waved his right arm and three soldiers ushered another trooper in the direction of the group outside the stockade. The trooper being compelled to join the two hundred was unarmed, his face white as a sheet.

"He's the one who fell asleep at his post," Jarvis explained, "permitting those fifty-two to escape."

Bertha took a step toward the fence, her fists clenched. "You'd best not do what I think you're gonna do!" she threatened.

Colonel Jarvis feigned a shudder. "You scare me to death, bitch! Would you like to come out here too?"

"Any time you're ready!" Bertha snapped defiantly.

"Yes, you probably would," Jarvis said. "But I'm afraid I'll have to disappoint you, my dear. Cheer up, though! You'll have a front-row seat, as it were."

"You don't have to do this," Blade stated. "You could release them. No one would ever know."

"Be serious!" Jarvis scoffed. "What do you take me for? I am a soldier and I have my duty."

"Is that how you justify it?" Blade angrily demanded. "By telling yourself you're just doing your duty?"

Jarvis only smiled and turned, facing the clustered bunch of prisoners and the fifty soldiers encircling them.

"Please!" Zahner pleaded. "I beg of you! Have mercy!"

Colonel Jarvis looked over his left shoulder, his slit of a mouth twisted in contempt. "Mercy is for weaklings! In case you haven't noticed, the law of life is the survival of the fittest! And we are the fittest!" He nodded at Captain Rice.

A hush fell over the entire compound as the prisoners suddenly realized what was about to transpire.

"Ready!" Captain Rice shouted.

Blade leaned forward. "I just want you to know, Jarvis, that if I ever get the chance, I'm going to personally see to it that you get everything you have coming to you!"

"You shouldn't take things so personally," Colonel Jarvis said over his shoulder. "Fighting men like us must develop a detached, aloof attitude toward scum like these. You must learn to be objective, Blade." He paused. "I might add that I'm finding you to be a bit of a disappointment. I'd heard so much about you and your renowned fighting ability, and now I discover you are little more than a simpering weakling."

"Aim!" Captain Rice yelled.

Blade couldn't recall an instance in which he had felt more helpless than he did now. He knew what was coming, but he couldn't prevent it, he was unable to save the two hundred doomed to be slaughtered. For a moment, he thought the fifty soldiers ringing the victims would perform the actual execution, but then he heard the metallic click of a bolt being thrown above his head and he looked up at the western sentry tower. There were four troopers in the tower, and one of them had the big machine gun aimed at the two hundred people below. Blade couldn't identify the make or manufacture of the mounted machine gun; he only knew it was impressive and undoubtedly deadly. If they were utilizing the mounted gun for their butchery, then the fifty soldiers surrounding the group were there to prevent anyone from escaping.

"Lordy!" Bertha mumbled, terrified. "Please don't let them do it!"

"*Fire!*" Rice screamed.

Pandemonium ensued.

Those within the barbed wire watched helplessly as horrifying carnage erupted outside.

The machine gun in the sentry tower opened up, the gun roaring as the heavy slugs ripped into the packed innocents below. Many of the two hundred attempted to escape their fate; they bolted in every direction, fleeing for their lives, panic-stricken, some voicing their fear at the top of their lungs as they shrieked and wailed. The fifty soldiers encircling the victims were enjoying themselves, shooting those who endeavored to escape before they could manage more than ten yards. Old or young, male or female, it didn't matter, they were indiscriminately massacred, their bodies being struck again and again and again, their faces contorted as they were hit, the slugs tearing through them, causing them to jerk and writhe and twist and squirm before they fell to the hard ground, lifeless. Even after they dropped, it wasn't over. The soldiers kept raking the group with fire, round after round pouring into the deceased, creating the illusion the dead forms were still alive as they flopped and jumped from the force of the impact.

The killing went on and on and on.

And finally ceased.

The silence following the gruesome execution seemed preternatural, as the troopers surveyed their handiwork and the prisoners in the compound gaped at the torn and bleeding bodies of their relatives and friends.

Colonel Jarvis faced the stockade, smiling. "Now you know I am not to be trifled with!" he announced. "If any of you give me any trouble whatsoever, I will do to you what I just did to them!" He glanced at Zahner and Bear. "You are their leaders. I will hold you accountable if trouble arises. Have I made myself perfectly clear?"

Zahner gazed up at the sentry tower, then at the corpses on the field. "You have made yourself clearer than anyone else I have ever known."

"Good." Jarvis nodded, staring at Blade. "I'll have Rice fetch you in an hour. My men are erecting a tent and we shall dine together."

"What makes you think I would join you for a meal?"

Blade demanded.

Jarvis started to walk off. "Oh, you'll come, all right, if motivated by nothing more than curiousity. See you in an hour." He departed, walking toward the trucks.

"Okay, men!" Captain Rice ordered. "Let's hop to it and clean up this mess! There will be no evening meal until it's done!" He strolled off, organizing the work detail.

"How could anyone eat after witnessing . . . that?" Zahner asked.

"Why'd they do it?" Bear inquired, looking at Blade.

"They were excess," Blade replied.

"Excess?"

Blade nodded. "Jarvis told me earlier there were about two hundred more prisoners than he could accommodate in his trucks. Now everyone will fit into the troop transports and the Army won't need to make two trips."

"I'm goin' to waste that sucker!" Bertha vowed.

"You'll have to stand in line," Blade told her.

"What's this about a meal?" Zahner queried.

"Beats me," Blade said shrugging. "Jarvis insists on having a meal with me. Maybe he wants to gloat some more."

"It's odd. . . ." Geronimo began, his brow furrowed.

"What's odd?" Blade wanted to know.

"I could be wrong," Geronimo elaborated, "but I get the impression Jarvis is treating us, and especially you, as if we're some kind of celebrities."

"You're off your rocker," Blade informed him. "The only reason we're still alive is because Samuel the Second wants to kill us himself."

"Could be," Geronimo agreed, "but haven't you noticed how hard Jarvis tries to impress you, how he's tacitly seeking your approval of his actions?"

Blade smiled. "Have you been reading the psychology books in the Family Library again?"

"Are you goin' to eat with that son of a bitch?" Bertha demanded angrily.

"Yes."

"Traitor!" she snapped.

"Bertha, I don't have any choice. They'd probably drag me off if I refused. Besides, Jarvis is right. I am curious. I may learn some important information that will aid us in escaping."

Bear swept his left arm around the stockade. "How can we get out? They've doubled the guard since the others got out under the fence the other night. And look at all that hardware. How can we get out of this?"

"We'll find a way," Blade assured him. "Where there's a will, there's a way."

"You Family types sure got a lot of cornball sayings!" Bertha remarked.

"If you think Blade is corny," Geronimo interjected, "just wait until you see Hickok again. If you peeled his ears, you'd have enough to feed everyone here."

"I don't believe you, man!" Bear snapped testily, annoyed. "You're cuttin' jokes after what just happened?"

"Humor nourishes the soul," Geronimo said, surprised by Bear's outburst.

Blade guessed that Bear was severely disturbed by the massacre, and he tried to assuage Bear's grief. "As Warriors, we've seen a lot of gory sights," he said slowly. "I'm sure you have too. If you think about it, about the brutality all around you, if you dwell on it and mope over it, it'll get to you. You'll be depressed all the time, and you'll become cynical and hard. The tougher things get for us, the more we tend to joke to safeguard our sanity, to prevent us from being emotionally ravaged. It alleviates stress if you concentrate on the lighter side of life."

"I think I got you," Bear stated, "but I don't think I could do it. I can't shrug things off the way you guys do."

"It's not that we shrug them off," Geronimo corrected. "We're affected by violence, just like you. Only it's our business, and we learned a long time ago to take it in stride, as calmly as possible. Humor helps immensely. Otherwise, you'd go nuts!"

"Hey! What are they doin'?" Bertha suddenly asked, aghast, pointing.

The soldiers were loading the bodies onto the trucks for transport to a disposal site. In the process of carting the corpses to the trucks, they were searching the bodies for any valuables. They were treating the deceased roughly and talking and smiling while they worked.

"If it's the last thing I ever do," Bertha pledged, "I'm going to get Jarvis for this!" She glanced at Blade. "Is Joshua with you this time too?"

Blade insured none of the troopers were close enough to eavesdrop. "Yes, he is. Why?"

"Because the last time you were here, he tried tellin' me all about this God business. . . ." Bertha began.

"You can't blame God for this," Blade said cutting her off. "Humans don't always do what the Spirit leads them to do. Some mortals even shut God out of their lives entirely."

"So you say," Bertha rejoined. "Me, I'm not so sure. I think if I bump into Joshua and he starts yakkin' about God, and how we live in a universe of love, as he called it, and goes on about how all of us are brothers and sisters . . ." She paused and smiled at a thought she had. "Then I think, just for the hell of it, I'm goin' to haul off and sock him in the mouth."

12

"I don't understand. . . ."

"What is it you don't get, pard?"

"Well, first you said we had to get out of here right away. Then you changed your mind and said we should sit here until dark. It's dark, and we still haven't moved. Why not?"

"Josh, has anyone ever told you you're a worry-wart?" Hickok inquired. They were seated in the SEAL, Hickok in the driver's seat, Joshua in the bucket seat across from the gunman. "We stayed put because I wanted to see if anyone would show up to check out all the shooting. No one did."

"So?"

"So that tells me no one is close enough to have heard the shots," Hickok reasoned. "It also tells me the Army must have done something to the Nomads, Porns, and Horns or they would have showed by now."

"Oh."

"We also waited until dark because we'll be able to move without drawing attention to ourselves," Hickok said.

"But won't you need to use the lights on the SEAL to

travel at night?" Joshua asked.

"Uhhhhh . . ."

"And won't the lights attract as much attention as if we were driving in broad daylight?" Joshua asked.

"Hmmmm. I never thought of that," Hickok admitted. "Oh well! We'll try something new."

"New?"

"Yep. We'll drive with the lights out. No one will see us then!"

"Isn't that dangerous?" Joshua queried. "What if we run into a boulder or a hole in the ground?"

"Relax. I'm driving, aren't I? It's gonna be a piece of cake," Hickok assured him.

Despite his bragging, the gunfighter was slightly nervous. He'd only driven the vehicle a few times, and the possibility of damaging the Family's primary means of transportation disturbed him.

Joshua sensed the gunman's uneasiness. "We could always travel by foot," he offered.

"We have to find Blade and Geronimo tonight," Hickok rejoined, "not next year."

Joshua leaned back in his seat. "I'm ready whenever you are."

"Don't rush me!" Hickok said irritably, agitated because he was in the process of mentally reviewing the proper operation of the SEAL and Joshua's comment had sidetracked him.

"I won't say another word," Joshua promised.

Hickok turned the key and the SEAL purred to life. He reached for the gearshift and hesitated. "This will be a mite tricky, doing this in the dark and all. Here goes." He gingerly shifted the vehicle into Drive. "You all set?" he absently inquired.

"Yes," Joshua responded.

"Then, away we go!" Hickok exclaimed, and pressed

on the accelerator.

The SEAL instantly lurched into motion, rapidly gaining speed.

Backwards.

"Blast!" Hickok fumed and tramped on the brake pedal.

Only a sturdy grip on the dashboard saved Joshua from flying into the windshield.

"I'll never understand why mankind gave up the horse for these complicated contraptions!" Hickok complained.

"Is something wrong?" Joshua questioned, striving to sound nonchalant.

"I accidentally shifted into the wrong gear because I couldn't see what I was doing," Hickok detailed. "Looks like I'll have to flick on the lights after all."

"That would be nice," Joshua said.

Hickok pulled on the light control knob and the dashboard lights lit up. "Hey! Look at this!" he exclaimed.

"Look at what?"

"Don't you see it? The dash lights are on, but the headlights are still off. You must have to pull this here knob all the way out to get the headlights on. Great! Now we'll be able to drive with the headlights off just like I wanted!"

"You still intend to travel without running lights?" Joshua queried apprehensively.

"Yep." Hickok glanced at the gearshift. "Look at this! What a dummy! I had the thing in Reverse instead of Drive. Isn't that a kicker?"

Joshua, thankful there had been open space behind the transport instead of a tree, nodded. "It certainly is."

The gunman shifted correctly this time and grinned at his companion. "Hi-Yo, Silver!"

The SEAL took off at a fast clip.

Joshua tensed, clinging to the dashboard, wishing he were back at the Home with his parents and friends. Why had he ever agreed to Plato's lunatic proposition to become the Family's ambassador?

Hickok carefully weaved the SEAL between the Nomad tents and continued south along Moore Lake. The driving wasn't as difficult as he anticipated; a full moon in the western sky illuminated the terrain nicely.

Joshua began to relax, marveling at the gunman's dexterity and reflexes. "You're doing very well," he complimented Hickok.

"Of course," the Warrior stated confidently.

The lake was quiet and peaceful, its surface tranquil, reflecting the light from the bright moon above.

Hickok rolled down his window and heard an owl voice its distinctive "who?" from a stand of trees to his left.

"What happens when we find Blade and Geronimo?" Joshua inquired.

"We free them," Hickok answered.

"What if we're outnumbered?"

"So what? Since when has that stopped a Warrior from doing his duty?"

Joshua stared at the gunfighter for a moment. "Hickok, can I tell you something?" he asked gravely.

"I reckon so," Hickok said. "What is it? You sound so serious."

"I know that you and I haven't always seen eye to eye," Joshua mentioned.

"You've got that right!"

"So I just thought you should know I'm really glad you are the way you are," Joshua said. "I sincerely believe you're one of the best Warriors in the Family, maybe the very best. I know I have criticized your frequently callous attitude in the past. I know I've lambasted your cavalier disposition toward the taking of other lives. But I've given the matter considerable thought, and I've reached the conclusion I wouldn't have you any other way."

"Does all of that mean you like me?"

'It means I like you," Joshua confirmed.

"Thanks, pard!" Hickok beamed. "I appreciate it."

"Actually," Joshua went on, "I've never disliked you. I've experienced considerable difficulty adjusting to the reality of life outside our Home."

"I know," the gunman acknowledged.

"I'm afraid my shock at encountering so much casual violence affected my personal relationships, particularly with you," Joshua stated.

"Why are you telling me all this?" Hickok asked.

"Because I want you to know how I feel. I don't want you to despise me because I've been, at times, such a . . . jerk," he concluded.

"None of us despises you," Hickok informed the Empath. "I'll admit I've been on your case a lot in the past, but that's because I couldn't handle all of your whinin' every time we killed someone. It took me a while to see that we look at the world differently, Josh, and just because we do doesn't make either of us wrong. You are the spiritual type, and you tend to view other folks, even those you've never met before, as your brothers and sisters. You're always ready to offer your hand in friendship. Heck, that's why Plato picked you as the Family ambassador. Me, I'm completely different. I'm a Warrior, and I'm naturally suspicious of everybody, particularly the people we run into outside the Home. I don't trust nobody until they show me they deserve my trust. As a Warrior, as someone responsible for protecting the Home and the Family, I've got to be this way. I'd sooner shoot someone in the head if they look at me crosswise than give them the chance to plug me in the back. I know it's the opposite of the way you look at things, but I hope you won't hold it against me."

"I'll never hold it against you," Joshua guaranteed.

"Good! Now that that's settled, let's go waste some wimps!"

13

The convoy of troop transports and munitions trucks was five miles out of the Citadel when one of the vehicles unexpectedly gained additional weight.

Yama.

After leaving the Mason ranch, he had headed due south until he had reached Interstate Highway 80. The traffic on 80 had been sparse; apparently few of the Civilized Zone inhabitants had wanted to travel any farther west than Cheyenne. He had kept going, bearing to the southeast, intending to enter the Citadel from the south, hoping the ploy would thwart any attempts to determine his origination point if he were apprehended. The sun was well below the western horizon by the time he had reached Interstate Highway 25.

The volume of vehicles had been incredible.

The vast majority of the nearly ceaseless caravan had been military vehicles of one kind or another: jeeps, troop carriers loaded with armed soldiers, supply trucks, a few noisy half-tracks, and two tanks. Once, a dozen flatbeds had driven past Yama's place of concealment behind a tree near the Interstate, huge artillery pieces mounted on the back.

He had wondered how he could successfully join the procession without being detected. The traffic had been moving at forty miles an hour, making a running leap into the rear of one of the trucks an extremely hazardous and unappealing strategy.

Yama had waited for over an hour at the side of the highway, and just when he had been convinced there was no other recourse but to attempt the running leap, the Spirit had smiled upon him.

The second of the two tanks had been passing his position, its motor clanking and wheezing as if from old age, when it had coughed and sputtered and the night had been rent by a loud clanging sound. The tank had shuddered, spouting smoke from underneath, and had ground to a stop, completely blocking the traffic behind it. The troop transports ahead of the tank had continued on their way, oblivious to its plight. Behind the tank had been six more flatbeds with missile launchers on the beds. The flatbeds had slowed and pulled up behind the disabled tank.

Yama had suddenly found himself abreast of one of the flatbeds. Except for the driver and a fellow rider in the cab, the flatbeds had been deserted. The base of each missile launcher had been covered with a heavy tarp as protection from the elements.

"What the hell is the holdup?" the driver of the first flatbed had bellowed.

A soldier had emerged from the stricken tank to examine the underside. "It looks like we blew our motor!" he had called to the flatbed driver. "Damn piece of junk!" He had kicked the treads in frustration. "If they don't complete that new factory soon, this whole Army will be as useless as a tin can with both ends missing!"

"Is there any way you can get your tank to the side?"

the flatbed driver had asked. "We can try and go around you."

"No problem!" the tank trooper had yelled. "Give me a minute and I'll throw it into Neutral. When I shout out the hatch, give me a push!"

"Got ya!" the driver of the flatbed had responded.

Yama had scanned the highway behind the final flatbed, encouraged to find the road free of traffic. But he had known the situation wouldn't last long, that soon headlights would appear from the south and ruin his golden opportunity.

There had been a call from inside the tank, and the first flatbed had inched forward until its front bumper nudged the tank. Slowly, its engine whining, the truck had been able to move the tank to one side, to the right, clearing a path for the other vehicles to proceed.

A head had popped out of the top tank hatch. "Thanks! When you get to the Citadel, would you let the Motor Pool guys know what happened and tell them to get their lazy asses out here on the double? The brass want this baby operational for the attack."

"I'll let the Motor Pool know first thing," the flatbed driver had promised.

The procession of flatbeds had begun to move out.

Yama had waited.

The first flatbed had driven past the tank, its gears grinding as it gained speed.

Not yet.

The second truck had curved by the tank and followed the first.

Not yet.

The next three flatbeds had done likewise.

Now!

Yama had darted from behind the tree as the last of the flatbeds had started to roll. He had glanced over his shoulder, staring southward.

He had seen the feeble gleam of approaching headlights in the distance.

Yama had run, covering the ground in a surge of speed, hoping the troopers in the cab were concentrating on the tank and not looking in their rearview mirrors. The flatbed had been doing about ten miles an hour when he had leaped, landing on the tarp spread over the base of the missile launcher.

His fingers probed around the edges and found a loose flap. In another moment, he was under the tarp and crawling toward the front of the truck. He was four feet from the cab when the tarp ended. Cautiously, he raised the edge of the tarp and glanced up.

There was a small window in the rear of the cab, open to allow for some ventilation.

". . . . feel sorry for that tank crew. As busy as the Motor Pool will be tonight, that tank will be stuck there until morning," one of the men in the cab was saying.

"I can't believe all the hardware they're using on this operation," commented the second man. From the direction of the voice, Yama deduced this one was the rider.

"All of this just to wipe out a lousy bunch of jerks on a few horses," groused the driver. "Doesn't make sense to me."

"The Cavalry has more than just a few horses," corrected the rider. "I hear tell they have seven hundred horsemen."

"Big deal!" scoffed the driver. "What good are seven hundred horses and guys with rifles and handguns going to do against all of our equipment, even if our stuff is on its last legs?"

"You know Samuel," said the rider. "He always has to play it safe. This time, though, I think he's planning to beat the Cavalry in one fell swoop. I don't think he wants a repeat of what happened in Montana with those damn Indians!"

"Yeah!" The driver laughed. "They would of beat us if it hadn't of been for the Doktor and his gas."

"I don't know if they would have beat us," disagreed the rider, "but they could have holed up in Kalispell a lot longer than they did."

"I wonder if Samuel sent the Doktor a thank-you note," joked the driver.

"Don't do that!" snapped the rider.

"What's eating you?"

"Don't make fun of the Doktor or Samuel. You know they have ears everywhere. They could even have this cab bugged!" stated the rider, sounding scared.

"Don't be such a crybaby!" laughed the driver. "I went over this cab with a fine-tooth comb before we left Denver. It's clean as a whistle."

"You hope."

"I know."

"Listen," said the rider, "can't we talk about something else? I get nervous discussing the Doktor or Samuel."

"Sure we can," concurred the driver. "I expect we'll have the rest of the night free, since they're not planning to move us out until tomorrow morning. . . ."

"Where'd you hear that?" queried the rider.

"I have my sources," the driver divulged. "Anyway, since we'll have the night off, why don't we visit this little lady I know? She'll give both of us a tumble at a discount."

"I don't know. . . ."

"What's the matter with you? Got the jitters over a broad too? Don't worry. She gets herself inspected at the clinic once a month, just like the Government says she should. I'm tellin' you, we can have a blast! She has the biggest . . ."

Yama flattened, ruminating on the significance of the information he'd learned. As part of his campaign to reconquer the territory formerly held by the United States of America, Samuel was gearing up for a major thrust against the Cavalry in South Dakota, against the only ally the Family currently had in their struggle to resist Samuel and the Doktor. The Cavalry must be warned! But how?

The flatbed was gaining considerable speed.

From the comments made by the blabbermouths, Yama gathered the Army was utilizing outdated equipment, possibly even from before the Third World War. Why would the Government be using such antiquated hardware? Didn't the Civilized Zone have the factories necessary to produce new military equipment? Was their problem a lack of manufacturing capability, or did it go deeper than that?

Could it be a lack of natural resources?

Yama mentally reviewed the area encompassing the Civilized Zone. He knew it embraced the former states of Kansas, Nebraska, probably most or all of Wyoming, Colorado, eastern Arizona, New Mexico, Oklahoma, the northern half of a state once called Texas, and, now that the Flathead Indians were eradicated, most of the state of Montana as well.

Quite a large tract.

But what sort of natural resources was available? The Government would need certain types of metals to build tanks and cannons and such, right? Were those metals available in the Civilized Zone?

Yama grinned.

Possibly, just possibly, he'd stumbled over informa- tion crucial to the Family's future.

Possibly, just possibly, Samuel and the Doktor weren't as militarily strong as everyone thought they were.

And hopefully he'd discovered the chink in the Civilized Zone's armor.

Yama raised the tarp and peered out.

The convoy was only a mile from the Citadel, according to a sign at the side of the highway.

Would every vehicle be checked as it entered the Citadel?

Before departing the Home for his spying mission to the Citadel, Yama had visited the enormous Family Library and researched every book he could find on the region, and specifically on Cheyenne. Unfortunately, Cheyenne, Wyoming, after World War III, was a vastly altered city from the one existing prior to the Big Blast. The tremendous influx of refugees and evacuees, combined with the necessity for improved security and fortification, had drastically transformed Cheyenne into a veritable fortress.

The Citadel.

Within minutes, the first line of defense was in sight, and Yama was awed by the structure.

The Army Corps of Engineers had erected a massive stone and mortar wall completely enclosing the city. The wall stood forty feet high and was three feet thick. Perched atop this wall were numerous gun emplacements and observation towers, enabling the soldiers to see for miles in every direction on a clear day. Four iron gates were established as the only entry and exit points, one such gate being positioned in the middle of each wall. The Army had hoped their huge wall would withstand a sustained mass assault, an assault which never came.

Cheyenne had been spared a direct strike from a

nuclear weapon, and the anticipated Soviet land attack
had failed to materialize. In fact, surprisingly, the entire
Civilized Zone had been spared from a Red invasion. No
one knew why. There were unsubstantiated rumors the
Russian Army had indeed invaded and occupied much
of the eastern half of the country, its advance inexplicably halted at the Mississippi River. But these
reports were unconfirmed, because the patrols sent east
to verify them never returned.

The convoy turned right onto another road. The sign
at the junction revealed they were now traveling on
College Drive.

Yama craned his neck and peered up at the huge wall
looming above them. College Drive was immediately
outside the wall. According to the intelligence he'd
received, Yama knew the wall extended to the west
several miles, completely enclosing the Francis E.
Warren Air Force Base and the United States
Experimental Station within its confines. The northern
boundary of the wall was once known as Four Mile
Road, and the eastern perimeter was only two miles
beyond North College Drive.

The first of the flatbeds reached the iron gate in the
center of the southern wall. All of the flatbeds slowed
and braked while the driver of the first truck conversed
with one of the guards stationed at the gate.

Yama glanced over his left shoulder, gratified to discover the nearest traffic behind them was at least a half-
mile to their rear.

". . . love coming up here," the driver was saying.
"Denver makes me feel so cramped, so crowded all the
time. At least here you have some elbow room."

What was he talking about? Yama wondered.

"Yeah," concurred the passenger, "I hear tell they
only have one hundred thousand or so on the graveyard

shift. Imagine that! I'd like to move here, some day, if the Housing Authority will allow it. The wide open spaces appeal to me."

"Me too," echoed the driver.

Yama crawled forward and risked a peek around the corner of the cab. The first flatbed was still stopped at the gate, the driver joking and laughing with the guard.

How much longer would they dally at the gate? Time was a crucial factor; he had to be out of the Citadel by daylight. He might be able to roam the city undetected at night, but Yama doubted he'd pass a close scrutiny in the light of day.

The first flatbed gunned its motor and drove into the Citadel.

Yama smiled. The Spirit was smiling on his enterprise. The guards were not bothering to check the flat-beds, and why should they? The Citadel had never been attacked nor the Civilized Zone invaded for over a century. Why should they expect any trouble now?

The second flatbed was passing through the massive gate.

Yama ducked and scurried under the tarp, pulling it over his head and holding the Wilkinson close to his chest. A moment later, the last of the flatbeds moved slowly forward.

Yama could feel the truck sway slightly as the driver turned left to enter the Citadel.

"Hey! How ya doin', Buck?" asked the driver.

"Fine. You got time for a brew or two?"

"Sorry. Not tonight."

"Catch me next time, then."

Evidently the driver knew one of the guards.

Yama counted to twenty and elevated the edge of the tarp.

They were inside the Citadel!

The flatbeds were driving north on a wide avenue, a thoroughfare packed with vehicles, again the majority of them military. Running along both sides of the avenue were sidewalks crammed with people. Yama realized the population density in the Citadel must be staggering. As a Warrior, when at the Home, he was obligated to work day shifts, evening shifts, and graveyard shifts on a rotating basis, and he deduced the same practice prevailed here. This made his task easier. In a crowd like this, he should be able to travel unchallenged.

The convoy kept bearing north for some time, its progress impeded by the crush of traffic. Finally, the flatbeds turned right on Pershing Boulevard.

Yama tensed.

They were almost there.

The Biological Center. The domain of the malevolent Doktor.

One of the Doktor's creations, a genetically spawned creature named Gremlin, had defected to the Family and provided extensive details on the interior of the Citadel. Gremlin had argued with Plato concerning the wisdom of sending a Warrior on a spying mission to the Citadel, contending the Warrior would never make it out of Cheyenne alive. Once convinced that Plato could not be dissuaded, Gremlin had then warned Plato that the Warrior should avoid the Biological Center. "At all costs, yes?" Plato had passed on the admonition to Yama after the Warriors had drawn lots to determine which one of them would perform the spying mission; Yama had drawn the short straw.

And there it was! Rising seven stories high, situated to the west of the V.A. Hospital, constructed of a black synthetic substance, rose the Biological Center. As with the rest of the Citadel at night, it was plainly illuminated by the dozens and dozens of street lights and spotlights positioned at periodic intervals. On the north, west, and south sides of the Biological Center were enormous parking lots, and the Army was assembling its forces on these lots in preparation for the assault against the Cavalry in South Dakota. Row after row of vehicles lined the parking areas; all of the jeeps, troop carriers, supply trucks, and others were gathered for the invasion.

The flatbeds pulled into a lot on the west side of the Biological Center and parked in a row near the south side of the lot.

Yama eased under the tarp and waited. He heard the driver and his companion exit the flatbed, slamming their doors and engaging in idle discussion as they walked off. In the near distance rose the sound of the vehicle traffic on the streets and avenues of Cheyenne. He also could hear someone shouting, although the words were indistinguishable.

As silently as possible, the Warrior slid out from under the tarp and crawled to the edge of the flatbed. The parking area was well lit, but he was concealed in the shadow of the missile launcher. He gazed around.

The parking lots were apparently deserted, except for the vast array of military equipment.

Yama dropped to the tarmac and walked around the cab of the flatbed.

Where was everyone? Indulging in a last fling before the war against the Cavalry?

Yama was amazed at how lightly the Army seemed to take its opposition. How could they afford to be so confident?

Whoever was doing all the shouting was still at it.

Yama casually strolled in the general direction of the Biological Center. He recalled Gremlin's warning and promptly disregarded it. The Biological Center was the Doktor's base of operations. In it, the Doktor produced his genetic deviates, his league of killers and monstrosities. From it, the Doktor exerted a profound, terrifying influence over the entire Civilized Zone. The Doktor, so the story went, was almost as powerful as Samuel the Second. Some claimed he was the real power in the Civilized Zone, that Samuel ruled as the Doktor's puppet.

Whatever the case, Yama thought with a grin, it was imperative to include the Biological Center in his scenic tour of the Citadel.

The Warrior had already passed several rows of trucks and was stepping into an open space between the rows when the voice assailed him.

"Hey! Hold it!"

Yama stopped, the Wilkinson at his right side.

"Hey! I'm talkin' to you!"

Yama turned, fingering the trigger on the Wilkinson.

Five soldiers were standing fifteen yards away, behind a supply truck with its tailgate down. One of them held an M-16.

"You hard of hearin', fellow?" demanded the trooper with the M-16.

"My ears function perfectly," Yama replied, stalling, his eyes darting right and left as he scanned for other soldiers in the vicinity.

"What are you? A smart-ass?" The trooper advanced on Yama.

14

"I trust you've enjoyed your meal?"

"My compliments to your cook. What was it? I've never tasted meat quite like it before."

Colonel Jarvis leaned back in his wooden folding chair and placed his hands over his slightly paunchy belly. "You've never eaten steak before?"

Blade, seated across from the officer at a small table in his tent, stared at the bone on his paper plate. "The Family normally consumes venison. Once, years ago, one of our horses was struck by lightning and we all had horse meat for several meals in a row. But I've never had meat like this. What animal was it from?"

"A cow."

"Did you bring the cow from Denver?"

Jarvis laughed. "No. Cattle are roaming loose all over the place. There's a big herd not more than ten miles west of the Twin Cities. I had some of my men bag one this morning. Rank does have its privileges, you know."

"So I see," Blade acknowledged.

Colonel Jarvis reached into his right shirt pocket and removed a thin cigar. "Care for a smoke?" He extracted a box of matches from his left pocket.

"No. I don't smoke."

"Of course. Ever the noble Warrior, eh? I'd imagine you don't have too many vices, do you?"

"Why should I? Vices impair your effectiveness and inhibit spiritual communion with our Creator. None of the Family smokes or drinks alcohol, although I understand both practices were widespread before the Big Blast."

"The Big Blast?" the colonel repeated. Then he nodded. "Oh. I forgot. That's how your people refer to the Third World War. Cute. But let me ask you something . . ." Jarvis said, his eyes narrowing as he scrutinized the Warrior, "about this Creator business. Do you really mean to tell me you believe in a God?"

"You mean to tell me you don't?"

"There's no such thing as God," Jarvis replied. "Everybody knows that. It's illegal to believe in a Supreme Being. You can be thrown into prison for just talking about it."

"What?" Blade asked in surprise. "I didn't know that."

Colonel Jarvis grinned. "Looks like you don't know as much about the Civilized Zone as you thought you did."

"How could they make it illegal to believe in our Heavenly Father?" Blade inquired.

"Easy. They passed a law."

"They can't do that!"

Jarvis smiled. "Why can't they? The Government has all the power, and when you have power you can do anything you want. About eighty years ago, I think it was, they passed a law outlawing all religion. They said our scientists had conclusively proven God does not exist. They said the fact that World War III took place shows the universe isn't dominated by a God of love. How could a God allow so many people to be slaughtered?

No. There is no God."

"You can't hold God accountable for the insanity mankind perpetuates," Blade countered.

"I had no idea you were such a philosopher."

"Everyone in the Family is encouraged to cultivate his or her religious nature," Blade explained. "We're free to adopt whatever beliefs we choose."

"Does everyone in your Family believe in a Supreme Being?"

Blade nodded.

"Amazing!" Jarvis stated.

Their conversation was abruptly interrupted by the arrival of Captain Rice at the tent flap. "Colonel!"

Jarvis twisted in his seat. "What is it? You may enter."

Rice walked into the tent and saluted. "Our patrol has just returned."

"And?"

Captain Rice shot a spiteful glance at Blade. "They found the two men sent after Hickok. Dead. They tracked him to the Nomad Camp. The four guards we left there are dead and the vehicle is gone."

Colonel Jarvis frowned. "Any sign of the vehicle?"

"None. We have two jeeps out looking now, but they haven't radioed in yet."

"Good. Keep me posted." Jarvis dismissed his subordinate with a wave of his left hand. "So," he said as Rice left the tent, "it appears your Hickok is going to be more of a problem than I thought. Where could he have gone?"

"Beats me."

"We'll find him," Jarvis predicted. "Knowing Hickok as I do, I expect he'll stupidly try to rescue you. When he does, we'll be ready for him."

Blade's mind was racing. So Hickok had reached the

SEAL! Good. Jarvis was right; Hickok would try to get them out. The gunman might be grossly outnumbered, but he had an edge. The Army was unaware of the SEAL's armament.

"Something on your mind?" Jarvis queried, noting Blade's reflective expression.

"I was thinking about your jeeps," Blade lied. "I didn't know you had any here."

"Three of them," Jarvis said. "We keep them on constant patrol."

"Something else," Blade mentioned, "I've been meaning to ask about. We took a radio from your men in Thief River Falls. We've tried to monitor your broadcasts with it, but we haven't had much luck. Why is that?"

Colonel Jarvis laughed. "We alter the frequency used on a daily basis according to a secret schedule, and we rotate the times of our regular broadcasts. Even if you went down the entire dial, the odds of stumbling across us at the right time and frequency are slim."

"We know," Blade agreed.

"We're not as dumb as you might think," Jarvis boasted with a smile.

"I'll never underestimate you again," Blade vowed, thinking of the massacre.

Jarvis gazed over his right shoulder at the night sky visible through the tent flap. "It's getting late and I have work to do." He faced the Warrior. "I've enjoyed our little talk immensely. It isn't often I get to associate with an equal. Say! I just remembered something I wanted to show you." Jarvis rose and walked to the tent opening and spoke to one of the two guards positioned outside.

Blade searched for a potential weapon. A lantern hung on the tent's center post, and there was a sleeping bag rolled up in one corner. In another corner was a rumpled green blanket. Blade debated using his steak knife, but rejected the idea.

"Wait until you see these," Jarvis said, still standing near the tent flap, waiting for one of the guards to return. "I couldn't believe it when we found them. I should be able to get a good price for them."

There was the pounding of running feet and Jarvis reached thru the opening.

Blade, his line of sight blocked by the officer's body, put his elbows on the table and rested his chin in his hands.

"Look at these!" Jarvis said elated, turning. "Aren't they gems?"

Blade straightened, startled.

Colonel Jarvis was holding an auto-loading rifle in his right hand, a Commando Arms Carbine with a ninety-shot magazine. In his left hand dangled two shoulder holsters containing Vega 45 automatics. "Ever seen anything like them?" Jarvis asked.

Blade almost nodded. He had seen them before. In fact, he had owned them, had taken them from the Family armory and brought them to the Twin Cities on the Triad's last trip here. He'd given them up for lost after they'd been confiscated by the Wacks. "Where did you get them?" he asked Jarvis.

"You wouldn't believe it," Jarvis responded. "After we attacked those crazies, the Wacks, at that hospital headquarters of theirs, we made a room by room sweep of the building. One of my men found these in one of the rooms on the second floor. I haven't the slightest idea how they got there, but I do know I can get a pretty penny for them after we return to the Civilized Zone."

"Sell them? Who'd want to buy them?"

"Anyone," Jarvis answered. "I can't sell them to civilians because it's illegal for them to own firearms, but it is legit for us in the service to own guns. A lot of officers like to collect old firearms like these. We can't manufacture them anymore, you know."

"You don't say."

Colonel Jarvis placed the Commando and the Vegas on top of the green blanket in the corner. "Yes, sir. Between these and the ones we took from you Warriors, I should add about five thousand to my bank account. I think I'll . . ." Jarvis began, then stopped, staring at the Commando. "That's odd."

"What is?" Blade glanced at the tent flap. There was no sign of the guards; they must be standing on either side of the opening.

"This gun . . ." Colonel Jarvis said absently. He knelt and retrieved the Commando, then lifted the green blanket.

Blade gripped the edge of the table, excited.

The A-1, the Dan Wesson, the Arminius, Hickok's Henry, and the other Warrior arms were all under the green blanket.

"Look at this!" Colonel Jarvis exclaimed. "The gun we took from you and the one we found at the Wack hospital look almost alike. Isn't that strange?"

"They both look like the Thompson submachine gun," Blade revealed.

"The Thompson submachine gun?" Jarvis reiterated.

"Yes. I think I read an article about the Thompson once. An ancient piece, if I recall." He looked at Blade. "You certainly seem to know a lot about it."

"The Family Library has an extensive section on firearms," Blade divulged.

"It figures," Jarvis commented. He placed the Commando and the Vegas under the green blanket. "I'd better see about returning you to the stockade or your friends will think you've turned traitor on them."

"They know I would never do that," Blade replied. Colonel Jarvis was tucking the blanket around the weapons, his back to his supper guest.

This was his chance!

If he could kill Jarvis silently, he could reclaim his weapons and . . .

"Colonel!" someone shouted, and a moment later Rat burst into the tent.

Jarvis stood, instantly enraged. "How dare you enter without my consent!"

One of the guards peered inside. "Sorry, sir! He slipped past us before we could stop him."

Colonel Jarvis motioned for the guard to leave, which he promptly did. "I repeat!" Jarvis snapped, glaring at Rat. "How dare you enter my tent without permission!"

Rat wasn't about to be cowered by the intimidating officer. "I just heard about those men you sent after Hickok! They're dead! You know what that means? He's coming! He's on his way!"

"So? What can he do against all of my men?" Colonel Jarvis asked. "Why don't you go ask Captain Rice for a drink? You could use something to steady your nerves, little man!" he said contemptuously.

Rat clenched and unclenched his fists. "You're makin' a big mistake, Jarvis! You should have killed Hickok and his friends the moment you had them in your custody. Look at this! You're having your meal with Blade!" Rat took a step toward the officer. "You jackass! Don't you know how dangerous these guys are? They play for keeps!"

Colonel Jarvis unexpectedly lunged, grabbing Rat by the front of his shirt and nearly lifting him from the ground. "So do I!" he warned. "If you'd care for a demonstration, it can be arranged right now!"

It was as if Rat's backbone turned to mush. He

blanched and recoiled from the officer's baleful glare. "Hey! Let me go! I didn't mean nothin'! Honest!"

"Mark my words, weasel!" Jarvis hissed. "Cross me again and it will be the last act you ever commit. Do I make myself perfectly clear?"

Rat nodded his head over and over.

Colonel Jarvis shoved Rat toward the tent flap. "Get out! And remember what I've told you!"

"Yes, sir! I'm sorry, sir!" Rat's chin was quivering as he backed from the tent.

"Disgusting filth!" Jarvis stated angrily. Then he glanced at the Warrior. "The presumptuous fool has ruined my mood! My men will escort you back and I'll see you in the morning. We'll be going for a little ride." Jarvis smiled. "Guards!"

Two guards entered the tent.

"Take this man to the stockade," Jarvis ordered. "Watch him! If he escapes, I'll have your balls for breakfast!"

The troopers stood aside to allow Blade to pass.

Blade rose and nodded at the officer. "I want to thank you for an . . . interesting . . . evening."

"Make the most of the time you have left," Jarvis advised. "I have a feeling you won't be eating too many meals after Samuel gets through with you."

Blade exited, marveling at how careless Jarvis could be. If only two soldiers were taking him to the stockade, he'd overpower them, return to the tent, and grab his weapons.

"Hold it!" directed one of the troopers behind Blade.

Four more soldiers appeared from behind a nearby truck. The tent was located on the grass near the parked troop transports.

"Take this scum to the stockade," the guard instructed, and one of the four nodded, pushing the

Warrior with the barrel of his M-16.

"Move it, jerk!"

Blade meekly complied, hoping to deceive the four guards, to convince them he was docile. He idly gazed up at the full moon, then at the nearby trucks. The transports were about fifteen yards distant, providing the closest cover. If he could reach the troop transports, he stood a good chance of eluding the soldiers. The troopers weren't about to fire into their own vehicles.

At least, he hoped they wouldn't.

Two of the escorts were immediately behind the Warrior, the third walked just to his right, and the fourth was staying alongside his left elbow.

Blade hesitated, stopping and glancing down at his left foot.

"Why'd you stop?" demanded the one to his left, poking Blade for the second time with his M-16.

Blade twisted his leg and used his right hand to elevate his left foot. "I've got something in my moccasin. Feels like a small stone."

"Ahhhh! Poor baby!" the one on the left cracked. "Does the teeny-weeny pebble hurt the big, bad Warrior?"

The other three soldiers laughed.

Blade grinned, surreptitiously scanning the area.

The stockade was brilliantly illuminated by the spotlights mounted on the four sentry towers. Most of the soldiers were gathered around campfires, cooking and relaxing. Those troopers standing near the barbed wire fence seemed bored with their duty. The soldiers in the sentry towers seemed to be keeping their eyes on the prisoners.

It was now or never!

"Get moving!" the soldier on the left barked. "You can take off your moccasins in the stockade. Do you think we want to catch a whiff of your smelly foot?"

"I guess not," Blade said, placing his left foot on the ground. "Although it would be a distinct improvement over your body odor," he added, calculating the remark would provoke another prod from the M-16.

It did.

Blade exploded into action at the same instant the barrel of the M-16 touched his left side. He swung his left elbow back and up, feeling it crunch against the trooper's nose even as he gripped the barrel of the rifle and spun, jerking the M-16 from the soldier's grasp and slamming the stock into the face of the trooper on his right, downing him, two of the four now out of commission.

The pair behind the Warrior were starting to bring their weapons into play.

Blade dove for the one on his left, knowing there was no way he could bag the one on his right before he was cut to ribbons. As he leaped, as his massive arms encircled his opponent and dragged him to the ground, Blade caught sight of the two soldiers in front of the tent. The tent guards were maybe ten yards off, and one of them suddenly perceived what was transpiring. He reacted automatically, whipping up his M-16 and firing a short burst.

There was a grunt and a gasp and the last of Blade's four escorts tumbled to the dirt.

The one in Blade's arms was still, stupidly, striving to use his M-16.

Blade drove his stony right fist into the trooper's mouth and felt teeth give. The soldier went momentarily limp, and Blade scooped up the M-16, rose to his knees, and pulled the trigger.

The two tent guards were charging on the run, and they were caught in the chest by the slugs, their bodies flipping backward and crashing to the hard earth.

Blade pivoted, staying on his knees to minimize the target he presented.

Three soldiers were approaching from the direction of the fence.

Blade angled the barrel of the M-16 to reduce the possibility of any of the bullets striking the captives in the stockade, and let loose with a short burst.

The three were struck in the head and died in a bloody heap.

A large gun abruptly opened up, one of the machine guns, the one on the western sentry tower.

Blade rolled backwards as the spot he vacated erupted in a spray of dirt and sod.

Soldiers were converging on the tent, drawn by the gunfire.

Blade crawled toward the troop transports, wondering if the sentry gunner had lost track of him.

No.

The machine gun chattered, the heavy slugs ripping a path through the ground not four inches from the Warrior.

Damn!

Blade rose, running at full speed, making for the trucks. He was within seven yards of the parked vehicles when he whirled and fired a burst into the nearest troopers, four of them approaching from the north. He saw them go down as he turned and raced for the transports, diving when he was yet a yard away and scrambling underneath the first truck as shots punctuated the night above him.

"Not at the trucks, you idiots!" Colonel Jarvis was bellowing, enraged. "We can't get home without them! Surround them! Surround them and flush him out! Go truck to truck if you have to but get him!"

Blade scurried under the second of the troop transports as boots pounded all around him.

The soldiers were hemming him in!

He was trapped!

"Bring flashlights!" someone was shouting.

"Watch yourselves!" another cautioned.

Blade glanced over his shoulder.

Boots!

He looked to his left.

More boots!

Doubledamn!

To be so close!

"Listen to me!" Colonel Jarvis yelled. "Listen to me! I don't care what Samuel wants! After what that bastard just did, I want him dead! An extended leave for the man who gets him! A month off with pay!"

"Did you hear that?" Blade heard a young trooper ask from somewhere near the cab.

"Sure did," replied a friend. "This sucker is as good as dead!"

"You got it!"

15

Yama was all set to cut the approaching trooper in two when a funny thing happened.

The soldier suddenly stiffened, snapped to attention, and saluted. "Sir! Sorry, sir!" He looked over his left shoulder at the four troopers standing behind the supply truck. "An officer!" he exclaimed, sounding petrified. "It's an officer!"

The four other soldiers immediately straightened, their arms held at their sides.

"I didn't see you were an officer," the one with the M-16 explained, "until I was right on top of you, sir. I wouldn't have called you a smart-ass had I known, sir."

Yama opted to bluff his way past these men.

"I certainly hope not," the Warrior said stiffly, "or you know where you'd end up, don't you?"

The trooper with the M-16 swallowed, his throat bobbing. "Yes, sir."

"What is your name?" Yama demanded.

"Corporal Gardner, sir!"

"Who did you think I was?" Yama pressed him.

"Just one of us, sir! A grunt like us! I thought I could get you to help us finish loading this truck so we could get out of here faster. I didn't see your bars until it was too late, sir."

Yama simulated making a momentous decision; he bit his lower lip and used his left hand to scratch his chin. "Well, Corporal Gardner, I'll let you go this time, but only because we both have a lot to do before we depart for South Dakota. Consider yourself lucky. I won't press charges for insubordination."

Corporal Gardner exhaled noisily. "Thank you, sir! It won't happen again, sir!"

"It had better not," Yama advised him, about to leave, when he noticed several large crates in the supply truck. "What is it you're loading up anyway?"

"Explosives, sir," Gardner respectfully revealed. "This is our last truck and we can take some time off. So far, we've loaded four trucks full of all kinds of stuff. Grenades, nitro, dynamite, mines, even a few of those rare tactical units, the small jobs that can lob a thermo about a mile or more."

Yama, puzzled by the references to "tactical unit" and to "thermo," wanted to ask more. He refrained for fear of displaying an ignorance inconsistent with his status as an officer.

"Anything else, sir?" Corporal Gardner asked, evidently eager to return to work and remove himself from the officer's presence.

"No. Carry on," Yama directed. He continued on his way toward the Biological Center, staying in the shadows of the vehicles to reduce the prospect of detection. Fortunately, he did not bump into any more late workers, and before he knew it he was there, at the edge of a wide sidewalk below the towering edifice. To one accustomed to the sedate pace of life at the Home, it was as if he had walked into a madhouse.

People were everywhere, great crowds of them, going

every which way, pressing against one another in their haste to reach their destinations. Men, women, and children; civilians and military types; some in fine clothes, some in rags; a compact commingling of humanity surging to and fro, intent on their own lives to the exclusion of all else.

Yama stared at the spectacle in bewilderment. Why was everyone in such a hurry? He looked down at his boots, then at the sidewalk not four feet away, confused. He gazed around at the parking lot, nearly deserted except for the vehicles and a few straggling soldiers, then at the sidewalk again.

He didn't get it.

Why were they all staying on the sidewalk, crammed together, when they could simply spread out and use part of the parking lot? It didn't make any . . .

Hold it!

Yama sensed he was being watched, and casually twisted, studying the passers-by, holding the Wilkinson close to his right side. Was he imagining things or . . . ?

There.

A tall man wearing a blue uniform and carrying a night stick was standing on a small, circular white platform, about three feet high, twenty yards north of the Warrior's position. The platform was located in the center of the sidewalk, forcing the pedestrains to bypass it on either side. The man was keeping an eagle eye on the crowd below his perch.

Yama knew the man in blue—weren't they called policemen?—was watching him closely and he wondered if he'd made a mistake or was about to make one. He couldn't afford a mishap, not when he was so close to his destination! Should he simply barge onto the sidewalk and trust he could lose the policeman in the throng? What if the policeman sounded an alarm?

Yama's predicament was unexpectedly resolved.

Another soldier appeared, walking from the parking lot toward the sidewalk.

Yama caught sight of the trooper out of the corner of his left eye and he followed the soldier's movement as inconspicuously as he could.

The newcomer on the scene didn't hesitate; he walked up to the sidewalk and stopped, directly across from the policeman on the white platform. At that particular point, Yama observed, the sidewalk tapered outward and formed a triangular-shaped section of cement. The soldier stood in the center of the triangle, patiently waiting, watching the lines of passing people. Suddenly, an opening presented itself and the trooper darted into the lane and was off, moving with the pedestrian traffic flow.

Yama detected a method to this madness. Those on the far side of the sidewalk were all moving to his left, toward the north. The people on the nearest half of the sidewalk were all walking toward the south, to his right. They were traveling in distinct patterns, although the initial impression had belied the fact.

The Warrior abruptly realized something else.

The shouting he'd heard earlier was still assaulting the ears. He'd been listening to it for so long, he must have subconsciously blocked out the words. Now they were crystal clear, and their source was self-evident. Thirty yards to the south was a metal pole, twenty feet in height, with a loudspeaker attached at the top.

". . .arrested for littering," the speaker was broadcasting, "Citizen Alfred E. Bradbury. Arrested for jaywalking, Citizen Norma T. Putz. Arrested for smoking, Citizens T.S. Doyle, Mary B. Martin, and Warren O. Sanderson. That concludes this edition of 'Criminal Corner.' The next report will be in thirty minutes. Ever remember: In Samuel We Trust."

Yama casually strolled toward the triangle, his mind utterly confounded by the sights and sounds around him.

". . .time for the hourly Civilized Zone Update," the loudspeaker was squawking, "and here with your news is Walter Carruthers, direct from Denver." There was a second of static, followed by a deep, resonant voice speaking in clipped sentences. "My fellow Citizens, good evening. This is a day to remember, a day that will go down in history. In his exalted wisdom, Samuel has decided to reabsorb the barbarians in the former state of South Dakota. As you are already aware, since you have been following these reports as required, a renegade band known as the Cavalry must be reabsorbed to save them from themselves. All of the Civilized Zone is behind our glorious leader in this enterprise; peace and stability will only come after what was once ours is ours again! However, because of the additional drain on our supplies, certain food and other items will face increased rationing during the course of the military campaign. Effective immediately, all Citizens will be permitted one ounce of chocolate every three months instead of every two. Movie credits will now be accrued at the rate of one credit for every eighty hours of satisfactory work performance, instead of every seventy-five hours. . . ."

Yama reached the triangle and stopped, striving to derive some logical meaning from the broadcasts.

". . .here with the latest Flashlines is Diane Evans."

The policeman wasn't taking his eyes off the Warrior.

". . .comes word from Topeka, Kansas, this evening of a despicable crime! The Morals Police report they have arrested nine parties, all involved in an anti-abortion ring known as The Breath of Life. These nine, five men and four women, have already confessed to terrifying activities against the State, against the Civilized Zone itself. These criminal offenses include distributing anti-abortion literature anonymously to pregnant women; spraying anarchist slogans on public buildings and other property; and inciting and perpetuating criminal insanity by distributing religious tracts randomly through the public mail. The prosecutor in this case says he is confident that all nine guilty parties will receive the death penalty. Elsewhere, in Tulsa, Oklahoma, four children will jointly receive the Citizenship of the Month Award from that city for outstanding service to their Government and fellow Citizens. The four, ranging in age from six to fourteen, collectively contacted the Crimestoppers Program and reported their parents for persistently saying grace at meals, a Class Nine Felony. All four children will receive an equal share of the two-thousand-credit reward in this instance. Congratulations to the Lancaster children of Tulsa, children with the courage to live the Golden Rule. Remember: Crime-stopping Begins in the Home!''

Yama ceased listening, at a complete loss to explain any of the babble. Morals Police? Turning in your own parents? It was utterly alien to his experience, as if he'd landed on another planet. He couldn't afford to waste precious time when he had a bigger problem to solve.

Namely, the staring policeman.

Yama knew he couldn't delay much longer; he had to enter the sidewalk soon or the policeman would come over to investigate his unseemly delay. He took a deep breath and girded himself, waiting for an opening.

The policeman was leaning forward, intently scrutinizing the man with the silver hair.

The loudspeaker suddenly went dead, absolutely devoid of all sound, even static.

Yama felt, rather than saw, a perceptible change in

the crowd, an ambiguous change in attitude and alert-
ness.

A raucous blast abruptly shrieked from the loudspeaker.

Twice.

Three times in all.

The reaction on the sidewalk was instantaneous and
inexplicable. The people stopped and packed into two
masses on either side of the lofty steps leading up to the
Biological Center, clearing a path from the glass doors
down to the parking lot.

Yama gazed up at the large doors, tinted black like the
rest of the seven-story structure, as they swung outward,
disgorging a veritable menagerie, a nightmarish
collection of genetic deviates walking in double file,
marching down the steps in synchronized precision.
Ten. Twenty. Thirty. Yama stopped counting. They
reached the sidewalk and turned to the left, their route
miraculously clear of all other traffic.

How did the Doktor do it?

Yama knew Gremlin well, even considered the
creature a friend. But the Warrior couldn't become
accustomed to the results of genetic engineering,
especially when those results could talk to you or eat
with you.

Or eat you.

All of the creatures in the Doktor's Genetic Research
Division were bipeds; beyond that, any similarity was
strictly coincidental. There were tall ones and short
ones, hairy ones and scaly ones, many more bestial than
human, some with exaggerated ears or extended fangs,
others with fiery red eyes or claws for fingers. Each of
them wore a leather loincloth and was fitted with a metal
collar around its neck, the collar the Doktor reportedly
utilized to monitor their activities and to electrocute

them for disobedience if necessary. Every one of them was endowed with keen animal senses and exceptional strength. According to the intelligence provided by Gremlin, the defector residing with the Family, there were fifteen hundred creations in the Genetic Research Division.

Fifteen hundred!

There was a murmur among the people on the sidewalk.

An imposing figure stood at the top of the stairs, a lean man looming head and shoulders over everyone, and everything, else. He wore a flowing white robe, the fabric covering him from his neck to his feet. His eyes were deeply set in their sockets and seemed to glow with an inner light. He grinned as he walked down the steps, exposing a mouth full of tiny, curiously pointed teeth. His hair was a dark black mane upon his sloping head.

Without being told, Yama intuitively knew this was the nefarious Doktor.

A young woman walked at the Doktor's side, attired in a brown robe. Her lovely features were serpentine, her skin yellow, and her narrow eyes a shade of lavender.

The Doktor and his consort descended the stairs and walked to the left, followed by as many genetically spawned creatures as had preceded them.

Forty soldiers, armed with M-16's and automatic pistols, brought up the rear of the procession.

The loudspeaker blasted three times as the last of the soldiers disappeared around a bend in the sidewalk.

Yama saw his chance.

The pedestrians were returning to the sidewalk, milling about in a disorganized fashion.

Yama quickly shoved his way through the throng and reached the bottom of the steps. He tightened his grip on the Wilkinson, feeling his scimitar rub against his back, as he ascended the stairs and made for the doors.

"Hold up, Citizen!" someone shouted behind him.

Yama slowly turned.

The policeman was walking up the steps, swinging his night stick in his right hand.

How would an Army officer address a policeman? Certainly not as a superior.

"May I help you?" Yama asked as the policeman reached the step below him.

The policeman's blue hat was pulled down to his ears, his graying sideburns flaring below his cheeks. His eyes were brown and attentive, his jaw rounded.

"Yes, sir," the policeman said. "I couldn't help but notice you back there. You looked like you weren't quite with it. Anything wrong?"

Yama mentally chided himself for his lack of self-control. "Nothing's wrong. Just feeling a bit ill, is all. My stomach."

"You'd better see the medics, then," the policeman advised.

"I intend to," Yama replied. "Thanks."

The officer nodded, smiling, and started to walk off.

Yama faced the doors.

"Say, Citizen," the officer inquired over his shoulder, "what unit are you with?"

Unit? How were the Army units designated? Yama recalled a comment Seth had made concerning the patrol at his ranch. "I'm attached as an auxiliary with the Genetic Research Division." He paused and glared at the policeman. "Why all these stupid questions? I have business inside and you are detaining me!"

Yama could read the policeman's features. The man was suspicious of the Warrior, but he couldn't put his finger on why. The policeman was racking his brain, trying to figure out what it was about Yama he didn't like, but he couldn't.

"I'm sorry," the policeman stated.

Yama nodded imperiously, walked to the doors, and stepped inside the sinister Biological Center.

16

The SEAL was parked in the trees on the west side of the road a hundred yards north of the stockade.

"We were fortunate those jeep patrols missed us," Joshua remarked.

"See? Aren't you glad I was running with no lights?"

"It was a fortuitous circumstance," Joshua admitted.

Hickok made a snorting noise. "Josh, the next time we come on a little trip together, remind me to bring a dictionary."

"Why?"

"So I can understand what the blazes you're talkin' about at least half the time," Hickok stated.

"You don't fool me," Joshua rejoined. "You were raised in the Family School, the same as Blade, Geronimo, and I. I'd warrant your vocabulary is as good as ours."

"Don't let it get around," Hickok quipped. "I wouldn't want folks to know how smart I am."

Joshua glanced at the stockade. "What do we do now?"

Hickok had his elbows on the steering wheel, his chin in his hands. "That's what I've been working on. I know our pards are in there, but there's a heap of soldier boys crawling over that place, and we've got to be a mite careful about how we bust them out."

"What can we do against so many?" Joshua queried.

Hickok patted the dashboard. "We have this baby."

"I've heard about the big discovery," Joshua mentioned. "Plato told me the Founder armed the SEAL and left behind a secret, coded instruction manual. Is this true?"

"Sure as shootin'," Hickok responded. "I was there when Blade read the decoded message from the Founder."

Joshua placed his left hand on the dash, frowning. "Even this mechanical marvel is tainted with the touch of war."

"Wow!" Hickok grinned. "That's a good one! Got a pencil on you so I can write it down?"

Joshua disregarded the barb. "Tell me. What type of armament does the SEAL have?"

The gunman pointed at four toggle switches in the middle of the dash. "You remember those? The four switches we could never use because Plato didn't know what they were used for and didn't want us to accidentally damage the SEAL?"

"I remember them," Joshua confirmed.

"Good. That one with the M next to it is the toggle switch for the fifty-caliber machine guns hidden in recessed compartments under each front headlight. Throw that switch and a metal plate slides up."

"What then?"

"The machine guns automatically fire. So don't bump that switch while I'm out taking a leak!"

"I'll try not to." Joshua grinned.

"The second switch, the one with the S, controls a dingus called a surface-to-air missile. This thing is mounted in the roof above the driver's seat. We can use it for, oh, taking care of loud-mouthed blackbirds or knocking nuts out of trees."

"You're putting me on," Joshua said.

"Would I do that?" Hickok retorted. "Anyway, that next toggle has an F for flamethrower. This doohickey is behind the front fender, right smack dab in the center. It spits flame balls about twenty feet."

"You're kidding?"

"That's what they told me," Hickok said. "That last switch there has an R for rocket launcher. This sucker is above the flamethrower, in the middle of the front grill. We found a whole room full of ammunition and rockets and tanks for the flame-thing and more instructions."

"If you have it memorized," Joshua stated, "then we should be all set to go."

"Who said I had it memorized?" Hickok replied testily.

"I recall seeing some books in our Library about military hardware," Joshua said, his brow furrowed. "Weren't those missiles and rockets and the like all big things? How can they fit in the SEAL?"

"What're you thinking of?" Hickok cracked. "A rocket to Mars? The missiles and stuff in this buggy are all miniaturized. I read once that right before the Big Blast, the scientists had refined the technology to where a terrorist could stick a nuclear device in his pocket. Imagine that."

"You don't suppose the Founder placed a nuclear device in here, do you?" Joshua innocently asked.

Hickok promptly sat back in his bucket seat. "Never thought of that." He studied the dash. "Naw. No way. We'd know it if there was one."

"We didn't know about the missiles and the rockets," Joshua said.

Hickok was about to reply when a commotion near the stockade caught his attention. "Well, look at that!"

Joshua looked in the same direction. "What's going on? It sounds like gunshots?"

"Blade."

"How can you know that?"

Hickok glanced at Joshua. "You're the Empath. You tell me who it is."

"I can't right now," Joshua said. "I require quiet if I'm to receive psychic impressions."

"You won't be getting any quiet for a spell, pard," Hickok informed him. The gunfighter started the engine and flicked on the headlights.

"What are you doing? They'll see us now!"

"Don't matter," Hickok stated. "Fun time is here!"

"Fun time?"

Hickok drove from the trees onto the road. "We're going to show these jokers what Warriors are made of!"

"What can I do?" Joshua nervously inquired.

"Sit back and relax. The SEAL's body is bulletproof, so I doubt you'll be hit. The Founder said the tires on this crate are almost indestructible, made of some kind of synthetic gunk. This'll be a piece of cake!" Hickok said, elated.

Joshua slumped in his seat. "Dear Father," he silently prayed, "please preserve your children in this time of combat. . . ."

Hickok crossed the road and floored the accelerator.

". . .and guide our souls during this tribulation. We do not want to do this. . . ."

"Let's get these turkeys!" Hickok shouted.

". . .but remain, as in all matters, ever subject to your will. Amen."

The SEAL was barreling toward the stockade at fifty miles an hour.

"Do we have a plan?" Joshua thought to inquire.

"This is it!" Hickok yelled, his excitement and enthusiasm overflowing. "It's them or us!"

Joshua shook his head. "Dear Spirit!" he whispered to himself. "I'm stuck in a vehicle of war with a crazy person!"

17

Blade heard a sudden outburst of automatic fire coming from the north, and the next instant the ground shook from a tremendous explosion. The ring of boots surrounding the troop transport dissipated, soldiers running every which way, orders being shouted, men shrieking and screaming as the firing attained a virtual crescendo.

What was going on?

He hastily crawled to the edge of the first truck and peered out, witnessing a scene of madness and devastation.

Smoke was everywhere. Army troopers were dashing back and forth and firing into the smoke almost at random. The northern sentry tower was in flames.

Blade eased from under the protective shelter of the truck and looked around. None of the soldiers were in his immediate vicinity. The machine-gunner in the western sentry tower was shooting at a target in the smoke.

What?

The smoke abruptly parted, revealing the SEAL in all its glory, its fifty-caliber machine guns blasting as it circled the area west of the stockade, mowing down soldiers in droves.

Hickok.

Blade rose and ran toward the tent. The Family gunman was deliberately drawing their fire, forcing the troopers to devote their complete attention to the SEAL, and judging by the volume of gunfire his plan was successful.

With one notable exception.

Blade was only three feet from the tent when the smoke briefly cleared, and there, standing in the opening, the Commando in his hands, was Colonel Jarvis, his features contorted in rage.

No time to turn aside and no place to hide!

Blade dove, his long arms outstretched, even as Jarvis spun, bringing the Commando up.

"Bastard!" Jarvis bellowed.

Blade crashed into the furious officer and they both slammed into the tent, into the table, upending it. They rolled on the ground, Jarvis gripping the Commando and striving to smash the stock against Blade's head.

"Bastard!" Jarvis repeated, his voice harsh, his eyes bulging, his veins prominent on his forehead. "Bastard!"

Blade found himself flat on his back, with Jarvis on top, the officer bearing down for all he was worth.

Where was that green blanket?

To his right or his left?

Blade heaved, his rippling muscles flinging Jarvis aside. The colonel struck one of the chairs and crashed to the ground.

Now!

Blade rolled to his right, his anxious fingers closing on the green blanket and lifting, and there they were, glistening in the light from the overhead lantern, his prized Bowies. Jarvis had removed them from their sheaths, apparently to admire their craftsmanship, and left them lying with the other weapons instead of resheathing them. A minor oversight, but a fatal one.

Colonel Jarvis had scrambled to his knees, the Commando leveling, as he twisted toward Blade, his finger already on the trigger.

Blade grabbed the handle of one of his Bowies and tried to rise to his knees.

Too late.

Jarvis had the Commando pointed at the Warrior's huge chest, a sneer on the officer's face.

Blade tensed, expecting the slugs to rip through his body.

"I was wrong about you," Jarvis taunted, reveling in his victory. "You're not my equal! You're just like all the rest! Uncivilized swine! Any last words for Samuel?"

Blade stared down the Commando barrel, wondering. Was it possible? "I have some last words for you," he told Jarvis.

Jarvis was surprised by the statement. "For me? What?"

"Did you clear it?" Blade asked.

Colonel Jarvis was confounded by the question. "Clear it? Clear what?"

Blade nodded at the Commando. "That. Did you clear it? The last time I used it, the thing jammed on me."

Jarvis snickered. "Fool! Do you think I'm that gullible? Do you think I'm an idiot?"

Blade slowly nodded, smiling.

Jarvis turned red and pulled the Commando trigger.

Nothing happened.

"That answer your question?" Blade said mocking him.

Jarvis was frantically pulling the trigger.

Blade rose to his knees, the Bowie in his right hand.

Colonel Jarvis pounded the Commando on the ground, then stared at the Warrior, wide-eyed, his mouth moving soundlessly.

Blade closed in. "I only regret I can't give you everything you have coming to you," he stated, his voice hard and low, "but this will have to suffice."

Jarvis tried to bring his hands up, to feebly save himself from his doom.

The hulking Warrior ripped the Bowie blade into the officer's stomach and twisted. Jarvis made a choking sound and clutched at the knife.

"This," Blade said, "is for all those innocent people you murdered today!" He steeled his arm and wrenched the knife upward.

The last sight Jarvis saw before he toppled into the long night was the sight of his own guts spilling over the ground.

Blade wrenched his Bowie free and stood. The clamor of shouts and shots outside drew him back to reality.

Hickok!

Blade knelt by the blanket and armed himself with the A-1, the Vegas, and the Bowies. He stuck the Dan Wesson .44 Magnum in his belt for added measure. He rose and saw the Commando at his left.

"Colonel Jarvis!" someone outside was yelling. "Colonel Jarvis!"

Blade knelt again and examined the Commando. He extracted the magazine and found the jammed bullet in the clip.

"Colonel Jarvis!"

Blade quickly reloaded the Commando, thankful the A-1 and it used the same caliber ammunition.

"Colonel Jarvis!" The voice was very close.

Nodding in satisfaction, Blade stood, the Commando held snugly in his right arm, the A-1 in his left.

"Colonel Jarvis! Sir!"

A soldier reached the tent and flung the flap to one side. He spotted the Warrior and attempted to bring his M-16 into play.

The Commando roared, bucking in Blade's arm, and the slugs caught the trooper in the chest, his back exploding outward as he fell.

Blade emerged from the tent.

Both the sentry tower at the north end of the stockade and the tower on the west side were demolished, spewing fire and smoke. The SEAL was stopped in the center of a circle of soldiers, and they were pouring everything they had at the vehicle.

Blade advanced across the field. He fired as fast as soldiers appeared, the Commando and the A-1 tearing them apart before they knew what hit them. Four troopers directly ahead were engaged in replacing the magazines in their M-16's. One of them spotted the Warrior and warned his companions; all four spun and were caught in a withering hail of fire. He downed nine more in five seconds.

Something plowed into Blade's left shoulder, stunning him and drawing blood. He knew he'd been hit, but he ignored the wound for the moment as he concentrated on wrapping up this operation. A group of soldiers suddenly appeared to his left, charging over a small rise.

Blade crouched, aiming the Commando, doubting he could hold them all off with just one good arm.

There were at least ten of them, and as they passed near the front of the SEAL there was a hissing and a puff of blue and the entire group was engulfed by a sheet of flame. Their death cries were awful.

Blade scanned the area, surprised to discover the

troopers were gone. The ones still alive, anyway. The ground was littered with dozens and dozens of bodies, some oozing blood from multiple perforations and others fried to a fine crisp.

The stench was staggering.

Blade rose to his feet, his ears ringing from the conflict. He could hear moans and groans coming from every direction; the sound was eerie. During his time as a Warrior, he'd seen a lot of fights, a lot of killing, but nothing like this. This was his first taste of all-out warfare, and he was feeling oddly uncomfortable as he faced the SEAL.

The driver's door flew open and Hickok emerged, his Pythons in his hands.

"Glad to see you could make it," Blade said. "I was beginning to think you were on vacation."

Hickok warily walked over to Blade, his eyes alertly seeking any indication of hostility from the bodies on the field. His lips were compressed, his expression drawn and haggard.

"Something wrong?" Blade asked him.

Hickok nodded. "I didn't like it."

"Didn't like what?"

Hickok motioned with his left arm toward the SEAL. "It wasn't a fair fight! These slobs never had a chance! All I had to do was sit there and flick a switch and I'd wipe out a dozen of them at a crack! Did you see the flamethrower? Those boys never stood a chance!" he repeated, sounding stunned. "I like it when I can face an enemy and go one-on-one. That's my ideal of a fair fight. This was . . . was nothing more than outright slaughter."

Blade knew what the gunfighter meant and agreed with him.

There was the thump of a door closing, and Joshua

jogged into view around the SEAL. "Blade!" he shouted. "You're okay!"

Blade rubbed his injured shoulder as Joshua reached them. "Not quite," he said. "I took one."

"I'll tend it immediately," Joshua stated, turning. "My medicine bag is in the SEAL. Did you see it?" he inquired, grinning, sweeping the field with his right hand. "Did you see it?"

"See what?"

Joshua, continuing toward the SEAL, glanced over his right shoulder. "Did you see Hickok? Wasn't he magnificent? He handled the SEAL like an expert! All that shooting and the explosions and everything and they never even touched us! Amazing!" And with that he entered the SEAL.

Blade eyed Hickok quizzically.

"Don't look at me, pard!" the gunman protested. "It's all his doing. Josh has decided he likes me."

"He likes you?"

"Yep. Just the way I am." Hickok saw a body nearby twitch and stopped talking, waiting to see if it would move again. Nothing. "How's the wing?" he asked Blade.

"Seems to be a clean hit, in and out," Blade replied, inspecting his left shoulder. "How about you?"

"Like Josh said," Hickok responded, "they never laid a glove on us. The Founder did a great job on the SEAL. Whatever he forked out was well spent. That plastic body must be practically impenetrable. The M-16's didn't even faze us. We could hear the slugs ricocheting, kind of like the buzzing of a bunch of angry hornets, but they didn't put a nick in the buggy."

"There were some bigger guns in the sentry towers," Blade mentioned.

"Yeah. I noticed them," Hickok said. "They rocked

the SEAL real good, which is why I took 'em out first. We were lucky. If they'd had grenades or a bazooka it might have been a different story."

Blade gazed at the SEAL, wondering what was delaying the Empath. "I still can't believe Joshua was excited over a fight," he commented.

"I think he's faking it," Hickok confided.

"Why?"

Hickok looked around to insure Joshua was still in the SEAL. "I reckon he's on a campaign to show us how helpful he can be. I think he knows he's been a monumental pain in the butt, and this is his way of making amends. Shhhh. Here he comes."

Joshua was running toward them, his leather medicine bag, supplied by the Family Healers, clutched in his right hand. "I finally found it!" he exclaimed as he rejoined them. "In all the commotion it slid under one of the seats. Let's have a look at your shoulder."

Except for wispy tendrils, most of the smoke had drifted from the field of conflict.

Hickok stared at the stockade. "Is she there?"

"She's there," Blade confirmed. "She's looking forward to seeing you."

"Maybe we can leave 'em in there another night," the gunman proposed. "We'll make like we're too busy checking bodies to pay them any mind."

Blade chuckled, then inadvertently flinched as Joshua probed his wound. "I don't think it would work."

"Why not?" Hickok wanted to know.

Just then, a loud male voice shouted at them from within the stockade. "If a certain party doesn't get his fat buns over here this instant and release us, then I'm going to tell another certain party some news the first certain party doesn't want the second certain party to know about a third certain party who shall remain nameless! *If you get my drift!*"

"That dingblasted Injun!" Hickok fumed, and stormed toward the stockade.

Joshua, in the process of cleaning Blade's gunshot with a clean compress and an herbal remedy developed by the Healers, grinned. "Was that who I think it was?"

"It was," Blade affirmed.

Joshua laughed.

"What's so funny?" Blade asked.

"I never realized it before," Joshua replied, "but you guys are a lot of fun!"

18

First observation: no guards.

Yama hesitated inside the Biological Center doors, astonished at discovering the lack of security. On reflection, though, it seemed eminently logical; who would be foolish enough to invade the lair of the Doktor and his Genetic Research Division?

Second observation: judging from ground level, the building must be a virtual maze. Eleven hallways branched off from a small reception area. A desk and a chair were positioned a few feet inside the doors, but the post was vacant.

So were the hallways.

Where was everyone?

Something whined to his left and Yama turned.

Third observation: never again judge Civilized Zone society by Family standards.

A row of four wide doors lined the walls to his left, doors lacking knobs or handles. Above each door was a lighted strip containing four letters and seven numbers: S-B-G-1-2-3-4-5-6-7-R.

What did it all mean?

The G in the lighted strip above the second door

suddenly lit up, there was a slight rumbling sound, and the door slid open.

A genetic deviate stepped out.

Yama noticed a bulletin board on a wall to his right and he headed toward it, forcing himself to stroll naturally, to avoid betraying any inkling of nervousness.

This G.R.D., as Gremlin had informed Yama they were called, was six feet in height. Its skin was covered with brown scales, and the spaces between its toes were webbed. A pair of huge, red eyes glared at the world from under a protruding brow. Its mouth was small, its lips thin and constantly twitching.

Yama reached the bulletin board and aligned his body so he could keep track of the G.R.D.

The thing walked to the outside doors and looked out. It frowned and glanced at Yama. "Did you see the Doktor leave?" it asked in a sibilant voice.

"You just missed him," Yama courteously responded, hoping his tone and inflection were normal.

"Damn it!" the thing hissed. "I'll have to catch him after he returns from the banquet tonight." It whirled and vanished down one of the hallways.

Banquet?

An announcement on the bulletin board drew Yama's attention: "TO ALL PERSONNEL: THIS IS YOUR FINAL REMINDER! YOU ARE ENCOURAGED TO ATTEND THE FORMAL BANQUET TONIGHT AT 2100 IN HONOR OF OUR GLORIOUS LEADER. THE RECEPTION LINE FORMS AT 2000. SEATING MUST BE ACCOMPLISHED BY 2030. THE PLACE: THE CONVENTION CENTER. BE THERE!"

Yama read another announcement tacked to the board below the first: "TO ALL PERSONNEL: PARADE AT 0600. IN HONOR OF SAMUEL II's

VISIT, AS PART OF THE PREPARATION FOR THE CAVALRY DRIVE, ALL MILITARY PERSONNEL, INCLUDING ALL BI CEN AUX, ARE REQUIRED TO PARTICIPATE IN A FULL-DRESS PARADE AT 0600. BE THERE!"

Yama thoughtfully stroked his chin. If he comprehended these messages, Samuel the Second was in Cheyenne for a banquet at the Convention Center. His visit was linked to the big push against the Cavalry commencing the next day. If the personnel in the Biological Center were encouraged to attend, it might mean the Doktor's den was understaffed. With fewer people—or whatever—crowding the halls, it increased the probability of a successful mission.

But which way should he try first?

He happened to look out the front doors, and immediately tensed.

That meddling policeman was returning with six armed soldiers. They were halfway up the steps already.

Yama moved to the reception desk, thankful the doors were tinted in the same fashion as the SEAL. If inside, you could see out, but those outside could not view the interior.

Which way should he go?

The decision was taken from his hands.

Yama walked to a hall on his left, then stopped as the clamor of a loud conversation carried down the hallway.

Others were coming!

The Warrior found himself hemmed in: in front of him, a confusing network of hallways; behind him, the policeman and the soldiers he had summoned; to his right, the bulletin board; and to his left, the . . .

The what?

Yama edged toward the four wide doors without knobs. The second door was still open, the G above the door flashing yellow. A memory tugged at Yama's consciousness, a recollection from his childhood, from his schooling years. He recalled lessons dealing with life before World War III, in particular a study of the mechanized marvels mankind had developed before the Big Blast. One of the books from the Family Library was spread open on the teacher's desk, revealing photograph after photograph of wonders of the scientific age: planes and jets, buses and trains, cars and trucks, motorcycles and snowmobiles, and something *really* incredible.

Portable closets.

Yama absently snapped his fingers, attempting to remember the proper name. It began with an E. . . .

Elevators!

Yama hurried into the open elevator. To his right was a series of letters and numbers corresponding to those on the lighted strip above the door, with each letter or numeral stamped onto a square white button. The buttons were arranged in a vertical row.

How did the elevator operate?

Yama glanced at the front doors.

The policeman and the six soldiers were only three steps from the top.

Yama quickly pressed the bottom button, the one marked with an S. Instantly, the door slid shut and the elevator rocked slightly as it began to descend.

Where was it taking him?

The elevator's descent was quiet, the motion smooth. As the door had closed, the button labeled with a G became very bright. The G grew dark after a few seconds, however, and the next button, the one marked with a B, lit up. After the elevator continued to drop, the next button, the S, flickered and illuminated.

What did the G, B, and S stand for?

The elevator abruptly stopped and the door rolled

open.

Yama raised the Wilkinson, alert for trouble.

A solitary hallway extended from the elevator, running straight ahead for twenty-five yards before it branched in two directions. The walls were constructed of cinder blocks, the ceiling of white tile, while the floor was covered with a thick red carpet.

The hall was deserted.

Yama edged from the elevator. There were closed doors on both sides of the hallway, four on his left and three on his right. The first door he passed was identified by a small sign reading: "Janitorial Closet."

Not exactly what he was looking for.

The next door bore a sign stating: "Bio Lab." Yama tried the doorknob and the door swung slowly open. Cautiously, he peered around the door, not knowing what to expect.

The chamber was huge and filled with table after table of scientific, medical, and chemical apparatuses. Dozens of workers, the majority of them from the Genetic Research Division and the rest human, were engaged in a variety of technical and experimental tasks. Some were toiling over smoldering test tubes, others mixing chemicals, and a group of four near the door was dissecting a dog, a collie.

Yama quietly closed the door before the occupants noticed him. He realized he must be in the very heart of the Biological Center, in the Docktor's inner sanctum.

The next door opened into a small office containing a desk, two chairs, and a file cabinet. No one was inside. The sign on the door revealed this office evidently belonged to someone named Clarissa.

Yama padded along the hallway and reached the next door. This door was locked and a bright red sign was posted at eye level. It read: "Keep Out!"

Now what could this be?

Yama knelt and examined the lock. He could shoot it open, but the shot would attract unwelcome attention to his presence. Trying to pry it open would take too long and leave marks.

The sound of cheerful whistling suddenly reached his ears.

Yama rose and hurried into Clarissa's office, leaving a slight opening between the door and the jamb so he could view the hallway.

A man in a white frock appeared at the junction, holding a glass bottle filled with a red liquid. The man reached the locked door, produced a key, and walked inside.

Yama waited a moment, then left the office, crossed the hall, and carefully entered the room. There was no sign of the man in the frock. This chamber, like the Bio Lab, was enormous, and like the Bio Lab it contained row upon row of tables. On these tables, however, were large glass vats filled with a clear liquid and something else.

What were they?

Yama moved closer to the nearest vat, observing at least a half-dozen tubes emerging from the vat and running along an overhead rod until they reached a massive piece of equipment positioned in the middle of the room. This latter item rose almost to the ceiling. Dozens upon dozens of tubes ran into it near the top, and the bottom third was a confusing array of switches, knobs, and blinking lights of varied colors.

Still no trace of the man in the white frock.

Yama reached the first vat and gazed inside. Although the liquid in the vat was clear, along the sides it was somewhat foamy, compelling the Warrior to squint as he looked within the vat. It took several seconds for the sight he was viewing to register.

It couldn't be!

Ordinarily, Yama was one of the more stoic Warriors, refusing to allow his feelings to show. It usually took quite a shock to elicit a reaction from him, and this time his mouth dropped, his eyes widened, and he inadvertently took two steps backward. Sheer disgust overwhelmed him and he suffered a nauseous sensation.

The grisly scene he beheld struck the Warrior to the very core of his being. As with every other Family member, Yama was deeply religious. The Founder of the survival retreat called the Home, Kurt Carpenter, had himself been a religious man. He had developed a program of religious instruction for Family members starting when they were yet infants. Carpenter had recognized that religion was indispensable to moral and spiritual growth, but he had wanted to avoid the formalized dogmatic doctrine, the perpetuation of fossilized creeds, so prevalent in pre-war society. Consequently, every Family member was permitted to cultivate exclusively personal spiritual beliefs, and the establishment of a Family religion was strictly forbidden. Despite the injunction against formalization, a certain generalized consensus did exist. Everyone in the Family believed there was a God, a Supreme Being, a Divine Light, the Way, Allah, or whatever term the individual Family member decided to use in describing the Maker and Shaper of the cosmos. Each Family member also accepted the fact every mortal was spiritually related to everyone else, was a son or daughter in one vast universal family. Consequently, the Family viewed life itself as especially precious, to be treated with the ultimate respect. Yama's reverence for all life was particularly keen, and consequently he was exceptionally unsettled by the contents of the vat.

It was a baby, no more than six months old, floating in the liquid in the vat, attached to a half-dozen intravenous tubes!

Yama couldn't bring himself to take another look. His utter revulsion sickened him. What was it Seth Mason had said? That the Doktor drank blood? Wasn't that the rumor? Well, one of the tubes running from the infant to the machine in the middle of the chamber was carrying a reddish substance!

What did it all mean? What was the Doktor . . .

"What the hell are you doing in here?"

Yama turned to his left. The man in the white frock was standing three feet away, his hands on his hips, glaring in obvious anger at the Warrior.

"What the hell are you doing in here?" the man repeated. "You know damn well this area is off-limits to everybody except authorized personnel! Let me see your pass!"

"Certainly," Yama replied sheepishly. He stepped over to the man and held out the Wilkinson. "Would you hold this for me?"

The man took the gun, closely scrutinizing Yama.

"I know I have it here somewhere," Yama said, reaching in his left pants pocket with his left hand while he scratched his head with his right.

"Hurry it up!" the man snapped, stamping his right foot.

Yama eased his right hand behind his neck and undid the leather strap securing his scimitar. He gripped the hilt before the sword could slide any lower. All the while, his left hand was groping in his left pocket.

"Do you have it or don't you?" the man demanded.

Yama removed his left hand, holding a coin. "I have this."

"A dollar?" the man scoffed. "Listen, buddy! You'd

better produce your pass, and fast, or you're going to lose your head!"

"I believe you have it reversed," Yama said quietly, and dropped the coin.

The man in the white frock was distracted by the falling coin; he watched it land on the floor and roll a foot before falling onto its side. "You'd better pick that . . ." he began, looking up at the silver-haired soldier.

Yama, the scimitar already held aloft over his head, swung, the razor-like blade arcing downward and connecting, slashing into the man in white, into his neck, and nearly severing his head from his body.

The man gasped once, his arms flapped against his sides, and he toppled to the floor, blood gushing from his ruined throat, covering him and the carpet both.

Yama wiped his scimitar on the white frock and replaced the sword in its scabbard, under his shirt, securing the hilt to the leather strap.

What could he do with the body?

He scoured the chamber for a plausible hiding place and came up empty. The closets were too small to hold a grown man. He considered tossing the body into one of the vats, but that would be too obvious. Finally, he dragged the dead man behind the machine in the center of the room.

It would have to do.

Yama went through his victim's pockets and found a set of keys attached to a metal ring. There was a handful of coins in the pants, some imprinted with "In the Name of Samuel" and others with "In Samuel We Trust." Different numbers were stamped onto the metal, some coins with a one, others with a five, and a few with a ten. He also found a wallet, which he stuck in his left back pocket until he could find sufficient time to examine its contents.

What should he do about the infants in the vats?

Yama thoughtfully walked to the front of the chamber and retrieved his Wilkinson. There was nothing he could do for the babies, he decided, not now anyway. He wiped the Wilkinson on the rug to remove some spattered blood. If he continued to search, he told himself, he might discover a room where records were stored. Surely somewhere in the Biological Center there had to be documents detailing the reason for this horrible room!

Vigilantly, he exited the chamber and locked the door. The hallway, for the moment, was deserted.

The next door was unmarked and unlocked.

Yama eased through the door, silently closing it behind him. This chamber was filled with tables loaded with cages. Cage after cage, each housing an animal of some sort. Mammals: mice, rats, rabbits, squirrels, chipmunks, raccoons, bats, and even some small cats, bobcats and domestic types. Reptiles: snakes, lizards, turtles, and several aquariums containing young alligators. Amphibians were also included: frogs by the score, salamanders, newts, and toads. In the rear of the room were large cages, towering above the rest, easily visible from the door.

The chamber was filled with animal sounds and a readily detectable odor.

Yama slowly walked down aisle after aisle, observing the wildlife and speculating on its purpose in the Biological Center. How did all these creatures fit into the Doktor's scheme of things? He approached the large cages in the back of the chamber. Two of them were empty, one contained a black bear cub, and the last one

held an unusual cat. Yama stared at the feline, curled up
on a bed of straw on the floor of the cage, and tried to
identify it. Its coat was a thick grayish-brown, its ears
were pointed, and it lacked a tail. As he was viewing it,
the cat abruptly opened its eyes, startling, penetrating,
vividly green orbs, and glared at the man.

There was nothing in here of major interest.

Yama turned toward the door.

"Going so soon, chuckles?"

The Warrior spun, his finger on the trigger of the
Wilkinson, thinking he'd overlooked a rear door.

"You're the nervous sort, huh, ugly?" The voice was
high pitched, the words spoken with a bit of a lisp, and
they were coming from . . . the . . . cat!

Yama gawked as the cat rose to its feet, standing on
two legs and defiantly staring at the Warrior.

"Cat got your tongue?" the thing asked, and laughed
at its own joke.

Yama saw he was mistaken. It wasn't a cat after all, it
was a man resembling a cat, about four feet in height
and not weighing more than sixty pounds, if that. The
thing must be one of the Doktor's genetically engineered
creations. It wore a leather loin cloth, but the metallic
collar normally worn by the deviates was missing.

"Well, let's get this over with!" the cat-man snapped.

"Get what over with?" Yama inquired, curious.

"Don't play games with me, soldier boy!" the cat-
man said harshly. "Get the execution over with!"

"Execution?" Yama repeated questioningly.

The cat-man made a show of gazing around the
chamber. "There must be an echo in here!" He-it
frowned at Yama. "I know why you are here. The Doc
told me tonight would be the night. So let's gt it over
with! I'm tired of rotting in this damn cage!"

"I'm not here to kill you," Yama informed the . . . thing.

The cat-man's eyebrows arched. "You're not? Then what the hell are you doing here, bub? I thought only the Doc and his zombies were permitted in here?"

"Zombies?" Yama reiterated.

The cat-man chuckled. "Boy, you jokers in uniform are still as brainless as ever! Zombies, idiot! That's what I call any of the Doc's little pet monsters."

Yama grinned. "Excuse me for saying this, but aren't you one of the Doktor's little pet monsters? Littler than most, I'd say."

The cat-man hissed. "If I wasn't behind these bars, bozo," he warned, "I'd tear you to shreds! These aren't just for show, you know!" So saying, he held up his hands. All eight fingers and both thumbs were tipped with tapered claws.

"What are you doing in that cage?" Yama asked.

The thing eyed the Warrior quizzically. "You don't know?"

"No."

"Then the Doc didn't send you to execute me?"

"Why does the Doktor want you executed?" Yama queried.

"Because I've been a bad kitty," the cat-man said sarcastically. "I tried to waste the son of a bitch!"

Yama took a step toward the cage. "You tried to kill the Doktor?"

The thing nodded. "Would have succeeded too, if that bitch Clarissa hadn't shouted and given me away! I'll get her, someday!"

"I don't understand," Yama admitted. "I thought the Doktor could control all of his creatures by using a metal collar of some sort."

The cat-man shrugged. "It works most of the time. But every now and then he produces one like me, one who won't take his crap, one who won't listen no matter how many times the bastard threatens us with the collar. If he can't keep us in line that way, he uses us for experiments or has us executed."

Yama nodded, comprehending. "And you thought I was your executioner."

"Say," the thing said, moving to the bars and gripping them in both hands, "there's something about you, chuckles. Something different." The cat-man sniffed the air several times. "I can't put my claw on it, but there's something strange about you."

Yama mentally debated the wisdom of revealing his identity to the creature. Was it likely the thing was lying about the reason it was confined in the cage? "Do you have a name?" he asked it.

The cat-man nodded. "I'm called Lynx," he said proudly. "Does the name mean anything to you?"

"No," Yama confessed. "Should it?"

"I'm famous," Lynx boasted. "My name was in all the papers and on every newscast for days. Whenever anyone tries to kill the Doc, or any of the bigwigs for that matter, it's news, chuckles. I took out fourteen of the bastards before they bagged me with a damn tranquilizer dart. Pricks! They thought I was one of the rebels!"

"What do you mean?" Yama probed. "Who are the rebels?"

"There's an underground movement," Lynx detailed, "an organized resistance to the Government, a group dedicated to the overthrow of Samuel and the Doktor. Everybody knows about the rebels." Lynx paused. "Except you, bub. And you didn't know about me either. If I didn't know better, I'd swear you weren't from the Civilized Zone."

"I'm not."

Lynx pressed against the bars, intently studying Yama as if he were striving to perceive the nature of his very soul.

Yama nodded. "It's been nice talking with you." He took a step away.

"Wait!" Lynx yelled. "Don't leave!"

Yama stopped. "Why not?"

"You're going to take off and just leave me to rot in this stinking cage?" Lynx demanded angrily.

"I'm on a mission," Yama replied. "Freeing you would complicate my assignment immensely. Besides, I'm still not completely positive I can trust you. For all I know, if I set you free you might try to kill me."

"What's your name, chuckles?" Lynx requested.

"Yama."

"Well, Yama, baby, I'll tell you what. You let me out of here, and I give you my word as a gentleman I won't cause you any grief. Fair enough?"

"No," Yama responded.

"No? What's wrong with my word?" Lynx asked, peeved.

"What if we run into some soldiers or other beings like yourself?" Yama pressed him.

Lynx snorted. "I'll rip 'em to shreds!"

"That's what I thought," Yama said. "It's not good enough."

Lynx cocked his head and uttered a peculiar trilling sound. "Sharp one, aren't you, bub? Okay. Let's hear your conditions."

"I'll release you from the cage," Yama stipulated, "if you will agree to my terms. One. You will assist me and guide me on a tour of the Biological Center. . . ."

"A tour?" Lynx laughed. "You want the deluxe or the tourist rate?"

"Two. You will follow my instructions implicity. Three. You will not attack anyone unless I give the word. Agreed?" Yama asked.

Lynx hesitated before answering. "You sure drive a hard bargain, pal," he finally said. "I don't see where I've got much choice so, yeah, I agree. Satisfied?"

Yama walked up to the cage and stared into Lynx's eyes. "If you cross me I will kill you," he stated in a low, soft tone.

Again Lynx made the trilling sound. "Yes," he said after a long moment. "I suppose you would. Don't worry, Yama. You have my word."

Yama nodded and produced the key ring taken from the man in the white frock. There were over a dozen keys on the ring, and he was on the seventh one before the lock clinked and the cage door swung open.

For a tense moment the pair eyed one another.

"Orders, boss?" Lynx asked.

"Follow me," Yama directed, and led the way to the door. Many of the animals displayed extreme fright as Lynx passed their cages, screeching and snarling or moving as far away from him as they could.

"Must be my breath," Lynx remarked at one point.

Yama peered into the hallway just in time to see two men in white disappear around the corner of the junction with the other corridor. Hurriedly, Lynx right behind him, he crossed the hall to the deserted office he'd found earlier.

"This is Clarissa's room," Lynx said as Yama closed the door. "The bitch who saved the Doc from my claws. What are we doing in here?"

"I require information," Yama mentioned. "We're

less likely to be disturbed in here than the cage chamber. Do you know what's in the room next to the cage chamber?"

Lynx frowned. "We call it the Baby Room, the room with all those babies in the vats. I take it you've seen it?"

"What purpose does it serve?" Yama inquired.

"It has something to do with the Doc's rejuvenation technique," Lynx divulged.

"I don't follow you."

Lynx leaned against the desk. "Do you know much about the Doc?"

"Very little," Yama admitted.

"Do you know how old he is?" Lynx questioned.

"How old? No. But I saw him outside earlier. I'd estimate his age at forty, forty-five tops. Why?"

Lynx snickered. "The Doc is one hundred and twenty-seven years old."

"That's impossible," Yama countered.

"You can stand there and look at me and talk about impossibilities? I tell you the Doc is one hundred and twenty-seven, almost one hundred and twenty-eight."

"But that would mean the Doktor was alive before World War III." Yama protested. "I don't see how. . . ."

"Look!" Lynx said impatiently. "You wanted to know about the Baby Room and I'm telling you. It has something to do with the Doc's longevity. Don't ask me what, because I'm no scientist. But everybody knows the Doc has an inordinate interest in babies with Type O blood. You want to know more, then ask him!"

"Those infants in the vats," Yama stated, almost shuddering at the memory, "are they alive or dead?"

"I think their bodies are alive," Lynx disclosed, "but I heard the Doc say once they're brain dead, whatever that means."

Yama thought a moment. "How does the Doktor create things such as yourself?"

Lynx shrugged. "Beats me. All I know is it involves genetic engineering. Beyond that, your guess is as good as mine."

"Doesn't anyone know?"

"The Doc. And he doesn't share his secrets with open arms. Clarissa knows a lot, but I don't know how much. Sorry I can't be of much help," Lynx apologized, "but I was one of the Doc's assassins until I saw the light. I didn't work in the lab."

Yama sighed in frustration. "It's all right. Do you happen to know where the Doktor might have a records room, a room with his personal notes and computations?"

"Sure do, chuckles. Two floors up. Want me to take you to it?"

"Let's go," Yama said, opening the door to the office.

They left Clarissa's private office and walked along the hallway to the junction.

"Which way?" Yama needed to know.

"That way," Lynx said, pointing to their right. "There's a flight of stairs at the end of the hall we can take."

"Remember what I told you about attacking others," Yama reminded the diminutive, feisty creature.

Lynx was opening his mouth to respond when the corridor was racked by the shattering wail of klaxons.

Yama crouched, cradling the Wilkinson. "What the . . ."

"The alarm!" Lynx shouted. "They must know you're here!"

The klaxons were alerting the entire structure.

"Which way, boss?" Lynx asked sarcastically.

Before Yama could decide, the door to the Baby

Room opened and two men in white stepped out, pistols in their hands. Beyond them, the doors to the first, third, and fourth elevators simultaneously slid open, disgorging four full armed soldiers apiece. The twelve troopers started jogging along the hallway, as the two men in white turned and spotted Yama and Lynx at the junction.

Lynx cackled. "Can I attack yet?" he yelled over the klaxons.

The two men in the white frocks opened fire.

19

Hickok reached the gate in the west side of the stockade and was greeted by a virtual sea of smiling faces.

"We knew you'd come back!" someone said.

"Took you long enough!" came from another.

"Get us out of here!" shouted a woman.

"Yeah," added Geronimo, standing beside the gate. "Get us out of here! I don't like being cooped up like this!"

Hickok shifted his gaze to the right, finding Zahner, Bear, and Bertha.

"Hello, Hickok," Zahner greeted the gunman.

"Hey, you loony sucker!" Bear beamed. "It's good to see your sorry ass again!"

"Hi, White Meat!" Bertha said, grinning from ear to ear. "I missed you!"

"Howdy, folks!" Hickok addressed them collectively. "Right nice to see you too. We don't have much time for small talk." He deliberately refrained from looking into Bertha's eyes. "Some of the soldiers got away and they may return at any minute. First we've got to get you out of this overgrown chicken coop."

"Blow the lock off!" a Horn recommended.

"Are you nuts?" Hickok retorted. "The bullet might ricochet and hit one of you. Hold the fort. I'll find something to bust you out with. Be right back." He whirled, catching sight of a pained expression on Bertha's face.

Blast it!

Just what he needed at a time like this!

He shut her from his mind and ran to Blade and Joshua. "I need to break the lock," he told the Alpha Triad leader. "Don't we have that metal doohickey in the back of the SEAL?"

"You mean the crowbar?" Blade asked him.

"That's it. I'll use it to pry the lock open."

"Good idea," Blade agreed, watching Joshua bandage his injury. "If that doesn't work, take our rope and tie one end to the rear fender on the SEAL and the other end to the gate and tear the thing down."

"Will do," Hickok said, starting to turn, holstering his Colts.

"Oh!" Blade thought to mention. "Your Henry is in that tent over there, along with Geronimo's weapons. Tell him. Then have everybody gather near the troop transports. And keep your eyes peeled for any soldiers."

"Want me to help you blow your nose too?" Hickok quipped, then raced for the SEAL. He quickly located the crowbar and returned to the gate. "Stand back!" he told them, and slipped one end of the crowbar through the loop in the padlock on the gate.

"If you're planning to use some muscle," Geronimo suggested, "you should lean on it with your head."

Hickok ignored him and exerted his weight on the crowbar. The padlock refused to budge.

"I still say you should shoot it off!" mentioned the Horn.

Hickok shot him a nasty look, then reapplied himself

to the crowbar. His sinewy muscles strained and strained, to no avail.

"Blasted lock!" Hickok muttered.

"Anyone have a deck of cards?" Geronimo asked.

Hickok leaned on the crowbar again.

"Here," offered someone behind him. "Let me try."

The gunman stood aside as Blade grabbed the crowbar in both huge hands.

"Be careful!" Joshua admonished, standing a few feet behind Blade. "You'll start that wound bleeding again!"

Blade pressed on the crowbar, his arms bulging with power. For a moment, it appeared as if the crowbar itself would snap in half.

"You can do it!" Bear said goading him on.

Blade grunted as he applied additional strength, gritting his teeth from the strenuous effort.

With a sharp metallic clang, the padlock snapped, the crowbar slipping as the padlock broke almost causing Blade to slip and fall.

Hickok caught his friend by the back of his belt and jerked him erect. "That's what you get for showing off!"

Blade flung the gate open. "All right! Listen up! I want all of you to form around those trucks, and I mean right now! Move it!"

The Nomads, Porns, and Horns immediately complied as Blade, Hickok, and Joshua stepped to one side. They were joined by Geronimo, Zahner, Bear, and a strangely quiet Bertha.

"Where is Reverend Paul?" Joshua inquired of Zahner.

"Dead," Zahner informed him.

Joshua seemed shocked by the news. "How tragic," he said sadly. "I liked him a lot. Who is the head of the Horns now?"

"I don't think they've had time to select one," Zahner revealed. "You might look up Brother Timothy. He was second in command under Paul."

"I'll do that now," Joshua said, and departed.

Hickok, continuing to avoid Bertha's probing gaze, nudged Geronimo. "You'd better come with me, pard."

"Where are we going?" Geronimo asked as he followed on the gunfighter's heels.

"Blade says our guns and your tomahawk are in that tent over there," Hickok said. "I don't know about you, but the sooner I have my Henry back in my hands, the better I'll feel."

Zahner faced Blade. "What do you want us to do?"

"I'll let you know in just a bit," Blade replied, moving toward the trucks.

"Wait for me," Zahner stated, and left with him.

Bertha and Bear remained behind.

Bear glanced at her, reading the sorrow in her face. "Well, what did you expect, babe? He'd throw his arms around you and give you a big kiss?"

"Somethin' like that," Bertha confessed.

"I kept tellin' you not to wait for him," Bear mentioned. "I told you no white boy is gonna fall in love with you."

"It's not that," Bertha said slowly, reflectively. "Somethin' is bothering him. I can tell."

Bear snorted derisively. "Listen to me, woman, and listen real good. Hickok ain't for you. Don't get me wrong. I like that honky. I like him a lot. But I know he isn't the one for you. And sooner or later you're gonna wake up to the fact too. When you do, old Bear will be here if you need me. You know how I feel about you, and nothin' will ever change that." He placed his right hand on her left shoulder and gently squeezed. "I can see you're in for a bad fall, and I want you to know I'll catch you if you want."

Bertha managed a wan smile. "Thanks, Bear. I appreciate it. Believe me, you'll be the first to know if I get serious about you. Right now I've got me some heavy thinkin' to do."

"I understand," Bear sympathized. He detected a movement out of the corner of his right eye and turned. "Say! Look at that! Blade is on top of one of those trucks. What's he doin'?"

Blade was perched on the canvas roof of the first troop transport, his arms raised over his head, the Commando and the A-1 both slung over separate shoulders.

Hickok and Geronimo, their weapons reclaimed, stood below their Triad leader.

"Your attention!" Blade shouted at the assembled mass. "Listen up! This is important!" He waited for the crowd to quiet, then resumed. "I believe all of you know who I am and the reason my friends and I are here. We promised we would lead you out of the Twin Cities to a place of safety. Orginally, we intended to conduct the exodus in the spring, when the weather would be nicer. Also, it would have given us time to prepare, to set aside extra food and other supplies to make your transition easier. Now that is all changed. Now it's impossible." He paused to insure they were paying attention. Everyone was riveted on his every word. "You saw what the soldiers from the Civilized Zone did to your relatives and friends today. You may know they were planning to take all of you to a place near Denver called a Reabsorption Center and enslave you. Do you want that to happen?" he asked.

Perhaps half of the throng responded with a desultory negative.

Blade scanned the people below him. "Listen!" he snapped. "My friends and I risked our lives for you! If you want to stay in the Twin Cities, that's fine with us! But if you don't, I need to know now! So I'll ask you again. Do you want the soldiers to take you into the Civilized Zone? Do you want to live under a dictator? Do you want someone else telling you what you can do and when you should do it? Do you?"

This time, the reaction was thunderous. *"No! No! No!"*

Blade waved for silence. "Good! Then pay attention! A lot of the Army troopers got away. They may return by themselves, or they could radio for reinforcements. Either way, we can't stay here any longer. We could try to hold them off, but our supplies are limited. They'd eventually overrun us. There isn't a place in the Twin Cities where we'd be safe. So here is what I propose. I say we pack ourselves into these trucks and head for our Home, for the place where Hickok, Geronimo, Joshua, and I come from. There are some small towns nearby. I guarantee you that my Family will do everything in its power to aid you in resettling. It won't be easy. Food will be scarce on the trip there, and the winter ahead will undoubtedly be rough. But my Family will see to it you have a roof over your head, and we'll share our food with you and help you in killing game. In the spring, we'll show you how to grow enough food to feed yourselves. So what will it be? Do we go?"

The night rocked with the chorus of *"Go! Go! Go!"*

"Good!" Blade yelled when they quieted. "Here's what I want you to do." He hesitated. "First, who's in charge of the Horns now that Reverend Paul is dead? I was told that Brother Timothy is the leader now."

"I am," a man in black cried out, a thin man with a thick beard. Joshua was standing next to him.

"Okay." Blade pointed to the right. "Timothy, I want you to have all your people form over there. I'll be with you in a moment." He looked down and spotted Zahner at the front of the assemblage. "Zahner, have your people gather over there." He pointed to the left.

"Will do," Zahner said.

"Where's Bear?" Blade demanded.

"Right here!" Bear shouted from near the stockade.

"Get the Porns together right there," Blade ordered, indicating directly in front of the trucks. "Let's go! Time is critical!"

"What do you want us to do?" Hickok inquired, looking up.

"After they've formed into their respective groups," Blade directed, "go to each one and take five men from each. Then scour this field and collect all the arms and ammunition you find. Don't miss a thing. Be sure and get those machine guns from the sentry towers still standing. Pile the weapons near the SEAL. We'll divide them up equally among the three factions. Remember. We can't afford to display any favoritism here. The slightest provocation could set them against each another."

"Do you think these trucks can carry all of us to the Home?" Geronimo queried.

"Jarvis intended to take them all the way to Denver," Blade reminded him. "Check. One of these trucks must have a spare supply of gasoline."

"How long do you reckon it will take us?" Hickok asked.

Blade calculated aloud. "It's about three hundred and seventy miles from the Twin Cities to our Home. If we push it, we can make a hundred miles a day, possibly more. So we could conceivably reach the Home within three or four days. The sooner the better. We'll be sitting ducks on the open highway."

"You figure the Army will try and stop us?" Hickok questioned.

"You can count on it," Blade affirmed. "Like Jarvis said, Samuel doesn't want us getting any stronger than we already are. I don't know how many troops they can muster between here and the Home, but whatever they've got they'll throw at us."

"Should be a mighty interesting trip," Hickok remarked.

"You've got that right," Blade concurred.

"Aren't you sorry now?" Hickok inquired.

"Sorry? About what?"

"Sorry that you didn't send Yama with us and go on that spying assignment yourself, instead of having all the Warriors draw lots? Just think! Instead of going through all of this aggravation, you could be doing just what Yama is probably doing right now. You could be taking it easy, strolling through downtown Cheyenne and enjoying the sights." The gunman sighed wistfully. "Yes, sir. Some folks get all the luck!"

20

Yama ducked to the right, pulling Lynx after him. He leaned against the wall and shoved Lynx in the direction of the stairs.

"Ahhhh, Mom!" Lynx protested. "I wanna stay here and play!"

"Move!" Yama commanded, marveling at Lynx's levity in light of the dire circumstances.

Lynx chuckled and hastened down the hall.

Yama counted to three, then swung into the junction, the Wilkinson leveled.

The two men in white were only five yards away, racing at full speed.

The Wilkinson burped, the nine-millimeter bullets, traveling at over two thousand feet per second, catching the two men in their chests before they could hope to react. Both went down as Yama leaped for cover.

The troopers advancing along the hallway began firing, their M-16's chattering, the slugs striking the walls and ricocheting wildly.

Yama ran, hugging the right-hand wall, passing closed doors on both sides of the hallway.

Lynx was twenty yards ahead, holding the door to a

stairwell wide open and gesturing for Yama to hurry.

The klaxons ceased wailing.

Yama was almost abreast of a large machine of some sort, a rectangular affair with a photograph of a drink covering the upper half and a row of glowing buttons aligned along the center, when his headlong rush was derailed by two simultaneous events. The soldiers reached the junction behind him and started shooting at the fleeing Warrior, even as a door directly in front of him opened and an elderly woman walked out.

Yama was unable to stop in time.

The woman shrieked as he plowed into her, the force of the impact spinning him around and knocking him into the drink machine.

Yama stumbled and fell to his knees, his gaze on the woman as she staggered, her mouth widening for a scream, a scream never heard because at that instant her forehead exploded outward as she was struck by the M-16 fire.

"Come on!" Lynx shouted encouragement.

Yama dropped to his elbows and knees and twisted, facing the junction.

The soldiers were just leaving the junction and bearing down on him.

Yama aimed and pulled the trigger, the Wilkinson recoiling against his shoulder, his shots finding their mark. Three of the men in uniform went down and the rest hesitated.

Lynx slid into the concealment of the stairwell.

Yama rolled, finding cover behind the drink machine as it was racked with gunfire from the M-16's.

Had Lynx deserted him?

Yama discarded the troubling thought as he popped out from behind the machine and pumped more rounds into the troopers.

One of them fell, his face bloody, screeching in torment.

Four down, eight to go.

Yama jerked behind the drink machine again as the soldiers intensified their assault. He glanced at the stairwell. If he tried to reach it, he knew he'd be cut to ribbons before he managed to go four feet.

The sound of the bullets striking the drink machine made it seem as if it was being attacked by a giant woodpecker.

Yama prepared to give them another blast.

"Spread out!" one of the soldiers yelled. "We've got him pinned down!"

That they did.

Yama attempted to lean out and fire, but a withering spray from the M-16's drove him back.

"Hey, chuckles!" someone called, and there was Lynx in the stairwell doorway, holding a circular object in his right hand. "Duck!"

Yama obeyed, flattening as Lynx lobbed the metallic object in an overhand motion toward the troopers.

The hallway rocked with a deafening detonation and concussion. Smoke choked the corridor and the agonized cries of the soldiers filled the air.

Yama rose and sprinted to the stairwell.

Lynx was waiting for him. "About time," he said. "I know you said you wanted a tour, but I had no idea you were going to take the scenic route!"

Yama looked over his left shoulder.

No indication of any pursuit.

"What was that?" Yama asked Lynx.

"A grenade," Lynx replied. "There's a munitions room one flight up for the auxiliaries. Only contains M-16's, some pistols, ammo, and a few grenades."

Yama noted that Lynx was still unarmed. "Why

didn't you get an M-16 for yourself?"

"Not my style," Lynx answered, grinning. "Besides, guns make me nervous."

"Your choice. Now get me to that records room, and fast!" Yama directed.

Lynx started up the stairs, the Warrior right behind him. "You did pretty good back there," Lynx commented.

"Lots of practice," Yama responded.

"Not as good as I would have done," Lynx said amending his compliment.

Yama smiled and stayed on his newfound companion's heels as they jogged up the stairwell and reached the desired floor.

Lynx paused at the door. "This place will be crawling with enforcement types, human and otherwise. We're outnumbered, but we have two elements working in our favor. These morons will be running around like chickens with their heads chopped off without the Doc to direct 'em, and I happen to know he's out, attending a big feed with Sammy. And also, I know this place better than most. So stick with me, pal. I'll hold your hand until we're out of this mess."

"Just get me to the records room," Yama stated.

"Here we go." Lynx winked at the Warrior and eased from the stairwell into the hall.

Yama kept his back to the wall as he stepped out. This corridor was forty yards in length. At the opposite end was clustered a crowd consisting of humans and creatures from the Genetic Research Division.

"Bluff the bozos," Lynx suggested, and boldly walked into view in the middle of the hallway.

Yama stayed by his side, expecting one of the group at the end of the hall to suddenly voice an alarm. Several of them did look his way, but they resumed their conversations without evincing any concern. Why should they? he reasoned. To them, Lynx and he seemed like any ordinary genetic deviate and soldier.

At the fourth door they reached Lynx stopped and grasped the doorknob. "Gee, chuckles, I forgot my key. Did you bring yours?" Without waiting for a reply, Lynx twisted the knob.

Yama heard a sharp snap and a grating, crunching noise as Lynx twisted the doorknob, and the lock mechanism, into scrap metal.

"After you, Mommy," Lynx said, flicking on an overhead light.

Yama entered the room. "How strong are you?" he inquired as he passed Lynx.

"If I don't bathe for a week," Lynx rejoined, closing the door after them, "I can down a fly at ten paces."

The records room wasn't very spacious, about twenty feet by twenty feet. File cabinets lined all four walls and a sturdy oaken desk occupied the center of the room.

Lynx's nose was twitching. "The Doc's scent makes me want to puke!" he said, grimacing in disgust.

Yama walked to the desk and examined the papers strewn over its top. Personal correspondence, magazine and newspaper clippings, classified intelligence reports, and sheets of mathematical calculations littered the desk.

Lynx pressed his right ear against the door. "Don't take all night," he advised.

Yama picked up a sheet marked "Top Secret." The paper contained a report on suspected rebel activity in a small Wyoming town. It also said a wanted rebel leader, a man called Toland, was believed to be hiding in the town. He stuffed the paper into his right pants pocket and scanned the room. His attention was attracted by a black leather pouch lying on a file cabinet behind the desk. He unsnapped the flap and drew out the contents, four thick hardbound notebooks with blue covers.

"I think we've got company, chuckles," Lynx reported.

Yama flipped the pages on the notebooks and discovered all four were filled, longhand writing covering each page. He searched for a name identifying the owner but couldn't locate one.

"They're going door to door," Lynx announced.

Yama thoughtfully stared at the notebooks. He had an unusual feeling about them, as if he sensed they were important in some respect. Acting on his vague premonition, he replaced the notebooks in the pouch and snapped the flap.

"Afraid our time is about up," Lynx said, his ear still against the door.

Yama hefted the pouch by its carrying strap and slung it over his right shoulder. He joined Lynx by the door.

"I can hear 'em," Lynx whispered. "They're about two doors off. When they open this one I'll make my move. Don't lose me." He paused. "Where did you want to go next?"

"With the whole Biological Center on the alert," Yama answered, "it would be useless to remain in the building. Can you get us outside?"

"Then what?"

"We'll play it by ear," Yama said.

"Fair enough, pal." Lynx sighed. "Too bad all I could get my hands on was a grenade! I'd like to bring this building down around their ears! Now if I just had a thermo. . . ." He stopped and motioned for silence.

Yama recalled hearing the word "thermo" before. What was a . . .

The door abruptly flew open and all hell broke loose.

Lynx sprang, his movements so quick it was difficult

for the eye to follow, leaping into the midst of four
soldiers standing outside the door. His arms flashed and
flailed, his claws ripping and shredding, and the
troopers were out of commission before they even knew
what hit them. Lynx went for their faces, for their eyes
and throats, growling and snarling as he attacked, his
keen claws drawing blood with every savage swipe.

Yama slammed into one of the staggering soldiers,
flinging him against the far wall.

Other troopers and members of the Genetic Research
Division were to their left.

"Get them!" someone bellowed.

Lynx suddenly grabbed Yama by the left wrist and
pulled him down the corridor toward the stairwell.

Three of the soldiers Lynx had jumped were on the
floor, two of them screaming and thrashing.

There was the crack of a pistol report and a bullet
buzzed over Yama's head.

They reached the stairwell and plowed into the door.
Lynx began up the steps. "Come on, slowpoke!" he
urged.

"Don't hold back on my account," Yama told him.

Lynx glanced over his right shoulder. "Yama, ol'
buddy, if I went at top speed you'd never catch up. I
don't want to lose you just when I'm starting to grow
fond of you!" He laughed.

They were two flights above the floor with the records
room when their foes burst into the stairwell.

"Which way did they go?" a trooper asked.

"Half go up," another proposed, "the rest go down."

Boots pounded on the steps below them.

Lynx immediately left the stairwell, leading Yama
along a vacant passageway. About halfway down this
corridor Lynx opened another door and they found
themselves in another, smaller stairwell.

"I was right," Yama commented. "This place is a maze."

Lynx led the Warrior on a dizzying, circuitous route through the mammoth Biological Center, first up one stairwell, then down another, always moving, going in one direction along one hallway and then reversing direction down another, selecting corridors he knew were infrequently used. When they did encounter others, on the stairs or in a passageway, they would stroll along, acting as innocently as they could, even greeting the people and genetic deviates they passed along the way.

Yama lost all track of time.

Lynx stopped periodically to cock his furry head and listen. They finally reached a narrow, unused stairway with a wooden bannister. "Keep your fingers crossed," Lynx said descending the stairs. At the bottom was a metal door with a lighted sign above it reading: "Emergency Exit Only."

"No one uses this," Lynx divulged. "They have to keep it unlocked to obey the Fire Code."

What was a fire code? Yama wondered. He braced himself as Lynx slowly opened the door, its hinges creaking from a lack of use and maintenance.

The emergency door opened onto a cement walkway. Evidently, pedestrians never used it, because it was deserted.

"What did I tell you?" Lynx asked, grinning in triumph.

They sauntered along the walkway until they reached a parking lot packed with military vehicles.

Yama gazed overhead. From the position of the moon he knew they were in the parking lot situated to the north of the Biological Center.

"What now, chuckles?" Lynx inquired.

Yama thought a moment. "You mentioned something

a while ago, something called a thermo. What is it?"

"Boy," Lynx snickered, "they sure raise 'em stupid where you come from, don't they? A thermo is technical jargon for a thermo-nuclear device."

"You want to drop a nuclear bomb on Cheyenne?" Yama asked in surprise.

"No, dummy!" Lynx shook his head. "I was thinking of one of the small tactical launchers, a lot like a big mortar only it fires a small missile with a tiny nuclear tip. They were real popular with the Army during World War III. The radiation spread is minimal, but it sures blows the crapola out of whatever it hits!"

Yama stared at the imposing edifice behind them. "What would a thermo do to the Biological Center?"

"There wouldn't be one," Lynx stated with obvious relish. "All you'd have left would be a gaping crater in the ground."

"How wide an area would it affect?"

"Oh, the Center and about a half-mile in all directions. Enough to take out the parking lots, at least. Say, why are you asking all of these questions, pal?"

"Because I think I know where we can get our hands on one of these thermos," Yama informed him.

"You ain't gettin' your hands on nothin', fella!" someone declared, the voice coming from their right.

Yama spun, regretting his carelessness.

It was one of the Doktor's genetically engineered creations, a G.R.D., endowed with a bulky body covered with light brown hair. It stood six feet in height and its face was decidedly canine in aspect, although the individual features were not as pronounced as they would be in a legitimate dog.

"I was wondering when you'd show up," Lynx stated.

"Oh?" the creature replied.

"I knew you were on my trail, Shep," Lynx said. "Out

of all of 'em, you're the only one who could have caught up with me."

Shep crouched and moved forward. "You didn't make it easy, I'll grant you that."

"You wouldn't want to let us pass and forget you ever saw us, would you?" Lynx queried hopefully.

"You know better than that!" Shep retorted. "I'm going to hold you here until the others catch up. They sent me ahead because my nose is the best there is."

"Next to mine," Lynx disputed him.

Shep glared at Yama. "Tell this fool to drop his weapons, Lynx, or he'll never know what hit him."

Lynx stepped between the Warrior and the approaching Shep.

"I don't require assistance," Yama informed Lynx.

"Yes, you do," Lynx said, never looking at Yama. "The Doc designed our bodies with a special attribute called accelerated repair. It's next to impossible to waste us unless you score a direct hit on the brain or heart. You might get Shep, but it would take a while and we don't have the time to spare. Shep is all mine, chuckles."

Shep smiled. "I was hopin' you'd resist, runt! I never did like your ugly puss much!"

"The feeling is mutual," Lynx rejoined.

Yama, about to raise the Wilkinson and aim at Shep's head, was too slow.

With guttural growls, the two G.R.D.'s hurtled at one another.

21

There was an unwanted delay in their departure from the Twin Cities.

At first, everything had gone their way. They had found spare gasoline cans in one of the trucks and two dozen crates containing canned food. Blade had distributed the weapons collected from the fallen soldiers equally among the three factions. Troop transport assignments had been made, with an average of thirty-three people per transport. They were all set to take off.

That's when the problem arose.

"Who's going to drive the trucks?" Zahner asked as the people were waiting for the word to load into the transports.

"Can't some of them drive?" Blade inquired in disbelief.

"Be serious," Zahner said. "Where would we learn to drive? There isn't a functional vehicle left in the Twin Cities."

Blade, stymied and chafing at the postponement of their run to the Home, called an executive meeting of the leaders and the Warriors. After a brief debate, it was decided each of the leaders, Zahner, Bear, and Brother

Timothy, would drive a truck, as would Joshua. Bertha was offered an opportunity but obstinately declined. With four of the troop transports accounted for, Blade instructed the leaders to each select four of their most trusted lieutenants for driving duty.

Zahner, Bear, and Brother Timothy left to make their picks.

"Will we be riding in the trucks or in the SEAL?" Geronimo inquired.

"We'll stay in the SEAL," Blade answered. "We'll roam up and down the convoy, help any stragglers, and watch out for soldiers."

"I made a head count of the bodies," Hickok mentioned. "If my math is up to snuff, about thirty of the troopers wimped out and ran off. That doesn't include those three jeeps you said Jarvis told you about."

"Thirty soldiers and three jeeps," Blade repeated, his brow furrowed. "They could jump us anytime, but my guess is they'll try and prevent us from leaving the Twin Cities or restrain us here until reinforcements arrive. I don't like it. Hickok, take ten armed men and establish a lookout post on the highway. If those jeeps come at us, that's probably the way they'll come. If you see anything, send someone on the run and let me know."

"You got it, pard," Hickok said, hefting his Henry as he moved toward a nearby crowd. "What will you be doing while I'm gone?"

"Geronimo and I will be teaching the drivers how to operate the troop transports," Blade disclosed, "which should be real interesting because neither of us have any practical experience with a manual transmission."

"Take your time," Hickok advised. "We'll hold the road." He ambled to the mixed group standing alongside the tent. "I need some volunteers!" he announced, and proceeded to designate the ten he required. "To the road!" he directed, waving them in the proper direction.

"What are we going to do?" a Horn wanted to know.

"We're goin' snipe hunting," Hickok revealed.

"We're what?"

"We're gonna keep our peepers peeled for unwanted company," Hickok elaborated.

They were twenty yards from the tent when a woman's voice rose behind them.

"White Meat! Wait for me!"

"Uh-oh," Hickok said under his breath. He grinned at the men with him. "Why don't you go on ahead. I'll be with you in a sec. Keep your eyes out for anything unusual."

Several of the men nodded their comprehension and they all walked toward the road.

Hickok took a deep breath and turned.

Bertha was only feet away, smiling, watching him uncertainly as she approached. An M-16 was slung over her right shoulder.

"Howdy, Black Beauty," Hickok greeted her, using his pet name for her.

"I figured we needed to do some heavy talkin'," she said bluntly. "Now's a good a time as any."

"Blade wanted me to stand guard on the highway," Hickok stated lamely.

"It can't wait." Bertha paused, locking her eyes on his. "I need to get something straight in my head. It's drivin' me nuts!"

"What is it?" the gunman questioned.

"You know damn well what it is!" Bertha exclaimed bitterly. "You've been avoiding me like the plague! Why? We don't see each other for months, and I don't even rate a hug when we finally do meet up. Why?"

"I . . ." Hickok began, before she cut him off.

"I've had a lot of time to think," Bertha said. "I've

thought about the last time we saw each other, and how you were actin' so cold. A real fish. Remember?"

"Yes, but . . ."

"After I talked with Bear I figured out why. You thought he and me was in tight. Am I right?"

"Yes, but . . ."

"Bear don't mean nothin' to me!" Bertha said, her tone softening. "He's a good friend, but that's it. Yeah, I know he's got the hots for me, but it ain't a two-way street. Do you see where I'm comin' from?"

"I think so, but . . ."

"But now that I've seen you again," Bertha said interrupting one more time, "I think Bear ain't the reason you're actin' so strange. What is it, White Meat? Don't be afraid to tell me the truth. I've been dumped on before. It's the story of my life. So? What is it? I got to know!"

Hickok placed his right arm around her shoulders, his sad blue eyes reflecting his inner emotional turmoil. "I'm sorry I avoided you," he said softly. "You know me. It isn't my style to run from anything in this world, but I didn't know how to tell you and not hurt your feelings."

"I knew it!" Bertha said sorrowfully. "I just knew it! You don't care about me the way I care about you! Am I right?"

"That's part of it," Hickok admitted. "I do care for you, Black Beauty, but as a real close friend."

"I don't believe it!" Bertha exclaimed. "You feel about me the same way I feel about Bear! I guess the joke's on me!" She gazed tenderly into his eyes. "But it ain't the end of the world! It means I still have a chance! Somewhere down the road you and I could still be an item! Right?"

"Wrong," Hickok blurted out, and then he mentally

berated his stupidity.

"Wrong? Why wrong?" Bertha demanded.

"I've only told you part of the reason we can only be good friends," Hickok elaborated, secretly wishing he could turn invisible and get the heck out of there.

"There's more?" Bertha took a step back, her hands on her hips. "What are you holdin' back? Did you find a girlfriend while you were away?" she asked angrily.

"Not exactly."

"What, then? And old flame show up and wrap you around her little pinkie?"

"Not quite."

"Then what the hell could have happened in two short months that's stoppin' us from showin' the whole world what true love is like? *What?*" she cried.

"I got hitched," Hickok said sheepishly.

"You what?"

"I was hitched proper."

"Hitched?" Bertha repeated, sounding dazed.

"Hitched. Tied the knot. You know. I got married."

"You . . . got . . . married?"

"Sure did," Hickok beamed. "The prettiest filly you'd ever want to . . ."

Bertha abruptly grabbed the gunman by the front of his buckskin shirt. "Your standin' there and tellin' me you got married? You took yourself a wife?"

Hickok, at a loss for words, simply nodded.

"A wife!" Bertha released the Warrior, her arms falling limply at her sides. "A wife!"

"I hope you won't take it too hard," Hickok offered in the way of condolences.

Bertha stared at him, her eyes narrowing. Before he could stop her, she unslung the M-16 and pointed the barrel at his head.

22

Yama was helpless to intervene, relegated to standing on the sidelines and observing one of the most spectacular fights he'd ever witnessed. The flow of combat was so swift, with the two G.R.D.'s shifting positions so rapidly, there was no way he could squeeze off a shot without running the risk of striking Lynx.

The two opponents were instinctual enemies, one the result of a human embryo genetically altered to produce a hybrid canine, the other a living embodiment of feline fury.

Shep was the larger by far, and ostensibly the stronger. He slammed Lynx to the cement walk and lunged, the claws on his right hand flicking at Lynx's eyes.

Lynx rolled to the left, his left arm slashing sideways as he did, his own claws raking Shep's shins and eliciting a howl of commingled pain and rage. Lynx leaped to his feet as Shep backed off several steps.

It was the first chance Yama had to fire, but the pair closed again before he could snap off a round.

Lynx and Shep went down in a thrashing, snarling, ripping, and tearing ball of fur, rolling this way and that, neither one gaining a decided advantage but both inflicting numerous severe cuts and gashes on each other.

Yama took his gaze from the conflict long enough to scan the area. This section of the parking lot was evidently deserted and the nearest major artery was the crowded pedestrian sidewalk almost seventy-five yards to the west. A hedge and a small stand of trees provided cover between the pedestrians and the battle royal. Yama concentrated on the fight.

The combatants had rolled into the parking lot, still embroiled in their intense life-or-death struggle.

Neither one seemed to have an edge. The fur and hair, not to mention the sweat and blood, were flying fast and furious.

Yama began to wonder how long the fight would take. Every moment they wasted increased the likelihood of discovery and apprehension.

Suddenly, Shep appeared to be getting the better of his opponent. He was obviously pressing Lynx, who sported a nasty wound on his right temple. In a blur of arms and legs, Shep managed to come out on top, astride Lynx's narrow chest, his legs pinning Lynx's arms underneath them.

"Now!" Shep hissed, and clamped his claws around Lynx's neck.

Yama, ready, brought up the Wilkinson, even as Lynx shifted. Lynx's hands were hidden from view under Shep's thighs, and Yama could only imagine what transpired as Shep unexpectedly straightened, his currish features distorted in unmitigated agony. He grunted and clutched at his loincloth, doubling over.

Lynx heaved, hurling his adversary to the pavement. In a flash, Lynx pounced, burying his pointed teeth in Shep's throat and then jerking backwards, rending the neck wide open. Lynx moved to one side, spitting blood and hair from his mouth.

Shep was experiencing convulsions, his left hand over his groin, his right hand pressed against his ruined throat. His mouth moved soundlessly until, with a final shudder and a quivering of his eyelids, he expired.

"So long, ol' Shep," Lynx said softly, more to himself than to Yama. His own breathing was ragged, the strain taking its toll. "You were tough. The toughest I've ever fought. Chalk up another one I owe the Doc for."

Yama walked to Lynx and touched his left shoulder. "We must be going," he prompted.

Lynx looked up and vigorously shook his head, as if striving to clear his mind of troublesome thoughts. "Yeah. Right, chuckles. I almost forgot. You were sayin' something about a thermo."

"Would you know how to use one if we found one?" Yama asked him.

"I think so," Lynx responded, sounding winded. "The Doc made all of us, all of his little pets, take classes on firearms and other hardware. The Doc doesn't trust old Sammy too much, and he knew even we couldn't go up against the Army unarmed. Where's this thermo of yours?"

"Are you up to traveling?"

"I could outrun you," Lynx bragged.

"Then let's go."

Yama headed due north, electing to swing around the sidewalk he'd encountered trouble at before. Unfortunately, the design of the immediate area thwarted his intention. The V.A. Hospital was located due east of the Biological Center. To the north, west, and south were the huge parking lots currently filled with military vehicles and equipment. The pedestrian sidewalk was situated to the west of the Center, but it actually ran

north and south. So there was no way Yama could get to
the west parking lot from the north parking lot without
crossing the sidewalk.

"What's wrong, bub?" Lynx asked when Yama
stopped and frowned.

Yama told him.

"Is that all?" Lynx chuckled. "Stick with me, kid.
You might learn something. Come on."

So saying, Lynx made directly for the thronged
sidewalk.

"Did you sustain brain damage in that fight?" Yama
facetiously inquired. "We can't cross that sidewalk.
We'll be seen. What do you have in mind?"

"You'll see, pal," was all Lynx would reply.

As they neared the bustling activity on the sidewalk,
Yama again speculated on the possible reason the people
were all crammed together instead of giving themselves
elbow room by using the parking lot. He posed the
question to Lynx.

"It's against the law," Lynx explained.

"You have laws governing where your citizens can and
cannot walk?"

"They're not my laws, chuckles. The Government
makes 'em, and the Government controls every aspect of
life in the Civilized Zone. I don't know if you're aware of
it, but the Government keeps a file on everybody. When
you were born, what schools you went to, if you're
married or not, how many kids you've got, how much
money you make and how much in taxes you pay, if you
ever broke a law, how much you weigh, how tall you are,
what color your hair is. You name it, the Government
knows it. Sammy doesn't miss a trick. As far as the
sidewalk and the parking lots go, it's illegal for a civilian
to use a military parking lot for any purpose, not even to
cut across. Hell, Yama, they even tell you which side of

the damn sidewalk you must walk on. You can only enter the sidewalk at designated entry points. If you should spit on the sidewalk, and you're caught, it's five years at hard labor. They've even got sidewalk cops to enforce their pedestrian laws." Lynx sighed. "I was born into a world gone mad."

"I had no idea you were such a philosopher," Yama remarked.

"You can't help but think about the way things are," Lynx said as they walked past a row of jeeps. "Not if you have a mind, anyway."

"I'm amazed the people put up with it," Yama stated.

"What choice have they got?" Lynx rhetorically queried. "The Army has all the guns. The Doc backs up Sammy with the Genetic Research Division, not to mention his other toys. A lot of people don't much like the status quo, but there ain't too much they can do about it. You dig?"

"What about the rebels?"

They were ten yards from the sidewalk. "There aren't enough of 'em. They're like a bee stinging a bear. The bee can irritate the bear no end, but there's no way that bee can ever whip the bear."

Yama scanned the crowded sidewalk as they drew nearer. No one was paying any special attention to them.

Lynx slowed. "Stay real close to me," he said. "We should be able to make it, no problem, provided none of these dummies saw my picture in the paper."

"I'll be right beside you," Yama promised. To play it safe, he pulled a fresh magazine from his right rear pants pocket and replaced the used clip in the Wilkinson.

Lynx walked right up to the sidewalk, never breaking his stride. When he was still a foot away, he cupped his hands around his mouth. "Make way!" he shouted. "Coming through!"

Yama was startled by the reaction of the pedestrians.

The people on the sidewalk stopped, only a few inadvertently bumping into others as the traffic flow abruptly ceased. A narrow space was cleared, and Lynx and Yama strolled across the walk to the west parking lot. No sooner were they clear of the sidewalk than the flow of people resumed.

"Incredible," Yama commented.

"It's no big deal," Lynx said as they continued bearing west. "You just gotta understand how the people feel about us, about the Doc's menagerie. They're scared to death of us. We're allowed to go where we please, when we please. Even the military is afraid of us. Give 'em another hundred years and they'll probably make us their gods."

"And you want to give up godhood?" Yama grinned.

"A slave by any other name is still a slave," Lynx declared harshly. "Enough of this yappin'. Where's the thermo?"

"The trucks we're seeking should be to the southwest," Yama replied.

They walked in silence, Lynx alert for soldiers, Yama scouring the vehicles for the munitions trucks he'd seen earlier.

"Can't you find 'em?" Lynx questioned after a while.

"There are so many trucks," Yama answered, "and they all look alike. I came across five soldiers loading explosives into some trucks. One of them said they had tactical units capable of firing a thermo a mile or more," he quoted from memory.

"Keep looking," Lynx urged. "If we can find 'em, we'll give the Doc something to remember us by."

Very few troopers were still in the parking lots. Most were either asleep in preparation for rising early the next day, or else enjoying a wild night on the town, one last fling before going into combat.

Yama stopped, something tugging at his mind.

"What is it?" Lynx asked.

"I think we're close," Yama said, studying the nearby vehicles. "I have the feeling I've seen this row of trucks before." He walked south along the row.

"Take your time," Lynx urged. "I didn't have a hot date tonight, anyway."

Yama turned, facing some supply trucks he viewed as vaguely familiar. "These may be the ones."

"Keep watch," Lynx directed, and darted between two of the trucks.

Yama could hear Lynx moving around in the backs of the trucks as he went from one to the other, hunting for the thermo they needed. About thirty yards to the south a trooper came into sight, moving in the direction of the Biological Center.

There was a thump and a crashing sound from within one of the supply trucks.

"Are you all right?" Yama called as quietly as he could while still making himself heard.

"Fine!" was Lynx's muffled response. "Tripped over a damn crate!"

Yama chuckled. He glanced at the Biological Center, thankful he was out of that horrid edifice, and wondered if the manhunt for Lynx and himself was still in progress. Probably. Would the Doktor be notified and hasten back from the banquet to personally oversee the search? Possibly. If so, and . . .

There was a whoop of delight from one of the supply trucks. A moment later, Lynx appeared. He was toting a large, rectangular metal box on his right shoulder. The box was at least five feet long and two feet wide. Tucked under his left arm was a narrow wooden crate two feet in length and only nine inches wide.

"You found it?" Yama asked.

"Yep. We're in business, bub. Now let's find us a jeep. Do you know how to drive?"

"I do," Yama assured him.

"Good. Let's get crackin'. They're bound to find Shep soon, if they haven't already, and when they do they'll know we're out here somewhere. They may order a general alert, and if they do this place will be swarming with Army types, cops, and G.R.D.'s."

They hurried, bearing to the south, passing trucks and flatbeds and several tanks and even some halftracks. But no jeeps.

"There's gotta be jeeps around here someplace," Lynx said with a touch of annoyance. "This thing is starting to get heavy."

Another fifty feet and they discovered a dozen jeeps parked in a neatly ordered row.

"Find one with the keys in the ignition," Lynx suggested. "There's bound to be at least one."

There was. The seventh jeep Yama checked had its keys in the ignition, ready to be driven off. The green jeep was outfitted with a roll bar, but it lacked a roof. A snap-on canvas top was rolled up behind the two front seats.

Lynx clambered into the back and deposited the metal box and the wooden crate on the floor. "Whew! I had no idea a tactical unit weighed so much!"

Yama sat in the driver's seat. "Which way do we go?"

"Do you know where Pershing Boulevard is?" Lynx inquired.

"Just south of this parking lot."

"Yep. Drive to Pershing and hang a right," Lynx directed.

Yama started the jeep and slowly drove south, turning on the headlights as he left the parking space. He carefully negotiated the many rows of parked vehicles before he reached Pershing Boulevard.

Lynx leaned forward. "Don't drive too fast," he advised, "and don't drive too slow. Either way, we'll have the cops on us. Stay at the speed limit."

"What's a speed limit?"

Lynx pointed at a white sign with black numbers near the parking lot exit to Pershing. "You see that sign over there? It says the speed limit is forty-five. That means you don't drive this heap over forty-five miles an hour. Got it?"

"I comprehend," Yama said. He'd seen a few such signs on his trip from the Home to Wyoming and been puzzled as to the purpose of a sign in the middle of nowhere with only a number on it. Most road signs and highway markers, after a century of abandonment, had blown over, rusted out, or faded to the point of illegibility. He turned the jeep right onto Pershing.

The vehicle traffic, like the pedestrian traffic, was very heavy, although it seemed to Yama the volume was slightly less than when he had arrived in Cheyenne.

"Keep headin' west until I tell you," Lynx said.

Their jeep traveled a mile from the Biological Center before Lynx recommended they turn down a side street. The traffic density thinned considerably, but the pedestrians still jammed the sidewalks on either side.

"Hey, Yama," Lynx said at one point.

"What is it?" Yama was concentrating on his driving.

"After we blow the Biological Center, and if we can get out of the Citadel, what are your plans?"

"I intend to pick up some friends and return with them to the place I came from," Yama revealed, still unwilling to impart any information concerning the Family and the Home.

"If we get out of this alive," Lynx said, "the Civilized

Zone will be too hot for yours truly. Do you think . . ."
he began, and paused. "Do you suppose I could . . ."

"Spit it out," Yama prompted when Lynx
inexplicably balked.

"Do you think I could come and stay with your people
for a spell? Would they mind?"

Yama perceived that his companion had been
embarrassed to pose the question. For what reason?
Was Lynx afraid of rejection? "Do you know a G.R.D.
by the name of Gremlin?" he asked.

Lynx appeared surprised by the query. "Yeah. I know
him. We're not the best of friends, but we've talked a
few times. Come to think of it, I haven't seen him in
some time. Why?"

"Because Gremlin is living with my people," Yama
elaborated. "We actually think of him as one of our
own."

"Gremlin? Living with you?" Lynx shook his head.
"No way," he stated emphatically. "The Doc removed
my collar because he knew I'd try to remove it and wind
up committing suicide. But the Doc never removed
Gremlin's collar. I would have heard about it. And if
Gremlin turned against the Doc, the Doc would have
fried him with a flick of a switch."

Yama glanced over his right shoulder at Lynx. "I
don't make it a habit of lying," he said, his tone low and
hard.

"I never called you a liar," Lynx replied quickly. "I
didn't mean anything by what I just said. I find it hard
to swallow, is all."

"Then you'll find this next tidbit even harder," Yama
predicted. "Gremlin isn't the only G.R.D. residing with
us. There's also one called Ferret . . ."

"Ferret!" Lynx exclaimed. "He's a pal of mine! I
heard he was dead."

"You heard wrong. Both Gremlin and Ferret are living with us and neither have their collars." Yama neglected to mention that Ferret was being held under house arrest because the Family wasn't certain they could trust him. Yet.

"Gremlin and Ferret . . . free," Lynx said, his voice abnormally soft and expressive. "It's my dream come true." He looked up and found a bright star overhead. "Maybe there is a God up there, after all," he mused.

"How much farther?" Yama inquired, snapping Lynx back to reality.

Lynx suddenly gripped Yama's right shoulder. "Turn! Turn right! Now!"

Yama spun the steering wheel, the jeep turning right into a quiet cul-de-sac devoid of other vehicles. The cul-de-sac ended in a small park, and even at this time of the night dozens of people were using the park, some strolling arm in arm, other walking and talking, and still others seated on the park benches, savoring the cool night air. The park-goers idly looked around as the jeep approached, and hastily glanced away once the occupants were identified.

Yama parked against the curb and switched off the motor.

Lynx put his left hand on Yama's shoulder. "Before we make another move, chuckles, let me give you some advice. If something should happen to me, head for the west wall of the Citadel. They will probably lock Cheyenne up tight as a drum after we play with our fireworks here, but you may be able to shoot your way through the west gate, or talk your way past the guards since you're in that officer's uniform, or . . ." Lynx gazed at the tactical unit, an idea forming. "Or you could bluff 'em. Pull up near the gate and tell 'em to open up or you'll launch a thermo into the wall. Believe me, they'll think twice before they open fire on you."

"I appreciate your concern," Yama told Lynx, "but it's a bit premature. We're going to get out of here together."

Lynx climbed down and lifted the tactical unit from the jeep. "Bring the wooden crate, sunshine," he said, and walked to the grass.

The people nearby studiously ignored him while many of them started to edge away.

Yama carried the wooden crate over to Lynx.

"This is the spot," Lynx announced, depositing the tactical unit on the ground. "I'll set it up here, but first . . ." He scanned the park and pointed at an elderly couple sitting on the bench fifteen feet away. "Hey! You two! Yeah, you! Come here!"

"What are you doing?" Yama inquired.

"Leaving our calling card," Lynx replied.

The elderly duo drew near, doing their best to hide their obvious terror. "Yes, sir?" the man timidly inquired. "How may we help you, sir?"

Lynx grinned, displaying his sharp teeth. "Citizen, I need you to do me a favor."

"Whatever you want," the man promised.

"Thought you'd see it my way. Listen up. I'd like you to go back to that bench and sit down. Stay there. After we leave, some soldiers are going to show up and ask everybody a lot of questions. I want you to give them a message for me. Will you do that?"

"What is it?" the woman asked.

Lynx winked at Yama. "I want you to tell them this. Say to them: Lynx and Yama send their love. Got that?"

"Lynx and Yama send their love," the man repeated verbatim. "I'll remember it," he pledged.

"Fine, Citizen. Thanks. Now go sit on that bench and watch the fireworks."

"Oh! There's going to be fireworks?" the woman said excitedly.

"The loudest and the brightest you've ever seen," Lynx confirmed. "Now go and sit down."

"Anyone ever inform you that you have a warped sense of humor?" Yama commented as the elderly couple departed.

Lynx laughed. "Let's get crackin'!" He knelt and began assembling the tactical unit.

Yama looked to the southeast. The Biological Center was clearly visible, rising above most of the surrounding structures.

Lynx worked quickly, his task facilitated by the light from a nearby street lamp. First, he unfolded a collapsible tripod from underneath the rectangular metal box and elevated the unit to a standing position. He swiveled the box, aligning it in the general direction of the Biological Center. The top of the metal box housed a retractable tube, or barrel, and Lynx extended this tube to its full three-foot length. The side panels on the metal box flipped outward, revealing vents on both sides of the unit. Lynx unhinged a panel covering the bottom third of the unit, displaying a miniaturized control board complete with colored lights, meters, silver switches, and buttons.

"Looks complicated," Yama remarked.

"Keep your fingers crossed, chuckles." Lynx twisted a button and the meters lit up and a loud hum emanated from the unit.

"You've done it," Yama congratulated him.

"Not yet," Lynx corrected. He picked up the wooden crate, his claws digging into the wood along one edge, and strained. With a resounding crack, one side of the wooden crate split open. Lynx placed the crate on the grass, removed the remnants of the splintered side, and extracted a gleaming missile. The thermo was two feet long and six inches in diameter. Four fins extended several inches from the base of the missile. "This is it!" Lynx stated. "We only get one chance."

"What's next?"

"We lock it on target." Lynx handed the thermo to the Warrior. "Place it in the tube with the pointed end up. Those fins fit into special grooves at the bottom of the tube."

Yama held the thermo aloft and peered down the tube on the tactical unit. He could barely distinguish the grooves at the bottom. Slowly, he eased the missile into the tube and aligned the fins with the slots. "Done," he announced.

Lynx was bent over the control board. "Let me see. This digital display here will give us the range if I flick this switch." He did, and the indicated display began showing a series of numbers. "We're just over a mile and a half from the Biological Center," Lynx disclosed. He punched several of the buttons and threw another switch. A row of six red lights brightened. "Good," he stated, and glanced at Yama. His right index finger hovered near a yellow button. "Once I press this button, there's no turning back. I've set the automatic timer for ten minutes. In ten minutes, this unit will automatically fire the thermo at the preset target."

"What about them?" Yama indicated the people in the park.

"Don't worry about them, chuckles. They won't touch this thing. Are you ready?"

"Do it."

Lynx pressed the yellow button and smiled mischievously. "I just hope the Doc is in when our surprise package is delivered."

"Speaking of surprises," Yama remarked, "we have company."

Lynx straightened and turned.

A black and white patrol car had turned into the cul-de-sac and was heading their way.

"Cops!" Lynx hissed. "Not now! We've got to get out of here!"

The patrol car stopped next to the jeep.

23

The blast of Bertha's M-16 within inches of his left ear caused Hickok to wince, even as he spun, raising the Henry to his shoulder, knowing she was too skilled a fighter to fire without justification.

This time she had it.

A soldier had been standing not more than ten feet behind them, prepared to fire, when her shot caught him in the chest and knocked him to the ground. Behind him, other troopers were advancing across the field toward the troop transports.

Hickok sighted and the Henry boomed. He heard a soldier scream as he was struck.

Bertha was firing indiscriminately.

Hickok grabbed her by the arm and pulled her down to the grass. "Stay low!" he warned her. "They can see you better if you're standing up."

The troopers had opened up, most of them directing their shots at the crowd near the tent.

"I'm gonna flank 'em," Bertha declared, and proceeded to crawl off.

Up on the highway, the ten volunteers had just reached the road when the first gunshots erupted.

Hickok, observing from his prone position, saw headlights abruptly come on, three sets of them, not more than twenty yards from his men. The ten were exposed in the glare of the headlamps as three fifty-caliber machine guns let loose.

"Get out of there!" Hickok shouted at the top of his lungs.

Too late.

The ten were unable to flee before being cut to ribbons by the big fifties.

With a roar, the three jeeps gunned their engines, leaving the highway and making for the stockade.

Hickok found himself directly in their path. He aimed the Henry at the spot where he assumed the driver of the first jeep would be sitting and squeezed the trigger.

The result was better than he could have anticipated.

The first jeep suddenly slewed to the left, apparently out of control, and slammed into the second jeep. There was a tremendous crash and the second jeep was knocked over by the force of the impact, flipped onto one side. The third and final jeep swerved sharply to avoid colliding with the other two.

Hickok rose to his knees, sighted, and fired, hoping to repeat his performance and nail the driver of the third jeep.

Evidently, he missed.

The last jeep bore down on the Warrior, its machine gun belching lead and flame.

The slugs were kicking dirt into the air all around him as Hickok dropped the Henry and stood, his Pythons streaking from their holsters. The Colts bucked in twin precision as he fired off the rounds, one revolver right after the other, eight, nine, ten rounds in rapid succession, and only ten because he seldom kept a round in the chamber under the firing pin.

The jeep was only six feet from the gunman, its fifty-caliber strangely silent, but still moving at a high rate of speed.

Hickok felt someone plow into his right side and he was yanked to the ground as the jeep hurtled past. He twisted and found his face next to Bertha's.

"Watch yourself, White Meat!" she exclaimed. "We want you in one piece when we get you home to the missus!" She pecked him on the cheek, grinned, and was gone.

Hickok rose to his feet, smiling. The focus of the battle had shifted nearer the stockade as the remaining soldiers conducted a futile assault on the defenders of the troop transports. Were the Army troopers attempting to knock the transports out of commission? They were plainly outnumbered and outgunned and it was only a matter of time before they were mopped up.

The two jeeps that had collided were in flames, while the third jeep had mysteriously stopped in the middle of the field and was sitting there, the motor idling.

Hickok holstered his Pythons. He detected the gleam of his Henry reflected in the fire from the jeeps and walked over to the rifle. As he stooped to retrieve it, a high, squeaky voice stopped him cold.

"Touch it and you're dead!"

Hickok slowly straightened and turned. "I was wondering when you'd show up."

Rat was standing to the right of the burning jeeps, an M-16 in his hands, a wicked look on his feral face. "You remember me, then?"

"How could I forget vermin like you?"

"Yeah! That's right! Have your fun while you can!" Rat cackled. "I've been waitin' for this chance for so long! I'm gonna repay you for what you did to Maggot, you prick!"

"Too bad I wasn't able to do the same to you," Hickok said goading him.

Rat laughed. "I love it! I just love it! I'm gonna waste you! Are you scared, Hickok? Afraid I might pull this trigger?"

Hickok feigned a gaping yawn. "Nope. I'm bored to tears."

"You're faking it!" Rat snapped. "You just don't want me to have my fun!"

"No. I'm just waiting for my friend, Geronimo, to put a bullet in your miserable head. He's right behind you." Hickok held his breath, hoping Rat would take the bait. It was literally the oldest trick in the book.

"You're full of shit!" Rat declared. "You must think I'm really stupid to fall for a gag like that!"

"You have no idea of how stupid I think you are," Hickok said.

"There's no one behind me!"

Hickok yawned again. "Want to bet your life on it?"

Rat's features mirrored his quandary. He didn't believe the gunfighter for a minute. At least, he didn't *want* to believe him. But a nagging doubt persisted in his mind. Maybe Geronimo was behind him. Otherwise, how could Hickok be so calm about his fate?

The issue was decided by the burning jeeps. One of the rear-view mirrors, overheated by the raging flames, suddenly shattered with a loud pop.

Rat, fearing the worst, whirled, firing the M-16 wildly. It took only seconds to realize he'd been duped. Geronimo wasn't behind him! He spun toward Hickok, continuing to fire the M-16, spraying the automatic at waist level.

The gunfighter was prone on the ground, the Henry to his shoulder. He saw Rat's mouth drop and his beady eyes widen in alarm. Perfect. The Henry thundered and recoiled against his arm.

Rat's forehead was caved inward by the impact of the 44-40 slug. The back of his head spewed blood, brains, and greasy hair in every direction. The M-16 flew from his hands as he slammed to the ground and lay still.

"Got ya!" Hickok elated, rising. He walked to his long-time foe and stared at the lifeless eyes.

The night was deathly still.

Blade and Geronimo materalized out of the darkness and reached Hickok's side.

"Are you okay?" Blade asked.

"Fine," Hickok answered.

Geronimo nudged Rat's corpse with his right foot. "He give you any problems?"

"Piece of cake," Hickok replied. "How about you? Finish off those soldier boys?"

"We got them all," Blade said, "then heard your shot and came running." He paused. "We can't waste any time. Take ten more men and watch the road. We're leaving here in an hour no matter what."

Bertha came running up to them.

"We've got to get back," Blade stated, leading Geronimo off.

Hickok faced Bertha, reading the concern on her features, the affection in her eyes. "No hard feelings?" he inquired.

Bertha shook her head, suppressing the inexpressionable sadness she felt in her heart. "No hard feelings," she acknowledged.

Hickok offered his right hand. "Shake on it?"

Her hand was damp as she gripped his and shook.

"Let's head back," he suggested.

They moved toward the tent in silence, Hickok experiencing a peculiar sense of remorse.

"Just you remember one thing," Bertha finally spoke

up, grinning devilishly.

"What's that?"

"If you and your wife ever have a fallin' out," she vowed, "I'm gonna be on you like flies on garbage!"

"Remind me to talk to you about your analogies sometime."

24

Nineteen miles northwest of the Cheyenne Citadel, resting that night after spending hours packing for their departure the next day, Adam Mason and his father and mother were relaxing on their front porch.

"I wish we didn't have to leave our home," Gail said, sorrow tinging her every word.

"We've been all through that," Seth replied. "We don't have any other choice. The Government will find us anywhere in the Civilized Zone. Yama is our only hope."

"If he returns," Gail retorted.

"He will," Adam chipped in. "I know he will."

"You hardly know the man, son," Gail rejoined. "None of us really know him, and yet we're all set to trust him with our very lives."

"We don't have any choice," Seth reiterated.

"I wish you'd stop saying that," Gail said.

Adam rose and stretched. "Don't worry so much, Mom," he advised. "Yama will take good care of us. He'll return. You'll see."

"I hope he hasn't run into any trouble in the Citadel," Seth commented.

"Yama can take real good care of himself," Adam asserted. "You saw that. Nothing can kill him."

Gail Mason suddenly cocked her head to one side, listening. "Shhhhh! Be quiet! Do you hear it?"

"I hear it," Seth corroborated.

"So do I," Adam ineterjected. "What is it?"

"Sounds like thunder," Gail mentioned.

"That's funny," Seth said. "There's not a cloud in the sky."

Adam, trying to get a fix on the distant rumbling, walked to the southern tip of the porch. "Look!" he exclaimed. "Come look at this!"

Seth and Gail hurried to the end of the porch.

"Dear Lord!" Gail cried.

The southeastern horizon was lit by a brilliant fireball.

"What is it?" Adam asked.

"I don't know," Seth admitted, "but whatever it is, I think it's coming from the Citadel."

Adam gazed at his parents with frightened, dilated eyes. "Could it be Yama?"

Neither one answered.

25

The attack, while it may have been anticipated, came from a completely unexpected source and caught them off guard and unprepared.

The convoy, embracing sixteen transports, one slightly shot-up jeep, and the SEAL, was two days out of the Twin Cities and stopped for an afternoon break at Floyd Lake, just east of Highway 59. The SEAL was parked near the water as Alpha Triad snacked on smoked venison and fresh water.

"I don't like it," Blade said to the others between mouthfuls. "We're making too many stops. We should have been much further by now."

"What did you expect with all the women and children along?" Geronimo countered. "Children need potty breaks more often than adults, and water is essential."

"I know," Blade acknowledged. "It's just that I have this uncomfortable feeling between my shoulder blades, like we're being watched or something is about to happen. I can't shake it."

"You're not the only one," Hickok disclosed. "I can't understand why the blasted Army hasn't hit us yet.

They've had plenty of opportunity. We didn't even see one measly soldier in Detroit Lakes, and we know they were using it as a monitoring post once. What's going on?"

"I wish I knew," Blade stated. "I'm responsible for the lives of all these people, and I don't mind telling you that this waiting is making me a bit antsy."

"We've got company," Geronimo mentioned.

Zahner and Bertha were strolling toward them. Bertha had opted to ride with Zahner.

"How much longer will we stay here?" Zahner inquired as the duo reached the Warriors.

"Until everyone has eaten and gone to the bathroom," Blade revealed. "I intend to drive as far as we can tonight. The sooner we reach our Home, the safer I'll feel."

Bertha leaned against the SEAL and playfully winked at Hickok. The gunman pretended he hadn't seen it, so she idly watched some white, fluffy clouds float by overhead.

"Any ideas why the Army hasn't tried to stop us yet?" Zahner questioned them.

"We were just talking about that," Blade replied. "Your guess is as good as ours."

"Hey!" Bertha interrupted, pointing skyward. "Look at that!"

They all peered in the direction she was indicating and saw a bright pinpoint of light high in the sky.

"I learned about them when I was in Montana," Blade detailed. "They're called satellites and the Civilized Zone utilizes them to spy on other communities and towns. There are a few still up there, orbiting the planet, left over from before the Big Blast. That's what that thing is. A satellite."

"Don't you remember?" Geronimo reminded them.

"We saw one before, on our first run to the Twin Cities. I even heard it."

Zahner chuckled. "You can't hear a satellite."

"What? How do you know?" Blade demanded.

"I don't know a lot about them," Zahner readily admitted, "but I can remember talking with my dad, years and years ago, about the technology they had before World War Three. He mentioned satellites. Said they circle the earth way up there. Way, *way* up there. No way could you hear one."

Geronimo, perplexed, was watching the spot of light in the blue sky. It was growing larger. "But I can hear that one," he said disputing Zahner.

"So can I," Hickok attested.

"I can too," Zahner confirmed. "Funny, though. I know my dad told me you can't hear a satellite with the human ear."

Blade was staring at the growing sphere of light. Was Zahner correct? Was it impossible to hear satellites? Why, he chided himself, hadn't he bothered to research satellites in the Family Library after he had returned from Montana?

The light abruptly arced downward, accompanied by a raucous screeching.

At that instant, Blade abruptly recalled a book in the Library dealing with the history of aviation. One photograph, in particular, stood out vividly in his mind, and he knew, then, what it was. He knew it wasn't a satellite, it wasn't a harmless contrivance used for high-altitude reconnaissance. It was something different, something deadly, a relic from the past sent to deliver a message of destruction from Samuel the Second.

It was a jet.

Specifically, a jet fighter.

The jet streaked in low over Floyd Lake, zooming over

the convoy vehicles parked near the southwestern shore. It rolled and banked to the west.

"What the blazes is that thing?" Hickok shouted.

"A jet!" Blade replied, glancing along the shore. With a start he realized how vulnerable they were; the troop transports, jeep, and the SEAL were sitting ducks, right out in the open, and the majority of the people were standing near the lake or, in the case of many of the children and a few of the adults, actually in Floyd Lake, swimming and splashing. Right at the moment, though, everybody was staring at the jet in wonder.

"Here it comes again!" Geronimo yelled.

"Get out of the water!" Blade cried. "Take cover!"

There wasn't enough time.

The jet swooped down out of the western sky, its guns blazing. Dozens of the refugees were mowed down where they stood. In a twinkling, the jet was gone again, banking for another strafing run.

Screaming in stark panic, the refugees were streaming toward a wooden section close to the lake.

"We've got to get the trucks out of here!" Geronimo said.

"Too late!" Zahner declared, pointing.

They all dove for the dirt as the jet angled in. This time the pilot zeroed in on the troop transports, the jet's guns booming, and as the jet flashed off to the right one of the trucks exploded, showering debris in every direction. Fortunately, none of the other vehicles were close enough to be caught in the blast.

"Follow me!" Blade commanded, and sprinted to the SEAL. He climbed inside, in the driver's seat, and studied the four toggle switches in the center of the dashboard, the armament switches.

Hickok, Geronimo, Zahner, and Bertha piled in after Blade, with Hickok taking the other bucket seat and

Geronimo, Zahner, and Bertha filling the back seat.

"What do you have in mind, pard?" Hickok queried.

Before Blade could respond, the jet was on them again. This time the pilot was aiming at the SEAL, and the five inside could feel the vehicle shake from the onslaught of the jet's guns. The SEAL's impervious plastic body, unlike the troop transports, was able to withstand the blistering attack.

Blade was trying to recall everything he could about the second of the four toggle switches, the one controlling the surface-to-air missile. The missile was mounted in the roof above the driver's seat. If he activated the switch, a panel in the roof would slide aside and the surface-to-air missile, a heat-seeking Stinger, would be launched. The Stinger, so said the instructions, had an effective range of ten miles.

"It's comin' again!" Bertha declared.

Blade rested his right hand on the toggle switch. Knowing the details of the Operations Manual was well and good, but the fact still remained that they had never tested the weapon and they had no idea if it would work as designed.

"Go for it!" Hickok urged.

Blade looked out his window and saw the jet bearing down from the west as before, coming out of the sun. Was the jet armed with missiles or rockets, as well as machine guns? If so, the SEAL would not survive a direct hit. There might be time to take cover! He started the engine and gunned it, the SEAL lurching forward as the jet passed overhead. The movement of the SEAL evidently disconcerted the pilot of the aircraft, because the devastating fire failed to materialize.

"Geronimo, keep your eyes on the jet," Blade ordered. "Cue me when it's about a mile off."

"Will do."

Blade drove the SEAL due north, putting distance between the SEAL and the remainder of the convoy, seeking a suitable spot where they could take cover.

"It's made a wide turn," Geronimo reported.

Blade saw a gully to his left, a wide one at the top of a rise, and he drove toward it.

"He's coming in fast," Geronimo announced, "about five miles out."

Blade had the pedal to the metal.

"Four miles."

The SEAL's colossal tires churned up the small rise.

"Three miles."

Blade wheeled the SEAL into the gully and slammed on the brakes.

"Two miles."

Blade gripped the toggle switch in his right hand.

"One mile," Geronimo stated.

"Now!" Hickok shouted.

Blade flicked the toggle switch, even as the jet roared overhead, not more than fifty feet above the SEAL. There was a tremendous explosion as something struck the gully above the SEAL. A shower of dirt and stones descended on the vehicle as a cloud of dust choked the air.

So!

The jet did carry more than machine guns!

But what about the surface-to-air missile?

"Nothing happened," Geronimo said.

That was when the entire SEAL bucked backwards and there was a loud retort from the roof.

Blade leaned over the steering wheel and spotted the small surface-to-air missile, the Stinger, in flight, arching upward into the bright blue sky on the trail of the jet. He threw his door open and jumped to the ground for a better view, followed by the others.

The pilot of the jet apparently knew the Stinger was after him. The jet was climbing as rapidly as the pilot could manage, gaining distance on the pursuing missile.

"The Stinger only has a ten-mile range," Geronimo noted anxiously. "If the jet can outrun it . . ." He left the sentence unfinished.

Blade was marveling at the supreme skill the pilot was displaying in his endeavor to avoid the missile.

The jet abruptly banked westward and the Stinger closed in and would have made contact with its target, but at the last possible instant the pilot rolled the jet and the missile passed under the aircraft. The pilot dived in a shrieking whine of the craft's engines, nosing the jet as steeply as feasible.

What was the pilot up to now?

The Stinger had turned and was soaring after the jet.

With consummate expertise, the pilot pulled the jet out of the dive just when it seemed the aircraft would crash into the ground.

The Stinger, close behind the jet, was slower to respond. Its sensors registered the jet arcing up and away and the guidance system compensated, the missile clearing a stand of pine trees with only feet to spare.

At full throttle, the pilot was fleeing in a vertical ascent. The Stinger was losing ground rapidly.

"He's doing it!" Geronimo said in alarm.

Blade glanced at the SEAL, wondering how they would escape if the jet returned to finish the job it had started. There was an unusual sound high up in the sky and he gazed up at the dogfight.

The jet was in serious trouble; it was making a coughing noise and depositing a trail of black smoke. It seemed to stall completely and hang in the air for several seconds.

The Stinger was eating up the space between them.

"Look!" Bertha cried.

The canopy of the jet suddenly fell away from the aircraft, and they could see a diminutive figure scrambling from the cockpit.

"Go!" Zahner yelled. "Get the hell out of there!"

Blade found himself doing the same thing, mentally rooting for the pilot to evade his impending fate. The man—or was it a woman?—had put up such a stupendous struggle, he or she deserved to live.

The Stinger, however, being artificial in construction and intelligence, was immune to the emotional pangs of compassion or a salute to bravery; it functioned according to a singular, preprogrammed purpose, and it fulfilled that purpose now.

The tiny form of the pilot was in the act of leaping clear of the jet when the Stinger hit. The blast of the impact utterly destroyed the aircraft in a sparkling, fiery cloud of annihilation.

"Back in the SEAL," Blade immediately instructed them. He waited until they were inside, watching the wreckage of the jet plummet to the ground perhaps four miles to the west.

"Funny they only sent one jet," Hickok remarked as Blade climbed behind the wheel.

"Maybe not so funny," Blade said disagreeing, starting the SEAL and backing from the gully. He headed for the convoy. "I've been doing some thinking, and I've come to the conclusion that Samuel isn't as powerful as we give him credit for."

"What makes you say that?" Geronimo asked.

"Think about it," Blade said. "Why have they waited one hundred years after World War Three to begin reconquering the United States? Why didn't they do it five years after the Big Blast instead? Or ten years? Or twenty-five? There's only one logical reason: they weren't strong enough."

"They must think they're strong enough now,"
Hickok noted.

"Oh, sure," Blade conceded, "Samuel intends to take
over the entire country in the coming years, but look at
how he's doing it. A piece at a time. Bit by bit. One
group here and another group there. Meanwhile, what
does he do? He keeps an eye on anyone living outside the
Civilized Zone, but he doesn't do anything to them
unless he decides they're a threat, like our Family. Even
now, when Samuel is trying to prevent us from returning
to the Home, what does he do? He sends a jet. One jet.
Not two. Not ten. Just one. Why doesn't he send more?
If stopping us is so important to him, why didn't he send
more jets? The answer is obvious. He only had one to
spare. Even the single jet he sent wasn't in top condition
or that pilot would have avoided our missile. It wasn't
the pilot's fault he failed; the jet itself was to blame. It
looked to me like the jet conked out on him." Blade
paused. "No, I don't believe that the Civilized Zone is
all powerful. Samuel the Second and the Doktor can be
defeated. All we have to do is find their Achilles heel.
When we get to the Home I'm going to have a long talk
with Plato and propose that we carry the fight to them
instead of waiting for them to come after us."

"Sounds great to me," Hickok said with enthusiasm.
"I've always said the best defense is a good offense."

"Haven't I heard that line somewhere before?"
Geronimo asked, grinning.

The SEAL was approaching the convoy. The truck
struck by the jet was still ablaze. The refugees had
gathered around the troop transports and were
ministering to the injured. Joshua ran up to the SEAL as
Blade braked and climbed down.

"Report," Blade told him.

"My initial tally," Joshua began sadly, "indicates twenty-nine dead and fourteen wounded."

"So many!" Zahner stated, joining them.

"Seven are in critical condition," Joshua revealed. "I don't think they'll reach the Home."

"Maybe we should stay put and tend 'em," Bertha proposed.

Blade became aware that all eyes were on him, awaiting his decision. He walked to the nearest troop transport and clambered onto the cab. "Quiet down!" he yelled, waving his arms over his head to attract their attention. "You've all just seen how vulnerable we are here. So long as we're tied to these trucks, whether on the highway or parked on the side, they can hit us whenever they want and wherever they want. They have the advantage. Well, I don't intend to allow this to happen again! So here's what we are going to do! Everyone will be loaded into the troop transports, even the injured, and we're going to take off. If you are hungry, eat now. I'd advise you to go to the bathroom now. Because we are not stopping again until we reach the Home! That's right! Unless there is a dire emergency, we'll drive until we reach our destination! No stopping! We'll drive all night if we need to, but I can promise you, come morning, we will be at the Home! Within a few days, we'll have you relocated in the town of your choice, in your new home. Are you with me?"

Zahner led the throng in a chant of *"Yes! Yes! Yes!"*

"Okay! Let's get moving!" Blade leaped to the ground.

Hickok was chuckling.

"What's so funny?" Blade inquired.

"Oh," Hickok said, grinning, "I was just thinking about how naturally talented a leader you are."

"Don't start," Blade warned him.

"I know how you feel about leading the Family," Hickok commented. "You've told us dozens of times you don't want the responsibility, and I'm with you one hundred percent."

"You are?"

"Of course, pard. Who needs our Family? They're small potatoes! If we take on the Civilized Zone and whip Sammy's butt, I say you should run for President!"

26

There were five of them, five people and as many suitcases piled into the green military jeep traveling east on a deserted stretch of Highway 11 in southern North Dakota.

"Tell it again!" the youngest occupant was pleading with the furry passenger riding in the back.

"Don't pester Mr. Lynx, Adam!" his mother admonished him.

"Please, Mr. Lynx!" Adam persisted.

"You heard your mother," Seth stated. He was seated across from the driver, Yama, while Gail and Adam rode behind them and Lynx was curled up with the luggage.

"It's no bother, bub," Lynx said to Seth. He smiled at the boy. "Like I told you, these two dumb cops came up to us and demanded to know what we were doing. I told 'em I'd just set up an air-pollution monitor. Didn't I, Yama?"

"That you did," the man in blue affirmed.

"Anyway," Lynx continued, "they didn't know if I was tellin' the truth or not 'cause they wouldn't known an air-pollution monitor from their . . . uhhhhh . . . elbow! One of 'em, though, keeps staring at me. I could tell he was going to place me, what with me being so famous and all. Aren't I famous, Yama?"

Yama smiled and glanced over his right shoulder. He was delighted at how well Lynx and Adam were hitting it off, although the boy's parents still entertained reservations about the G.R.D. Both Seth and Gail had protested against bringing Lynx along. Gail, in fact, had reacted strongly when she had first seen him; she had promptly fainted. It had taken Yama over an hour of intense persuasion before the Masons acquiesced and consented to make the trip as planned. "Yes, Lynx," Yama answered, "you are famous. And exceedingly humble."

Lynx ignored the remark and resumed his tale. "Sure enough, this copper makes me, and the two of 'em go for their guns."

"Gosh! What did you do then?" Adam inquired, fascinated.

Lynx hesitated, reluctant to relate all of the extremely bloody details. "There were only two of 'em. They didn't stand a chance! I . . . took out . . . one and Yama got the other one, and before you could say lickety-split Yama and I were in our jeep and drivin' like mad for the west wall. I tell ya', midget, I never saw anyone drive like old Yama! I think we ran down over a hundred people by the time we got to the west gate!"

"Ahh! You did not!" Adam said skeptically.

"Smart little tyke, ain't you? Okay. We *almost* ran over a hundred. We drove through the gate just as the thermo went off. And that's all there was to it. The rest you know. We showed up at your place, picked you up, and bingo! Here we are!" Lynx gazed at the stark landscape. "Course, don't ask me where here is."

"Wow!" Adam said in awe. "You beat all those soldiers and everything! You must be a great fighter!"

Lynx puffed up his chest a bit. "Well, yeah, midget, I guess I am."

"Do you think you destroyed the Biological Center?" Seth asked Yama.

"I believe so," Yama responded. "And probably a good portion of the Army as well."

"If you didn't get the Doktor," Seth stated, "he'll come after you with everything he's got."

"It might be the other way around," Yama said.

"I don't follow."

Yama patted the pouch he was still carrying. "I may have the information my Family requires to deal a decisive blow against the Doktor."

"I pray you have what you need," Seth declared.

"I don't have everything I need," Yama mentioned.

"You don't? What are you missing?" Seth inquired.

Yama looked in the rear-view mirror at his newfound feline friend. "A sturdy pair of earplugs."

Make the Most of Your Leisure Time with
LEISURE BOOKS

Please send me the following titles:

Quantity	Book Number	Price
_____	_____	_____
_____	_____	_____
_____	_____	_____
_____	_____	_____
_____	_____	_____

If out of stock on any of the above titles, please send me the alternate title(s) listed below:

_____	_____	_____
_____	_____	_____
_____	_____	_____
_____	_____	_____

Postage & Handling _____

Total Enclosed $ _____

☐ Please send me a free catalog.

NAME _____
(please print)

ADDRESS _____

CITY _____ STATE _____ ZIP _____

Please include $1.00 shipping and handling for the first book ordered and 25¢ for each book thereafter in the same order. All orders are shipped within approximately 4 weeks via postal service book rate. PAYMENT MUST ACCOMPANY ALL ORDERS.*

*Canadian orders must be paid in US dollars payable through a New York banking facility.

Mail coupon to: **Dorchester Publishing Co., Inc.**
6 East 39 Street, Suite 900
New York, NY 10016
Att: ORDER DEPT.